◆ Telling Stories ◆

The moment I saw the two policemen I knew perfectly well I wasn't going to tell them anything.

'Marie-Christine Masbou?' said the tall one in the leather jacket, and I made not the slightest attempt to contradict him. Why shouldn't I borrow Chris's name for a few days until I felt ready to face things? She didn't need it. I decided to tell them neither who I was, nor who I wasn't. Let them tell me, I thought. Let them decide. And I did have the copy of the *Mail* open on my knee – that bit at least is true. So if they'd wanted to, they could have seen the photograph easily enough; they could have read the article. It was up to them to make the connection. I simply went along with whatever they said. It seemed easiest.

Valerie Windsor lives in Cheshire. She is the author of many radio plays (for which she has won awards, including the Giles Cooper) and television plays. Her stage play, *Effie's Burning*, was performed at the National Theatre and on BBC1. She is currently a writer for Channel 4's *Brookside*. *Telling Stories* is her first novel.

◆ Telling Stories ◆
Valerie Windsor

Mandarin

to Mick

A Mandarin Paperback
TELLING STORIES

First published in Great Britain 1993
by Sinclair-Stevenson Ltd
This edition published 1994
by Mandarin Paperbacks
an imprint of Reed Consumer Books Ltd
Michelin House, 81 Fulham Road, London SW3 6RB
and Auckland, Melbourne, Singapore and Toronto

Reprinted 1994

Copyright © by Valerie Windsor
The author has asserted her moral rights

A CIP catalogue record for this title
is available from the British Library
ISBN 0 7493 1534 2

Printed and bound in Great Britain
by Cox & Wyman Ltd, Reading, Berks

◆ THE END ◆

One Thursday afternoon in Paris, I left my husband. After sixteen years of what everybody agreed was an unusually successful marriage, I stood up in the pause between the ordering of the coffee and its arrival, and left him sitting there at a pavement café in the rue François Premier.

I try to think what it was that made me do it, and I have no idea. I mean what specific thing made me choose that moment rather than any other. But I'm using the wrong words: I didn't 'choose' at all. It simply happened. It was an odd afternoon. I don't know what was the matter with me. It was windy: either the wind or the noise of the plastic chair scraping the pavement started a strange sensation in the bones of my head. Tony chose the café: one of those *salons de glace* where they serve expensive cocktails.

'Will this do?' he said. 'Here?' and he flicked at the seat with his handkerchief. 'Don't sit down yet,' he said. 'They haven't been wiped.' But I deliberately sat down anyway, without looking, even though I was wearing a white skirt. It annoyed me to hear him fussing about such things. A man should not fuss about such things. A man should not even notice them. I didn't. So

◆ 1 ◆

was he implying that I should; that because I so patently failed to notice them, he was forced into doing it, against his will? The odd sensation in my head turned into a thin, high buzzing as if a wasp were trapped in the hollows of the skull.

'What will you have?' he asked.

It was June, I think. May or June, I forget which. But cold. Warm enough to sit at a pavement café, but cold enough to want something hot to drink.

'Coffee,' I said.

He was reading the menu. Behind him was a bank of potted plants with spiky orange flowers.

'Plastic,' said Tony turning to look.

'Are they? I don't think they are.' I leant over to touch one. I wanted it to be real. I wanted it to be alive, and as vicious as it looked. But he was right, of course: it was plastic. The buzzing in my head grew worse.

'What's the matter?' he asked.

I lied. 'I think there's a wasp.'

'Where?'

'I don't know.'

Any kind of uncertainty infuriated him. 'Well, either there is or there isn't.'

'I don't know what the matter is,' I said, pressing my fingers against my temples. And then the waiter came.

'*Deux cafés*,' said Tony, without even glancing at him. I had to do all the smiling for both of us: I had to make all the submissive gestures, the ones that meant, 'We are English, we are on holiday, please forgive us for these inadequacies, please understand the meaning of my anxious smiles.'

The waiter smiled back. He was a very young man, a boy. 'D'accord,' he said and wiped the table.

Tony leaned back in his chair and breathed out. 'Well, this is nice,' he said. And that was all. That was the sum of what happened between us. There was no atmosphere. The unpleas- antness of the previous day when I had got us lost in Neuilly because of incompetent map reading was forgotten. And by mutual understanding we never allowed the surfaces to be disturbed by any mention of the unsatisfactory nightly rituals which, by some failure of imagination, I could never connect with love.

I sat there with my hands folded in my lap, and the buzzing in my head grew thinner and higher, a whining electrical noise in the bone. I stood up. I could feel a damp patch at the back of my skirt.

'Where are you going?' Tony said, embarrassed by the sudden noise as my chair fell on to the pavement.

'To the Ladies.'

He pointed to the back of my skirt. 'You sat in something.'

'No,' I said, because I was tired of him being right. 'It's blood.' It wasn't, of course. I don't really know why I said it. To make him anxious, I suppose. And it worked: he *was* anxious. I have a last image of his face: the look of fear struggling with exasperation.

He set my chair back on its legs. 'Do you want me to come with you?'

'No, I'm fine.' His kindness embarrassed me. 'I just need to go to the Ladies.'

And, truly, I had meant to do just that: to sit and breathe quietly for a moment, to be alone, to dab the worst of the stain off my skirt. That was truly all I was planning. Inside, the waiter stood behind the counter putting paper umbrellas into ice-creams. I said: '*Excusez moi, est-ce que vous avez des toilettes?*' My French was not very good then, schoolgirl French. I was capable of phrasing any number of useful questions but could seldom grasp the answers they provoked. The waiter pointed to a white door at the end of the bar.

'*Oui, Madame. Par là. La première à gauche.*'

I pushed the door open. There was a short, dim passage ahead of me. On the wall, I remember, was a poster advertising Corsica. I thought how exciting it would be to go to Corsica.

Now. This minute. In the foreground a growth of violent pink flowers was smothering a ruined column: there were no plastic flowers in Corsica.

While I was standing there playing with these pointless and irrelevant thoughts, a man, his stomach bulging over the top of his trousers, came out of a kitchen shouting something about twelve flutes. You see how clearly I remember all these details? I realise now he was talking about bread, but at the time it seemed part of the oddness, and I nodded to myself as if this was all just as I had expected. He opened a door at the end of the passage and left it swinging open behind him. Light from the street poured on to my poster. Through the door I could see a car trying to get out of a parking space. A cold wind funnelled into the passage. Someone from the kitchen shouted, '*Eh, la porte. Fermez-la.*'

Obediently I hurried down the passage to do it. I am a very obedient person. I can't help it. The man who was trying to get out of the parking space had lost patience now: a van was blocking the narrow side street. I stood in the doorway watching for a moment and trying to get my bearings, and then, without making any clear-cut decision about it, I started walking. I told myself I needed air: I needed to clear my head. Five minutes, I said, that's all. I shall just pretend for five minutes that I'm really going somewhere, somewhere like Corsica for example, on my own. After all, I argued, I'm grown up: I'm thirty-six years old. I can do what I choose. I am quite old enough to go to the end of a foreign street by myself. It was strange how daring it felt. I started to count up the number of times I'd been alone in a foreign place and could think of none, except, of course, when I was in the lavatory or going up to our room in some hotel; never in a street, or at least never without the consciousness of having to meet Tony in half an hour, or of having to get back because Tony would be getting anxious. Never really alone. How extraordinary, I thought, laughing out loud – I *think* I laughed out loud, I'm not sure – how extraordinary that he should be sitting there on the pavement waiting for me, imagining that I was still in the Ladies' room. I walked past the shouting drivers. I felt very light and strange. After a moment, I came out on to the road that ran parallel with the rue François Premier. This was surely far enough. Nobody seemed to notice me. I thought: Perhaps I have become invisible. My head certainly seemed unusually clear, as if the whining noise had bored a hole into it. I remember thinking, very rationally, that invisibility was a conceit of fairy tales: far more likely, I thought, far more likely that I was not really there at all, that all this was no more than a piece of vivid wishful thinking; that in reality I'd finished in the Ladies' room long ago and was back sitting with Tony at the plastic table, that he hadn't even missed me. Well, how could he have missed me if I was still there? As far as he was concerned I was never missing: I was a part of his consciousness. I existed only because he needed me to exist. Beyond that, I probably had no solid reality. I was immediately tempted to go and look, to turn back – because I'd gone quite far enough now – and check that I was, in reality, safely sitting at the table with him, drinking my coffee, listening to him read the menu.

I could have done that, but I didn't. I walked on. Just a little further, I said to myself. Only to the next intersection. Just a little further. And I felt quite safe, because of this theory of mine about not really being there at all. In the corner of my brain I was quite convinced of it. So I was surprised when a woman bumped into me and I felt the solidity of my body collide with hers. I stood there, shocked by the amount of real physical space I took up on the pavement. The bones of my head buzzed with pain. I apologised and hurried on as if I were late for some appointment. I was beginning to feel frightened. I couldn't understand what I was doing. Well, I will go as far as the fifth tree, I said, and then I'll turn back. But I was so preoccupied, I lost count. All right then, this time I will go as far as the tenth tree. But after I'd counted to seven the trees stopped and I was standing at the edge of the pavement and had to cross a very wide road junction, as wide as a river in flood, so wide I couldn't see clearly what was on the other side. I couldn't see anything very clearly. My eyes were blurred. If I am not really here, I said without conviction, then nothing can hit me: but instinctively I was watching the traffic and waiting for my moment to cross, so I knew this was a ridiculous conceit as well, and that of course I was really there. Besides, my head was now very painful and I understood that the reason I couldn't see clearly was because my eyes were full of tears.

After a while I came to a park. I sat on a bench and swallowed some aspirins I'd found in my bag. Aspirins might dull the curious feeling in my head. I didn't know what I was doing in this park. I grew cold with embarrassment. By now Tony would be getting anxious. He'd have discovered I was not in the Ladies. He'd be searching for me. I got up and started running, stumbling into flower beds and tripping over my own shoes until the park stopped and I was in a street full of smart shops. I drifted into a department store and wandered round, getting my breath back and looking at gloves, which were things I never ordinarily wore because I was always losing them. I toured the perfume counters and sprayed my wrists from the trial bottles.

'*Madame désire quelque chose?*' a salesgirl asked.

'No,' I said, backing away. 'No. Nothing.'

A thin, whispery voice in my head told me I was behaving like a madwoman. You'll have to go back sooner or later, it said reasonably enough, so go back now. But it was a very distant voice, and instead I started humming to block it out and took the escalator to another floor, where I tried on a turquoise silk dress with a black bodice. And then I went up and down the escalators several times and finally left by a completely different door from the one I'd come in by. This seemed to me a very clever tactic. They won't catch me now, I said, though I'm not quite sure who I meant by 'they'. Tony and the waiter, I suppose. I imagined them running distractedly up and down the streets looking for me. Or perhaps I meant the police, although it was far too soon for Tony to have contacted them. And anyway, what nonsense, he wouldn't be chasing about the streets after me: he'd be sitting in the hotel, waiting. He'd be brewing up a thick, dark, punishing silence. I knew those silences. I knew the power of his anger.

I saw myself walking through the revolving doors of the hotel, my head at an unnatural angle, self-consciously pretending this is how I always walk through revolving doors in case he's in the foyer waiting for me. But all this was too exhausting to think about. I couldn't go back yet: I didn't have the energy to spin the complex web of lies I'd need to comfort and confuse him with, so I just kept on walking. There didn't seem to be any alternative.

I had no idea where I was going. I crossed major roads. I stood on railway bridges staring down at the gravel between the sleepers. I wandered through windy subways where swastika signs and OAS were scrawled in red paint. In English someone had written 'I am Death'. I had no idea what it meant but it seemed significant, it seemed part of a bigger conspiracy over which I had no control. It was obviously connected with the odd feeling in my head and with twelve flutes and violent-coloured flowers and the noise of a chair scraping on a pavement. I walked under flyways and past traffic lights. I walked through a district where neon lights flashed 'GIRLS' and 'Le Peep' and 'Club Poussiquette'. A dark girl wearing jeans and a white shirt stood in a doorway of a place where men paid to look through a small hole in a booth and see a naked woman, or at least that part of her which most interested them. She looked clean and ordinary. Perhaps she was just the cashier. A man with tobacco-stained skin fell into step with me. He smiled and held his cigarette between his teeth. He muttered things in my ear. He made suggestions. I understood none of the words. He wore a blue suit and a gold medallion instead of a tie. He was threateningly close, his body moving exactly in rhythm with mine. I was very afraid. I didn't know how to shake him off. I walked faster. He walked faster.

'*Je suis anglais*,' I said, as if this would explain something. I blushed at the mistake. '*Anglaise*,' I mumbled.

It occurred to me that he was offering me money. Or perhaps I had misunderstood, and rather than offering it to me he was asking for it. '*Cent cinquante francs.*' I caught that much. Something like that. Then 'OK, OK, *deux cents francs. Deux cents francs.*' He touched my arm and whispered more things in my ear.

'Fuck off,' I said. My voice trembled. I was not used to saying things like that out loud.

He shrugged and fell back. He was laughing at me. I started to run: I dared not look back. My legs shook. I went on running until I began to feel sick.

It grew colder. The muscles in my calves ached. My feet burned. I walked along street after street of peeling stucco, rusting iron shutters, ancient advertisements for Cacolac and Dubonnet. The wind whipped the litter out of the gutter. I had no coat. I had nothing. But still I went on, past warehouses, past a meat-processing factory where the men were coming out of the gates and crossing to a car park. Is it that late? I thought. A woman with a loaf of bread strapped to the back of her bike cycled past me. People were going home. I should go home as well.

I could hear someone's television. A woman was weeping, her voice slightly crazed because the volume was too high. The music swelled to match her hysteria. Plates clattered. There was a smell of frying bacon and garlic. At the hotel they'd be starting to serve dinner. I ought now to be lying on the double bed, half-watching the drama of the weeping woman on the television in our room, while Tony showered and considered whether or not he was in the mood for shellfish. That's what I *ought* to have been doing, and I didn't know why I wasn't. I had no idea why I was wandering about these foreign streets, my stomach stretching with hunger, my head empty. I must telephone someone immediately. I must telephone the hotel. No, a taxi firm – I must get a taxi. For a moment it all seemed very clear, but then the sharpness of the conviction began to fade a little and anyway I couldn't find a public telephone. I wandered in circles for a quarter of an hour looking for one before I saw the sign Café-Bar-Restaurant du Centre. It was written across the width of an olive-coloured building in faded blue paint. There were telephones in cafés. Du Centre of what? I wondered, standing on the pavement outside, staring up at the cracked façade. It looked shut. The fly-blown *Tarif de Consommations* had fallen off the window and was trapped against a grubby lace curtain. I pushed the door, not expecting it to open, but it did, so I went in.

Two men sat at a table playing cards and drinking red wine out of minute glasses. I don't know why I was so obsessed with all these details: I could describe everything to you, everything – what the woman behind the bar was wearing, the adenoidal breathing of the child who hovered close to the card players.

'*Vous avez un téléphone, Madame?*' I said. The two men looked up and stared at me with indifferent curiosity. '*Téléphone?*' I repeated.

'*Vas-y,*' said the woman fiercely. I thought she was talking to me, but she dashed out from behind the bar and slapped the child's hand. '*Vas-y.*' And then to me: '*Là-bas, Madame.*'

I picked up the receiver and was putting money into the slot, when I realised I had no idea what the number of the hotel was. In England I could have rung Directory Enquiries, but even if there were such a thing in France – which presumably there was – I didn't know what it was called, I didn't know what number to ring. I listened to the dialling tone for a long time and did nothing. Under a pile of papers on a shelf I saw a battered telephone directory. I stared at it out of the corner of my eye as if I were afraid it might suddenly move, because only then, only if I caught it moving, would I have to acknowledge it was really there. Then, very carefully, I put the receiver back on the hook. My money jangled back. The relief of not phoning made me feel weak. Well, there you are, I told myself, lying, you tried. You did try. I imagined myself saying it to Tony: 'I tried to ring you, but I couldn't get through.'

'*Est-ce que vous avez une chambre?*' I asked the woman behind the bar. I was surprised to hear myself say it. I was surprised how easily it slid out of my mouth.

She asked me for how long I wanted it.

'*La nuit seulement*,' I said.

She shrugged, and unhooked a key from the board. '*Numéro cinq*,' she said.

I followed her up a flight of uncarpeted stairs. Her legs were discoloured with old bruises and misshapen wormy knots of varicose veins. I wondered what had happened to her that the supply of blood should have become so painfully contorted. She was not an old woman.

'*Quatre-vingt-dix francs la nuit*,' she said, opening the door of the room. '*Ou quarante francs l'heure*.'

'*La nuit*,' I said. '*Je suis en vacances*,' I added. She nodded. She didn't believe me. Of course not. I had no luggage, no coat. People *en vacances* had luggage: they did not stay in places like this. The child who had followed us upstairs stood in the doorway staring at me and sucking her thumb. There was something wrong about her: something missing.

'*Viens*,' said Madame, but the child took no notice and went on staring and stroking her nose with a lascivious little smile. In the end I had to shut the door on her.

There are certain rituals to be observed in strange hotel rooms. I observed them all. I opened the window and folded back the shutters to see what was outside: a courtyard where a rusting van was parked beside some dustbins. I ran the water in the basin and watched it gurgle down the plughole, I read the notice behind the door, I looked in the wardrobe, I examined the sheets, I lay on the bed and stared at the cracks in the ceiling. I think I had expected that as soon as I was alone, as soon as I stopped walking, I'd be able to cry, and that this would bring me so much relief I'd be able to think clearly again, but nothing happened. I simply lay there, first on my back, then on my stomach, looking at the balls of dust on the floor. I said to myself: What do you feel? And the answer really was nothing, nothing at all except a vague discomfort which might have been fear, a sense of frozen emptiness as if a parasitic worm had eaten everything away, flesh, blood, nerve ends, everything except the bone. I could feel its pale segmented body stir with hunger.

Well then, you must face the truth, I told myself.

The truth is I am a liar. I always have been. You can believe nothing I tell you. It's a concept I've always had difficulty with, the truth. It slides about so much. Face the truth, I said firmly to myself: but instead I found myself making pictures out of the damp stains on the wall. 'Perhaps you're ill,' I whispered out loud. I could think of no other possible explanation for what I was doing. It was a comforting thought. It relieved me of any responsibility. I am very, very ill, I whispered, trying out the sound of it. There is something very wrong with me.

Outside the door, the child with the lascivious grin shuffled and sang tunelessly to herself through her blocked nose. It grew darker. I was afraid to turn on the light. I wanted to pee but I was afraid to move from the bed. I heard myself whispering aloud. 'I don't know what to do' – repeating it over and over again. I couldn't go back. At some point or other I'd already decided that. But I couldn't go forward either. So this was as far as I went: this room was my boundary. I started hunting frantically in my bag as if there might be something in there that would solve the problem for me. I had three aspirins, a comb, a bottle of toilet water, a bag of spilt make-up, approximately £20 in French money and two £5 notes, two credit cards, a library ticket and a driving licence, a dusty Polo mint smelling of perfume, some loose change among the grit and fluff at the bottom and a couple of shredded tissues. Tony had my passport safely back at the hotel. I swallowed the aspirins and ate the sweet and sat there on the bed rocking backwards and forwards, my elbows pressed hard into my stomach and both fists stuffed against my mouth to try and hold in the rising panic.

After a while – I don't know how long – I realised the whining in the bone had stopped. And beyond the room there was silence: no banging doors, no thumping of water in the pipes, no traffic. In the darkness, I pulled the chair across the room and used it to balance on while I peed into the wash-basin. 'I am lost,' I whispered. It sounded very like the truth. I said it again, louder. 'I am lost.'

I must have slept. Of course I must, because I dreamed. And if I wasn't asleep, then the noise of a downstairs door slamming shut couldn't possibly have woken me, which it did. The door banged, then I heard men's voices whispering and the sound of feet on the stairs. I was instantly alert. I knew who they were. I froze. I listened to them walking up the corridor towards my room and waited for them to stop outside my door. I'd been expecting them, so it was almost a relief to know they'd finally come. Ridiculous to imagine that you could simply disappear without having first made elaborate plans. People were always found nowadays. One newsflash on the radio would do it. The gendarmes were probably already inundated with phone calls about me. Madame would certainly have called them. 'Yes, an Englishwoman. Without any luggage. Behaving very oddly.'

So I picked up the key and went to open the door for them, but the footsteps went on past *numéro cinq* to the end of the corridor. I was confused. I pressed my head against the door to listen. I heard some mumbling and what sounded like swearing, but I couldn't catch any of the words. I heard the sound of someone trying to turn a door handle. They've made a mistake, I thought, they've got the wrong room, and I nearly went out on to the landing to explain this to them. I was even phrasing the French in my head – '*Non. C'est moi que vous cherchez*' – when a man said, 'Etienne?' in a loud, urgent whisper. '*Dépêches-toi, uh?*' and then something else which I didn't catch because he spoke too fast and in slang.

So they hadn't come for me. Not yet. They would, though. Eventually they'd come. It was inevitable. You can't hide for long in a foreign country without money, without friends, at the very least without a working knowledge of the language. Anyway, there'd be a photograph of me in the morning papers. Which photo? I wondered, but Tony is not the sort of man to keep a snapshot of his wife in his wallet, so it would have to be my passport photo. I hate it. Every time the light flashed in the booth, my eyes blinked shut. I look as if I'm dead: as if I am a corpse propped up against the pleated orange curtain. Even Tony thought they were bad and he usually quite likes photographs of me. I don't. I hate them all. 'Is that me?' I say, drawing back. 'Is that really what I look like?' What confuses me is that there's no consistency. Except, of course, there must be, because Tony always recognises me. 'That's a good shot of you,' he says, and I peer at it trying and failing to find anything I accept as being incontrovertibly me. I feel no connection at all with the person he seems to recognise so easily.

'I don't really look like that, do I?' I say and he takes my concern for vanity.

The men had gone, taking Etienne with them. I heard them pass my door and go downstairs. Outside an engine started up. The room was grey now, thickly grey as if full of fog. I washed my face with cold water. In the fly-blown mirror everything looked grey: my face, my eyes, the walls. I twitched the cover straight on the bed, and carrying my shoes so as not to make too much noise on the stairs, went down into the bar. I left a 100-franc note under my key by the coffee machine and let myself out on to the street. I had no plans, so I simply started walking again.

At first I thought the main road would be dangerous. I thought I'd just find somewhere safe to cross and then continue on side streets. I behaved like a criminal on the run, turning my head away whenever a lorry passed, as if I had no right to be there. But then the wild possibility of hitching a lift occurred to me. It was not something I'd ever done before. I sat on a wall for a moment, covertly watching the traffic and weighing up whether or not I'd dare take such a chance. There was still very little on the road. On the opposite pavement, the sun had touched the windows of a car showroom so that it appeared to be on fire. It was going to be a beautiful day. I wondered if Tony had slept: if he was up yet or whether he'd spent the night in some police station. But it was too painful to think about Tony: I couldn't bear to think about his pain. I had a sudden, a desperate longing to be sitting at a hotel table with him eating croissants and drinking coffee, but I cut it out: as soon as it came I sliced it away and concentrated hard on emptiness and on thinking about nothing.

'I am ill,' I reminded myself as I crossed to the far pavement. 'Very ill.'

Several cars passed me, one after the other. I stuck my hand out in an ambiguous gesture, so that if one of them stopped I could still change my mind at the last moment and pretend I was waving to someone. They all drove past. Ahead I could see a large signpost. I cupped my hands over my eyes and strained to see what it said. Toulouse, I read. A car drew in to the kerb beside me, a French car with one driver. I panicked.

'No,' I said, as the driver leaned across and opened the door.

My French deserted me completely. 'No, I'm sorry. It was a mistake.'

'You're English?' She looked very young. She had short, spiky blonde hair and wore jeans and a denim jacket. 'Where are you going?' she asked.

I had no idea. 'Toulouse,' I said. It was the first place that came into my head.

'I can take you as far as Figeac,' she said, 'if that's any use.'

The fact that she was a woman made the whole thing possible, even respectable. And because she was English she was unlikely to have seen a French paper. It seemed a piece of enormous good luck, as if it were meant, as if it were yet another in the train of significant events.

'Thank you,' I said and got in beside her. She watched while I settled, her hand on the gear. I thought perhaps she was regretting her impulse. I could see her wondering if I was all right, or if I might after all turn out to be dangerous. I smiled at her.

'Toulouse?' she said, letting out the clutch.

'Yes,' I said. 'To see my sister.' I thought a sister might reassure her. It reassured me. I've always wanted a sister. In dreams I often have one. When I was small she inhabited other parts of my life as well as my dreams. I even mentioned her to people, but they either laughed or looked uncomfortable so I gave that up. Sometimes I hear myself saying to strangers, 'Oh really? Yes, that's what my sister thinks', or 'How funny, my sister likes that too.' But this has nothing to do with the sister who inhabits my dreams. This is more to do with needing someone on whom to project experimental ideas. If I'm not certain what response is expected of me, I test the water by dipping an imaginary sister into it. What I would really have liked is to have had *two* sisters. I would have liked to have been the third, the youngest, the one who made all the right choices and won all the consequent good fortune.

The spiky blonde woman in denim nodded and drew out into the traffic.

I sat back and let myself be driven. An industrial zone streaked past us – blocks of flats, prefabricated supermarkets, Intermarché, Leclerc, Magazin But.

'Can you map read?' she asked. 'Only as soon as we're out of Paris I want to get off this road.'

There was a Michelin book of maps on the back seat.

'Where do you want to head for first?' I asked.

'Orleans.'

I found Orleans on the map and then looked for Figeac. I hoped it was a long, long way away, an eternity away, so I could stay in the safety of the car for hours. 'How long does it take to get to Figeac?' I asked.

'It depends,' she said. 'Are you in a hurry?'

She was concentrating on overtaking a lorry. She drove fast, hovering too close to things she wanted to overtake, but I wasn't frightened. She zoomed past the lorry. Ahead the road was clear and opening out into flat countryside.

'No hurry at all,' I said.

'I'm Chris,' she said, when we were on the minor road. 'Chris Masbou.'

'Masbou? What's that? Is that French?'

She nodded. She was older than I thought. At first I'd assumed she was about nineteen or twenty, but I could see now that her hair was dyed and she had a haggard, slightly battered look. Her skin was drawn and tired. I revised my opinion of her age. 'My father was French,' she said. 'I'm not.'

'Marina,' I mumbled in return. It wasn't, of course, my real name. Not, at any rate, the name people knew me by. It was the name I used to call myself in fantasies when I was a child. 'James,' I added. 'Marina James'. I made the James bit up as well. It feels like a clean, firm, empty name to me. It carries nothing with it. I do have a name, of course. Everyone does. But it's never really fitted me. 'Marina James,' I say to strangers in trains, knowing I'll never see them again. I don't do it very well. I can see they're not convinced. I have a proper surname too. Except it's really my father's name so it doesn't count as anything very personal. And then, when my father died and my mother remarried, it was my stepfather's name. And later still, when I married, it was my husband's name, so it was never really mine. I never think of it as mine.

Hurriedly, before she could make any comment, I asked, 'Are you on holiday or business?'

'A bit of both,' she said. She jabbed her finger at the open page of the map. 'I want to get off the N20,' she said. 'I don't want to go through any big towns. No towns at all, preferably. The thing is, I'm not used to a left-hand-drive car.'

I was surprised. She seemed very competent to me. She drove with casual and slightly aggressive skill. That was the thing that most struck me about her: her confidence. It was fine by me: I was happy to find the slowest and most tortuous route going. I relaxed back into my seat. The sun and my sense of encapsulated safety made me feel sleepy, but I concentrated hard on the map because I wanted to impress her. After a couple of hours we stopped in a small village for breakfast. She parked under trees outside the church and we crossed the square to a Café de Sport.

'I have no money,' I mumbled, with my head turned away so the girl who was serving wouldn't hear.

Chris was ordering coffee and croissants.

'What, none? You mean none at all?'

'Well, yes, but very little.'

'You have to eat,' she said reprovingly. The skin on her neck was lined and looked a little grubby. I revised my estimate of her age again. She must be at least thirty.

The café was full of men. At the end of the bar by the juke-box a man was taking some kind of bets, racing bets. We sat at the end of a full table. The man beside me was reading a paper. I hurt my eyes trying to read the headlines without moving my head. When the croissant came I ate it in three mouthfuls without tasting one of them.

'Do you want another?' Chris asked. She caught the girl's eye immediately. Her French sounded as easy and natural as if it were her native language.

'You speak French fluently?' I asked.

The idea seemed to surprise her. 'Good God, no. I speak it very badly. Do you?'

I shook my head.

'It's all right,' she said when the second croissant came. 'I'm paying.'

The man beside me drained his cup and started fiddling in his pocket for money. I willed him to leave the newspaper. I closed my eyes and willed him. Some young men at the next table turned round. They stared at me and whispered. I didn't know whether it was because they were intrigued at hearing English spoken or because they thought they'd recognised me, or even both. I pretended to drink so they couldn't see my face.

The man beside me stood up. 'Leave it,' I willed. And then in case that wouldn't work: '*Laissez-le*.'

He said goodbye to someone. He was rolling the newspaper up into a tube. A man who had just come in and was standing at the bar turned round. '*Ah, ça va?*' he said, his face lighting up. My man dropped the newspaper on the chair and edged himself out, his hand extended to shake hands with the man at the bar. I waited until neither of them was looking, then slid the paper on to my lap.

Chris was watching me. She was amused. 'We could have bought one,' she said.

'I don't usually do this sort of thing,' I said, feeling myself go red.

She laughed out loud. The young men turned round again, their eyes speculative. I stared at the paper in my lap.

'Excuse me,' I said. 'I have to go to the Ladies.'

It was one of those where you crouch over a hole. It smelt vile. I leafed frantically through the paper, my hands trembling. I had to force my eyes to look properly: they kept glazing with fear. There was nothing. No photograph, and as far as I could tell no article, not even two lines, not even 'English Woman Disappears in Paris.' Well, of course not, I thought, ripping through the pages again, to make sure. Of course not. It's too soon. It will be in tomorrow.

When I got back, Chris was paying the bill. I leaned against the wall by the juke-box, sleepy with relief, and waited for her. I was still safe. For another whole day I was safe.

We drove on as before, through flat wheatfields. There were poppies all along the side of the road. 'I thought poppies grew on blood,' I said.

'Blood?' she said. 'No, just where the land's been disturbed. It doesn't matter how. They just grow anyway.'

This seemed to me such a large view of things that I smiled at her. 'Thank you,' I said. And then added hurriedly, 'For breakfast. And for the lift. Thank you very much.'

She smiled dismissively as if I'd said something stupid, which I had. 'I needed a map reader,' she said.

'Yes, but I don't usually do this sort of thing. Hitch lifts from strangers.'

'I can tell,' she said.

And that was all we said for miles, except for 'Bear left at the next fork', or 'Straight over at the crossroads.' I wasn't sure whether I found her silence peaceful or unnerving. I could see she was one of these totally confident people who know about everything: how to overtake lorries, how to order breakfast in a French café, the habits of wild flowers. I couldn't think of anything interesting to say. Every so often, I glanced at her. In profile her face was sharply defined as if somebody had cut it out with a razor. That was how I wanted to look. I wanted to be small and have spiky hair and skin pulled tautly over a fine bone structure. I wanted to wear old jeans and a denim jacket, and even with a slightly grubby neck, *still* manage to make everybody else look wrong.

'Is there any way,' she said, after a long silence, 'to get across the Loire without going through somewhere big?'

It was clear that she'd picked me up not for my company but as a navigator; and as I badly wanted her to like me, I gave the problem serious thought. I managed to get us across the river and out into open country again without going through the centre of anywhere. The landscape changed. Some miles south of the river we passed one of the minor châteaux, a private one almost completely hidden among trees. There was a brief glimpse of the whole frontage: white stone, and fairy-tale turrets with silvered roofs.

'Oh,' I said, craning my neck, enchanted by it, and consequently lost my place on the map. 'Left,' I said when I meant right; and the road petered out in the cobbled yard of a farm. I was very flustered. I expected Chris to be irritated with me, but she shrugged it off as an amusing mistake, the sort of thing that might happen to anyone.

'The fact is,' I said, while she was expertly reversing at speed out of the lane, and because my navigational error had reminded me uncomfortably of Tony, 'the fact is I've just left my husband.'

Saying it out loud, defining what I had done, made my gut grow hot and loosen with fear.

'I thought there was something,' she said. Well, of course she had. People like me do not hang about in the industrial suburbs of Paris without any luggage at six o'clock in the morning waiting to hitch a lift. 'Your sister in Toulouse,' she added, 'will you stay with her or go back to England?'

'I don't know,' I said. 'She has problems of her own.' (Chief among which was her insubstantiality.) 'She has three children,' I added, as a detail which might pin her down a little.

'Two girls and a boy.'

'It's a nice place, Toulouse,' said Chris, and we lapsed into silence again until, when my train of thought was on something else altogether she said, 'You're very lucky. I always wanted a sister.'

'I always wanted a sister too,' I said, witlessly.

She turned and looked at me. 'You've got one.'

'No, I mean another one,' I said. 'I always wanted there to be three of us.'

It was true. Once upon a time there were three sisters, and the youngest sister was good, and unfailingly selfless and obedient, and worked hard, and had tiny feet and consequently, as always happens, married the prince and lived happily ever after in a castle with pepper-pot towers. I like that story. I always have.

At about half-past four Chris said, 'Do you mind if we stop for a bit?'

The roads were becoming increasingly tortuous, bend after bend through thick woodland and low, humped hills. She turned off on to a sandy forest track and drove a little way down until the road was out of sight.

'I didn't sleep much last night,' she said. She adjusted her seat until it was almost flat, screwed up her jacket for a pillow, settled herself and closed her eyes. 'Wake me if anyone comes.'

I assumed she meant if a tractor came and she needed to move the car.

'Yes, OK,' I said.

She fell asleep almost at once. I didn't know what to do. I had to do something to stop myself from thinking. I flipped through the book of maps and then watched Chris's face as she slept. The mascara on her eyelashes was smudged and had gathered in gritty black deposits along the creases of skin on her eyelids. Tony had once told me that small creatures live in one's eyelashes, or was it in one's eyebrows, anyway creatures large enough sometimes to be seen by the naked eye. I studied Chris's eyelashes hard in the hope of seeing something move there, but nothing did. I thought that we were like huge walking cities, like continents, like densely populated planets spinning in empty space. Bigger fleas have lesser fleas, etc., etc., and so on *ad infinitum* on a scale which has no beginning and no end, which grows from an infinity of minuteness and disappears into an infinity of vastness. In which case, I thought, nothing that I did or didn't do, or wanted or didn't want, could possibly matter very much in the scale of things. The fact that I had no money, no passport, no idea of what I was doing, or how I'd ever get myself back to reality again – all this, on the scale of infinity, was too trivial to make any mark at all.

I watched the seconds on the car clock change. How long a second was. I yawned and tried to make myself comfortable. I told myself I was exhausted, but it was impossible to sleep. My mind tore from one thing to another. I could think of a hundred things and all their possible permutations in the time it took for one second to give way to another. The sun burned through the car window. I opened the door quietly and slid out. I had this obsession with movement: I couldn't sit still. I left the track and started walking into the wood where the grass was long and soft and brilliantly green in the clearings. Above me the leaves glittered and shook in the sun. I walked deeper and deeper into the wood. The grass grew sparser. Dead leaves shuffled under my feet. I thought if I walked far enough I would come to the end, but always ahead the slim white perpendicular trunks stretched into the distance. So I carried on walking, on and on, disturbing birds and ripping my white skirt on the thickening brambles, and I thought about ends and beginnings and other metaphysical inanities, which at least stopped me from having to think about anything relevant.

After a while, it occurred to me that I'd been walking for a very long time and was probably lost. The word 'lost' fascinated me. It was a terrifying and seductive word. 'I am lost,' I whispered, listening to the meaning of it. It seemed to excuse everything, because it implied that none of it was my fault. It implied an inconceivable kind of freedom. More comfortingly, it implied the possibility of being found if the freedom grew too frightening. A kindly forester might eventually find me asleep on a bed of leaves and carry me away to his cottage where he'd wrap me in blankets and feed me on bread and milk and other childish things. And everybody would be so pleased and relieved to have found me – by 'everybody' I meant Tony – that they'd forget to ask what on earth I was doing there alone in a French wood, 200 miles or so south of Paris.

I was deeply involved in this fantasy when, pushing my way through a thick patch of brambles, I suddenly found myself right back on exactly the same stretch of sandy track I'd set off from. I was only about fifty yards away from the car. It was hard to know whether the discovery that I'd been walking round in a huge circle was a relief or a disappointment. Chris was still asleep, her mouth open and a small trail of silvery dribble on her chin.

'Oh God,' she said, jumping awake. She blinked in a confused way for a moment until she'd grasped who I was. For a moment she looked quite frightened. 'Oh God,' she said, 'what time is it?'

'Five to seven.'

'Shit.'

She backed the car down the track and we drove to the next small town, to eat. She stopped at what I thought was just a garage with a forecourt of parked lorries, but next to the garage was a seedy looking Relais Routier. She strode in as if she'd known the place all her life, as if it belonged to her, so I followed. Heads turned. The room was full of men: drivers, sitting at long, oilcloth-covered tables. I'd never been in such a place. Tony and I went to restaurants with names like Le Lion D'or and candles on the table and red checked curtains in the window, anonymous places with what Tony called 'local colour'.

'All right?' Chris said. 'Here?'

She sat down and started fiddling with the salt cellar and looking round.

'Fine,' I said. Why not? Everything was in her hands now. I'd given up until we reached Figeac. Until then I'd just sit back and let things happen.

Chris ordered two pastis. 'Drink it,' she said. 'It'll do you good.' She poured water into my glass and the mixture went cloudy. I liked the way she decided things for me, it made me feel safe, so I drank, although I loathe aniseed, and immediately I felt light-headed: it was as if I were observing everything through glass.

With the meal we had a *pichet* of red wine. '*Vin compris*' it said on the stained piece of card on which the set meal was handwritten in indecipherable, looped French. I grew warmer. I began to enjoy the steamy atmosphere: I liked the way the pan of soup was taken from table to table, I liked the noise of the men's voices, the sound of the coffee machine, the clink of glasses, the laughter. I liked being with Chris. After the crudités and the soup we ate rabbit in mustard sauce. Chris ordered another *pichet* of wine. She kept refilling our glasses.

After a while everything she said seemed funny. I remember I laughed a lot. Every so often, I had a vague twinge of memory about something I knew I would prefer to forget, but I never allowed it to grow beyond that: I never let the thought grow big enough to be identified. If it squirmed I took another mouthful of wine and drowned it at birth. Somebody put a record on the juke-box. Happiness swelled inside me until I couldn't tell whether it was happiness or food that was making me feel so full.

'Normally, you see, I would never set foot inside a place like this,' I explained to Chris. It was only her presence there that made mine possible at all.

'You keep saying that,' she said. 'You keep saying you never do things.'

'Because I don't,' I said. I leant back in my chair and looked

♦ 24 ♦

round the restaurant with interest. I had the protection of complete passivity. It was all her responsibility, not mine. She was in charge. 'I would never dare,' I said, 'not by myself.'

Halfway through the second *pichet*, I wondered briefly if she was planning to drive on afterwards, and was about to ask her about it when she filled my glass again and I forgot.

'Oh no,' I said. 'No more. Really.' But I didn't mean it, and she knew I didn't. We smiled at each other.

'So – you've left your husband?' she asked.

'Yes,' I said. My cheeks ached. I had to control a powerful desire to laugh. I was determined not to laugh unless she said something intentionally funny. It seemed to me that to laugh at nothing would be a sure sign that I was drunk. Or mad. Or both. 'Yes,' I said. 'In the rue François Premier.'

'The rue François Premier?' she repeated in amazement. 'And is he still there?'

Tears poured down my face. Wine regurgitated up my nose. 'I don't know,' I said, almost hysterical with laughter. 'I don't know.'

Faces turned to look, eyes stared, mouths opened.

Chris wiped her eyes with the back of her hand. 'God,' she said, 'the details of life are so ridiculous.'

I nodded.

'And you just walked out on him with nothing?' We had begun to calm down. There was that flat moment after laughter when nobody knows quite how to follow it. 'When was that?' she asked.

'Yesterday.'

'So that's why you look such a mess.'

'I am a mess,' I said.

She looked at me sharply. 'No, I mean your skirt and everything,' she said. 'You'd better borrow something of mine.'

'I wouldn't fit into anything of yours.'

'I'll find you something. You can't turn up at your sister's looking like that.'

'The truth is,' I said, my voice trembling on the edge of laughter again, 'the truth is I haven't got a sister.'

'Yes, you have,' she said. 'In Toulouse.'

'No, I haven't. It was a lie.'

The *patronne's* daughter brought cheese and left it on the table for us. Chris cut herself a sliver from a piece that looked like a black triangle dusted in icing sugar.

'Have some cheese,' she said and I cut myself a piece of everything because I didn't know what to choose: I wanted everything.

'So where *are* you going?' she said.

'Nowhere. I don't know.'

'I'd ask you to come and stay with me for a bit – ' she said.

This was not at all what I meant. 'Oh no,' I said, mumbling with embarrassment. 'No, really. Please don't think ... I didn't mean ... '

' ... but I'm staying with relatives myself. So I can't really ... '

'No, of course not.'

'Only the thing is,' she said, 'I don't really know them.'

'Your relatives?' I was confused.

'Well, I know them, of course, but not very well. We used to come over on holiday until my father died, and then ... ' She speared a piece of cheese and ate it. 'I was about eight. I haven't seen them since. Except my Uncle Gaston. I see him sometimes.'

Two drivers came in with a young woman wearing tight jeans and scuffed white high heels. She was very pretty. She had blonde hair which was piled carelessly on top of her head. Darker tendrils escaped down her neck. She was very aware of herself.

'Otherwise,' said Chris, 'there'd have been no problem.'

She turned and stared in the direction I was looking, at the blonde girl who was talking in a loud voice, showing off, twining her arm round the neck of one of the men she had come in with.

'Prostitute,' said Chris, turning back.

'Pardon?' I said.

'She's a prostitute. She works the routes.'

'You *know* her?'

Chris laughed. 'No, of course I don't know her. I just know what she is. It's obvious.'

I had a very good view of the girl from where I sat. I watched her covertly.

'So what are you going to do?' Chris asked.

'I don't know.' I didn't want to think about these things now. 'I had thought,' I said, to put her off, 'of going to Corsica.'

'Corsica?'

'I saw a poster. It looked nice.'

'It is nice,' she said. She seemed to know about everywhere: Toulouse, Corsica ... 'You could hitch down to Marseilles and get a boat. It wouldn't be difficult.'

'Yes, it would,' I said. 'It would be impossible. I've got no money.'

'Oh, money.' She dismissed money as if it were the least of anyone's problems.

'And no passport,' I added, which seemed to me to be a pretty well insuperable obstacle. 'My husband's got everything like that.'

The *patronne's* daughter came to offer us dessert. She hovered at the table and then shyly asked us if we were English. She said she was studying English at school.

'No, Dutch,' Chris said smoothly. 'We're Dutch.'

I stared at her in surprise.

'Oh, I'm sorry. I thought I heard you speaking English,' said the daughter in French. She was embarrassed.

'We were, yes,' said Chris. 'We practise a lot. We're translators. From Arnhem.'

'Why on earth did you tell her that?' I asked when the daughter had gone to get our ice-creams.

Chris shrugged. 'Because I didn't want her practising her English on us.'

Her instant ability to put someone off the track made me laugh. 'I do that too,' I said, but she seemed not to hear. She slouched back in her chair, her fingertips in her jeans pocket, and looked at me speculatively.

'So tell me about yourself,' she said. 'Who are you?'

What an impossible question. No one had ever asked me that before. She rephrased the question. 'What do you do?'

I considered lying, but I was too drunk to have instant access to my usual stock of lies. I could have told her that I ran a small carpet-cleaning business, which is a story I sometimes tell strangers in trains, but I didn't. What *do* I do? I get up, I live through the day, I go to bed, I dream. Sometimes I get the living and the dreaming muddled. Time passes. Nothing seems very real. I clean the house and cook. I take up hobbies and drop them. I work. The truth, is – and this *is* the truth, although it feels just as unlikely as anything else – the truth is I am a secretary. I work for a firm of accountants: but I certainly didn't want to admit this to Chris. I didn't want her to know that I was nothing more than a housewife on the one hand and a secretary on the other. 'What do *you* do?' I asked instead.

'Commodities,' she said. 'I'm a commodity broker.'

I nodded. That made sense. That would account for her easy confidence, and her knowledge of how the world worked. 'You must be very clever,' I said. She started to talk about her work, but my eyes had wandered away to where the blonde girl was making a lot of noise about what chair she was going to sit in.

'She fascinates you, doesn't she?' Chris said.

'Is she really a prostitute?' I asked. In England I would have whispered it, but in a foreign country one has a certain immunity: one can speak very freely.

'You're going to say you've never seen a prostitute before,' Chris said. 'Where've you been all your life?' As if mixing with prostitutes and hitching lifts and eating in seedy restaurants were the norm, as if this was what everybody did.

'In Hanley,' I said, slightly piqued.

'Hanley? Where's that?'

The *patronne's* daughter brought our ice-cream.

'If you want a passport,' Chris remarked casually, licking her spoon, 'I might be able to sort something out for you. Have you got any travellers' cheques on you?'

I shook my head.

'Credit cards?'

The blonde girl, the prostitute, was sitting with her two escorts at a table near the door. I could only see the movement of her head as she fawned over one of them, ruffled his hair, whispered in his ear.

'But if I use my credit cards surely I can be traced,' I protested.

Chris's eyes opened wide. 'By whom? By your husband? So what? By the time he catches up, you'll be miles away.'

Despite all I'd eaten, a hollow feeling was opening up in my stomach.

'And anyway,' Chris was saying, 'if he does catch up with you, so what? You're a free agent.'

'No,' I said. 'I don't think I am.'

'Of course you are,' she said impatiently.

'What exactly do you mean "a passport"?' I asked.

'What do you think I mean?'

The truth was I didn't know. 'A forgery?' I suggested.

'Forget it,' she said.

She ordered a cognac with her coffee. I sat there, snubbed, my cheeks burning. I hunted blindly in my bag for the remaining 100-franc note.

'Oh, for goodness's sake,' she said crossly. 'Put it away. This is on me.'

'You bought breakfast,' I protested.

'So what?' She drank the brandy in quick gulps. 'Well, whatever you decide to do, you really can't do it looking like that.' She drained her coffee cup and stood up. 'Wait here. I won't be long.'

She walked across to the bar to pay the bill and then went

out into the darkness. I played with the idea of being abandoned: I imagined I heard an engine starting, I imagined Chris driving away without me. I waited, stirring a spoon round my empty coffee cup. On my face was a glazed, self-consciously pensive smile. I was wondering whether I'd dare accept a lift from any of these drivers. It was a kind of solution. It had a certain logic. I could spend my life driving up and down France, going nowhere in particular, round and round in continuous circles, accepting hospitality from lorry drivers. When Chris came back, which of course eventually she did, she was carrying a loose black bundle. 'Go and put those on,' she said. 'The skirt's got an elasticated waist. It might fit. I'll wait for you in the car.'

Standing up was quite difficult. After the first dizzying warmth of the pastis it felt as if the more I drank the more sober I became: but when I tried to get to my feet, the room reeled and I had to grab the table to steady myself. I fixed my eye on the door marked '*Toilettes*' and would not allow myself to be sidetracked by anything other than the necessity of reaching it without stumbling or drawing attention to myself. There was no one else in there. I glanced in the mirror. My face looked blurred and distorted and alarmingly pale. My hair was wild. I leant forward so that my face and my reflection were almost touching to see if things were any better in close-up, but then I couldn't find the whole of my face, only parts of it – a huge bloodshot eye, a squashed, pitted piece of skin, a black nostril with a string of mucus caught on a hair. I backed away. I threw water over it all, cold water from the tap, and kept my eyes shut so that I wouldn't have to look at it any more until I was safely locked in the toilet. I peed for what seemed like an age: I thought it would never stop. My white skirt was ripped, stained with wine, and badly creased. It smelt stale. I took it off and put on Chris's skirt. The elasticated waist stretched almost to breaking point. A black T-shirt fell out of the bundle. I pulled off my blouse. There was no bin, so I rolled my discarded clothes into a ball and pushed them into the corner.

When I unlocked the door and came out, the blonde girl, the prostitute, was standing in front of the mirror rearranging her hair while she waited. I didn't know whether or not I should speak to her. I didn't know what she would expect. I smiled nervously at her reflection. 'Pardon,' I said. I stood beside her with my handbag perched on the wash-basin, and took out my bag of make-up. She said something in her husky voice, something in French that I didn't understand.

'Pardon?' I said again, this time apologising not for being so long in the loo, but for not understanding. I hoped she grasped the difference. 'Je suis anglaise,' I added, just in case.

'Anglaise, uh?' She laughed. I was still very nervous. I patted my swollen, pale face with powder. It looked worse. I brushed my cheeks with blusher. My reflection grew more grotesque. She smiled at herself. I watched her in the mirror, touched by her prettiness. She had the most perfect teeth. I couldn't reconcile the way she looked with anything else about her: her raucous voice, her loudness, the way she earned her living.

Our reflected eyes met. I looked away hurriedly and took my comb out of my bag. She slid past me in the narrow space to the lavatory and said something else I couldn't catch. Her body brushed against mine.

Instead of going in and shutting the door behind her she stood there in the opening and repeated whatever it was she had just said. I felt myself growing hot. 'Je ne comprends pas,' I said.

'Vos vêtements.' She pointed to them, a shameful little bundle in the corner.

'Ah, oui,' I said. 'Yes.' I wanted to explain that I had left them there intentionally, that I didn't need them any more, but I got confused with all the pronouns. She looked at me with faint disgust, as if she had caught me out in some socially unacceptable practice, so I found myself forced into the humiliating position of pretending that I'd forgotten the clothes were there. 'Merci, Mademoiselle,' I said, assuming effusive gratitude. I squeezed past her to pick up the bundle. A switch clicked: sudden darkness. 'Bon soir, Madame,' she called cheerfully. A door banged. I knew immediately what had happened. And if my head hadn't been so thick and heavy, if I hadn't stumbled against the door, I might perhaps have run after her and stopped her. Or perhaps not. I don't know. It didn't seem very important. I found the switch and turned the light on again. My handbag, which had been sitting open on the wash-basin, had gone. I washed my hands, and wondered idly what I was supposed to do without any money at all and without any make-up.

When I went back into the restaurant there was of course no sign of the girl or of the two drivers. Outside, in the lorry park, Chris was leaning against her car looking green in the neon lighting from the garage sign.

'You took a hell of a time,' she said.

'My bag's been stolen,' I told her in a matter-of-fact way.

She peered at me. 'Your what?'

'That girl – the one you said was a prostitute – she stole my bag.'

'Cheeky bitch,' Chris said. 'I saw them go. She said bon soir to me.'

'It doesn't matter. It didn't have anything in it,' I said. 'A hundred francs. My library ticket. Some make-up.'

'And your credit cards.'

She slammed her door shut and started the engine. 'Get in,' she said. The tyres skidded on the gravel.

'Are you all right to drive?' I asked.

'Are you suggesting I'm not?' She turned the lights on. Ahead, the trees bent curiously over the road. The air smelt sharp and cool. Pale moths fluttered towards the headlights and smashed themselves against the windscreen. I felt very sad. I rolled down my window at some point and tossed the bundle of stale-smelling clothes into the hedge.

'Actually,' said Chris, 'I feel a bit sick.' She sat forward in her seat, clutching the wheel and peering hard out of the windscreen as if she couldn't see. 'All those fucking trees,' she said.

I found it hard to follow the map and read the road signs in the dark. I kept losing my place. 'Left or right?' Chris said.

'I don't know,' I said. 'One or the other.' This made her laugh. It never made Tony laugh.

We turned left and the road rapidly disintegrated into a rutted lane and disappeared into a field. It was impossible to turn. Chris made a mess of reversing the car. 'Shit,' she said. She drove far too fast back down the lane. The car bumped and lurched into potholes and over dried tractor treads. I braced myself against the dashboard.

'You're driving too fast,' I told her.

'If you don't like the way I drive, get out,' she said.

The car lurched up over the bank. There was a bang, and then a violent scraping noise as the side of the car hit and bounced off a stone wall.

'Oh hell,' said Chris. 'What now?'

She stopped the car and got out to examine the damage, touching the crumpled metal gently as if it were bruised flesh. A long series of white scratches ran the length of the side.

'I'll drive,' I said.

'Oh, that's something you *have* done before, is it?' she said nastily. She let her body collapse against the bonnet. 'The trouble is, I'm so tired.'

The trouble was she had drunk too much but I didn't say so. I had drunk almost as much myself, but the cold air had sharpened my mind, and the loss of my handbag made me feel pleasantly light and insubstantial. I wore black clothes and had no possessions at all, nothing to pin me down. I was part of the darkness. 'Let me drive,' I said.

I had never driven a left-hand-drive car before and it felt odd: I had to think about what I was doing. I drove with exaggerated care to the end of the lane and turned left. I concentrated on the road ahead, on the small section of it I could see at any one time, like a chicken hypnotised by a ribbon of chalk.

'I ought to turn off somewhere,' I said to Chris. 'If we keep going this way we'll hit the N20 again.' But Chris was asleep, her head flopped on her chest. I remember very clearly thinking that this was ridiculous: we were neither of us fit to drive and I had no idea where I was going. I remember deciding that as soon as I came to a suitable place, I would stop the car and we could both sleep until the morning. But almost at once I saw the 'Stop at 50 metres' sign, and there ahead was the N20 with a huge sign pointing to Limoges in one direction and Toulouse in the other, so I turned towards Toulouse. The road was straight and wide and I lost all sense of the strangeness of a left-hand-drive car, all sense of nervousness. The speedometer rose. I had no idea what speed I was doing because it was in kilometres per hour but it felt fast and very free and quite safe. I overtook cars, I overtook caravans, I overtook lorries. I laughed out loud because I thought maybe the girl who had stolen my bag was sitting up in the cab of one of those lorries cursing me because she'd got nothing but a grubby make-up bag and a 100-franc note. I was passing an oil tanker and still laughing to myself, when there was a sudden appalling bang, a noise like the world exploding, and then the car slipped away from me as if the road had turned to ice, and slithered and spun out of my control. Oh dear, I thought, dispassionately and inappropriately. It happened so fast I had no time to think anything else. Except that the very last moment, when I was blinded by the lights of the oncoming lorry, lasted it seemed for years. For years and years. It wasn't, if you're interested in these things, a matter of one's life flashing before one's eyes – flashing is entirely the wrong word. It was, in fact, very leisurely. But nor was it the strange, slow-motion explosion of glass and metal and fragments of body that you see on films. It wasn't like that at all. The last moment extended for so long that I had time to think about Tony and how the police would have to tell him that I was dead, and about the irony of dying now after such a good meal. I even had time to laugh a little at my absurd metaphysical speculations earlier on in the day about there being no such thing on the infinite scale of things as beginnings and ends, which was particularly funny because here it was. Without any ambivalence or room for quibbling, here it was. This was it. The End.

◆ Limbo ◆

The place where I finally found myself – after a long time of being nowhere at all – was completely white. I lay cocooned in whiteness.

No, that's confusing. First, I ought to explain what happened. What happened was this: travelling at about 90 miles an hour on the N20 north of Cahors we had a blow-out. The bump against the stone wall had fatally weakened the tyre. The car skidded and came to a sideways halt on the opposite carriage-way directly in the path of an oncoming juggernaut. Chris, who was sleeping, was killed on impact. She probably never even woke up. Her thin, tough body was sliced almost in half and her head and shoulders crushed into a splintered pulp. I had forgotten, of course, to put my seat belt on, a piece of characteristic forgetfulness which in this case probably saved my life: I was catapulted through the smashed windscreen, and landed on the road inches away from the wheels of the juggernaut, which ploughed on for another hundred yards, pushing the hire car ahead of it out on to the verge. I lay unconscious on the tarmac, bruised, cut, broken, but alive.

The following day – though of course I knew nothing about this at the time: I only learned about it much later, piecing the facts together from old newspapers and magazines – the following day, a woman by the name of Dominique Vayrac was arrested in Poitiers for trying to obtain money with a stolen Mastercard. The name on the Mastercard had attracted the attention of an alert bank teller. Over his breakfast coffee, he'd just been reading about the disappearance of an Englishwoman on holiday in Paris. Later in the same day, a farmer found a bundle of clothes in a hedge. These were subsequently identified by the Englishwoman's husband as being those his wife was wearing on the day she disappeared.

Mlle Dominique Vayrac, who described herself as a 'touring artiste', told the police that she had found the credit cards in a handbag which she claimed to have discovered in the lorry park of a restaurant about nine kilometres away from where the clothes were discovered. The bag had been thrown on to some waste land, she said. She denied absolutely having stolen it. She also denied ever having seen the Englishwoman to whom the cards belonged.

The *patronne* of the restaurant remembered two foreign women coming in to eat on the Friday night, but she was sure they were Dutch. The police showed her a passport photo of the missing woman. She wasn't sure, she said: it could have been the same person, but to tell the truth she'd been too busy to take much notice, and anyway she was fairly certain that the two women she remembered were sisters. The police asked her what gave her that impression. Had they said they were sisters?

No, she said.

Did they look alike?

No, but then sisters don't necessarily, do they? No, it was something else about them, but she couldn't put her finger on it. Anyway, they weren't English. They were Dutch. The daughter, who had served them, confirmed this. They came from Arnhem, she said.

Well then, could either one of them have stolen the Englishwoman's handbag? the police asked.

It's possible. They certainly behaved very oddly.

In what way?

The *patronne* was hard put to explain in what way they had behaved oddly. It seemed to boil down to the fact that they had laughed a lot.

A police search was immediately mounted in the Limoges area. Rivers and ponds were dragged. The press maintained a morbid interest in the outcome of these activities for several weeks.

In this white place where I found myself, I floated quietly. I smiled and kept my arms folded on my chest. My hair drifted behind me. Somewhere in the distance was a beautiful noise. I was never quite sure whether it was voices singing, or some sort of orchestra. I don't think I consciously identified the noise as music. I don't think I identified it as anything. It was simply, almost unbearably beautiful. Occasionally I was aware that something hurt, but I wasn't sure what. I wasn't sure whether it was an actual pain or whether it was a deep sadness, or whether it was something to do with the exquisite nature of the noise, but it never lasted long.

Once I heard a voice say quite clearly, 'Miss Masbou?' but I was so far away that I didn't bother to answer. Anyway, it wasn't my name, so why should I? They weren't talking to me. My name was something quite different. I tried to think what it was and couldn't remember. It didn't matter. I didn't need one.

Another time when I was drifting quietly down a long reedy stream, I came without any warning to a shallow pebbly stretch: my back scraped along sharp stones, along jagged, razor-edged rocks. A sudden excruciating pain shot through my body from my neck to my feet. I cried out. I was outraged. But then distantly I heard the sound that might have been singing, and the stream grew deeper again until it was a dark pool where I floated gently through streaming weed and let the water warm and soothe me.

Once I remember catching in my mind a small frond of thought, a name: Tony. But it meant nothing to me and I let it disentangle itself and drift away into the dark water, where it sank.

It was very pleasant, this mindless, gentle state of perpetual drifting. I was very happy. I lay almost on the bottom of the deep pool, below the currents, below any possibility of movement, resting quietly on a bed of feathery weed, where I was dreamily suspended in time, when suddenly, and entirely against my will, I began to rise, slowly at first and then faster and faster until I was shooting uncontrollably upwards through the water. The pain of being forced against the tug of gravity was more than I could bear. I didn't want this: I wanted to go on floating with my hands folded on my chest and my hair trailing behind me. In my fury at being disturbed, I kicked and thrashed and fought, but on I went dizzyingly spiralling upwards. I opened my mouth to shout and it filled with water. I spat and choked. The pain was an intolerable pressure over my entire body. I thought I would burst. There was a breaking noise like glass shattering, and I shot through the surface and lay flapping on a bed as dry and hot as fire.

I was in a vast white room, a room with high walls sloping wildly upwards into infinity, a room as immeasurably vast as my pain. In fact it seemed to me that the room *was* my pain; it precisely measured its boundaries. A woman in black was walking towards me from the door, and every step she took across that interminable distance was agony to me. I closed my eyes and concentrated on floating. On flying. On anything but this unbearable solidity.

'*Doucement*,' the woman said softly. '*Doucement*.'

I opened my eyes and tried to focus on her, to see who it was, but the effort was too exhausting. She took my wrist in her hand. It hung limply and very far away. Wires and tubes trailed from it into distant machines. I wept with pain as if I were a child, as if weeping would make someone with the power to take the pain away sorry for me. I cried for my mother who was long buried. I wanted someone to come with hot-water bottles and comfort, but no one came. I cried because after all I was still there; second after intolerable second I was still there; because I had lost the beautiful sounds and the ability to float; because I couldn't bear so much pain.

Much later a man in a white coat appeared.

'Good evening,' he said. 'How do you feel?'

He spoke in English, but it didn't help. The meanings of words took so long to register; they made such curious juxtapositions. 'How do you feel?' What an absurd and touching series of sounds. I repeated them to myself.

How do I feel? I feel with every part of my skin, with my ears, with my throat, with my tongue. I feel with my gut, with my bones, with the hairs on my arms ...

He touched me on the hand. 'Miss Masbou?' he said. 'Are you awake?'

'No,' I said, denying that my name was Masbou.

He sat down. The noise of the chair scraping on the wooden floor made even my teeth hurt.

He sat there in silence for a moment. Slowly he began to come into focus.

'Do you remember what happened?' he asked after a while.

I wanted to speak but I had trouble making the words come. The only word that seemed available to me was no.

'You were in an accident,' he explained. 'Forgive me, I should, of course, introduce myself. Dr Verdoux. Guy Verdoux.' He spoke slowly as if he understood my difficulty. 'A car accident,' he said. 'You were driving a car you hired in Calais. Do you remember that?'

'No,' I said, denying that I had ever hired a car in Calais.

'One of the tyres blew. You skidded.'

'Yes,' I said. This bit at least was right.

He seemed pleased. He patted my hand.

With enormous effort I started to ask a question. 'The girl ... ' I began.

'Miss Hughes. Yes. Was she ... ?' He paused and cleared his throat. 'Did you know her?'

'No,' I said, distressed at all this nonsense, this muddle of words which meant nothing. Who was Miss Hughes? Who on earth was he talking about? He must have got two separate accidents muddled up. 'No, not ... No ... '

'Katherine Hughes. Yes. She was travelling with you.' He nodded at me encouragingly.

'No,' I said. I tried to explain that it was the other way round, that I had hitched a lift. 'Hitched ... ' I said, although as soon as it appeared in my mouth the word sounded completely meaningless, ' ... hitched ... '

'Oh, I see. I see. She was a *hitch-hiker*.'

I began to get angry with him.

'No! I was the ... I ... '

'Take your time. It's all right. It's the drugs.'

His kindness made the tears well. I needed to talk to Chris. Chris would sort it out for me. I couldn't. I couldn't concentrate; the pain got in the way. I couldn't seem to make words work properly.

'Where is she?' I asked. I struggled to sit up, but nothing moved.

He patted my hand very gently and explained with exquisite tact, his eyes fixed on my knuckles, that unfortunately – he lowered his voice – unfortunately Miss Hughes had been killed in the accident.

'No,' I said, because this was getting ridiculous, this was getting completely out of hand, I was losing all grasp of what was happening. 'No, not Hughes. Chris. Chris Masbou.'

For some reason this response seemed to please him. 'Good,' he said. 'Well done.' He shone a tiny torch in my eyes and blinded me. A grey shape moved behind him. 'Sister Marie-Thérèse will give you something to make you sleep now.'

I closed my eyes. I didn't need anything to make me sleep. I was already exhausted.

'No,' I said, but no one seemed to be listening to me, and shortly afterwards the pain drained away. I became as light as air and rose from the bed and hovered high up above the furniture. When I next woke it was daylight. Overnight, the room had apparently grown smaller and the walls were now quite straight and ended properly, as walls should, in a ceiling. A nun sat in a chair near the window, sewing.

'Everything hurts,' I said to her indignantly. The pain had stopped being overwhelming and had become an unrelenting nuisance.

She turned to look at me. '*Je regrette, Madame, je ne parle pas anglais.*' She put down her sewing and left the room. A few moments later Dr Verdoux arrived. He was very young and had thin ginger hair, a detail I hadn't noticed before.

'Good morning,' he said. 'Are you feeling better?'

'Everything hurts,' I complained.

He examined the various machines to which I seemed to be wired and looked at the chart at the end of my bed. He pulled back the cover. I was swathed in bandages and plaster.

'Tell me exactly where it hurts,' he said.

That was simple enough. 'Everywhere,' I said.

'Good,' he said. It didn't seem at all good to me and I said so. He smiled and started digging his pen into my feet. 'So what I want you to do, Miss Masbou, is to tell me if you can feel this.'

'No,' I said, very firmly.

He looked alarmed. 'You can't feel it?'

'No, I mean my name is not Masbou. I'm not Chris Masbou.'

His pen hovered above my right foot. 'Not ... ?' He frowned. I couldn't understand why it was so difficult for him to grasp. It was so obvious. 'All right then,' he said after a moment, 'all right then, so what *is* your name?'

I opened my mouth to tell him, but nothing came. I couldn't remember. For the life of me, I couldn't remember what my own name was.

'Longer than Chris,' I said at last, which was as much as I could manage.

'That's right,' he said. 'Marie-Christine.'

'No. *She* was Chris ... the other woman.'

A worried look crumpled his face. 'I'm sorry, I don't understand you. Are you trying to tell me you're Katherine Hughes?'

'No, of course not.' For an intelligent man he was amazingly stupid. 'I've never heard of this Katherine Hughes.'

He touched my left foot very gently with the pen.

'Katherine Hughes was the girl who was in the car with you,' he said. The one who was killed. The hitch-hiker.'

This was all beyond me.

'It'll come back to you soon,' he said kindly.

I tried again, suddenly, without thinking. 'My name ... ' I began, but it was no use. I thought if I suddenly jumped out at it I might catch it unawares, but it simply wasn't there.

'Can you feel that?' he asked, running his nail along my sole.

'I can feel everything,' I said.

He sat on the bed and pulled my eyelids apart.

'Try again,' he said kindly, peering into my head. 'Tell me who you are.'

I shook my head. 'I don't know.' The tears gathered in my eyes.

'No, please, Mademoiselle, don't upset yourself,' he said. 'It's perfectly normal. It often happens with severe concussion. It'll all come back in a day or so.'

I smiled thinly at him through the tears.

'But the fact is,' he went on, 'your name *is* Marie-Christine Masbou. It's on your passport.'

This was even more confusing. 'Is it?' I said.

'Well, of course. That's how the police identified you. From the passport in your handbag – '

But I didn't have a passport. And surely I didn't have a handbag either: surely it had been stolen.

' – which they still have,' Dr Verdoux was saying as he examined my sore, swollen face.

'Can I get up?' I asked. I had begun to panic about what all this pain meant. Not only was he obviously a very good doctor, this ginger-headed young man, but he also spoke almost fault-less colloquial English and he understood the difference in meaning between 'can' and 'may'. He put his hands in his pockets and stared at his feet. He said he suspected there might be some lasting problems: probably not of mobility, he thought, although he couldn't yet be certain whether I'd recover a full range of movement; possibly of recurring pain; certainly of scarring. He cleared his throat. 'Well, anyway,' he said, 'we'll see how things go. The important thing is that you're still alive. You've been extraordinarily lucky.'

When he'd gone, I thought about that – about this business of still being alive. I felt distinctly *un*lucky. I much preferred the state of non-being, of floating quietly, of drifting. I liked having no weight, no guilt, no consciousness. How ironic that Chris, who seemed to find the burden of consciousness so much easier to carry than I did, had effortlessly, and by my agency, managed to achieve what I so longed to return to and couldn't. All afternoon I lay thinking about Chris, whose identity everybody but me seemed to have trouble in grasp-ing. I relived in my head our whole journey together. I'd forgotten nothing. I remembered in detail her sleeping face, her impatience with me, her thin legs striding into the res-taurant, her slightly grubby neck, her hands on the wheel. I thought about her confidence, her ability to cope with things, her assumption that the space she occupied was right-fully hers. All afternoon I mourned her. The curtains billowed away from the open windows: the sun warmed the pale, tiled floor: the nun sat with her head bowed and the needle moving in a slow, deliberate rhythm, and I mourned.

Later in the day they disconnected me from the machines and the tubes and the plastic bags which had kept me filled and emptied. They brought me a bowl of soup. I thought about the last meal we had eaten together, Chris and I, and about how disproportionately important she'd become to me, how deep was my sense of loss. I'd known her only for one day, and yet it seemed as if she had been on the edges of my dreams for years, as if I'd always known her but had somehow failed to meet her in the flesh before. I thought about her for hours. Well, there was no one else to think about: no one else was at all clear to me. Everything before I met Chris was still a muddle, like a television picture with faulty vertical hold. I kept almost catching it, only for it to start slipping away again. I didn't mind. I didn't really try all that hard. I was quite happy suspended there without a past. So the evening drifted on. I lay on my bed semi-drugged with the stuff they brought me for the pain, and continued quietly to mourn my friend.

That night I dreamt about Tony. I dreamt he came to see me in the hospital. He was tight-lipped and trembled slightly the way he did when he was either very angry or very excited. 'Your skirt is stained,' he said. It was an accusation. 'It's blood,' I told him. And it was. I pulled back the cover to show him. I was lying in a pool of it. It was all over my hands. It welled up and trickled into small pools on the floor. He stood there with his hands over his eyes. 'Are you crying?' I asked him. I was very surprised, and quite frightened. I tried to comfort him. 'It's all right,' I said. 'It's not serious.' But the moment I said it I thought: No that can't be true. It must be serious. Look at it. The whole floor was stained with blood.

In the morning, I woke up and immediately remembered everything: the rue François Premier, my name, everything.

I think perhaps I've given a very unfair picture of Tony. How do you imagine him? He's tall. He has dark, very straight hair and healthy-looking skin, and he wears glasses. He has enormous energy. He's like a terrier: that's the best way to describe him. He won't let things go. He goes on and on worrying at them until all the life has been shaken out of them. What does he do? He's Deputy Marketing and Sales Director for an engineering firm in Stoke-on-Trent. He likes his work. He complains that it's too full of stress and pressure, but stress and pressure are what excite him. His passion is anything mechanical. He loves wheels and cogs and piston heads and manifolds. It's not simply that machines are precision engineered and follow a rigid grammar of rules, it's far more than that. I understand it. I know what appeals to him about an engine: it has the glamour of power.

I first met him in Coventry. It seems an unlikely place to meet anyone, but I did. I was there with my mother and stepfather. Coventry was just the sort of place where my stepfather liked to stay. I can't remember now whether it was a weekend away, or an overnight stop *en route* home from the south coast. My stepfather was interested in cities like Coventry: he was still obsessed by the Second World War. He had been a bomber pilot: one of the young and glamorous doomed who waved bravely as they climbed into their fragile machines and flew off to bomb targets all over Europe. The trouble was that unlike the majority of his friends my stepfather had come back again. He survived. It was a terrible anti-climax for him. In fact, from then on so was everything: the England he came back to, the Europe he had saved. They were all gone to the dogs, he said. Peace, he implied, was synonymous with the moral degeneration of the human race. In his middle age, for reasons I have never understood, and suspect that he never really understood either – some instinctive, old-fashioned gallantry, perhaps, towards frail young widows – he married my mother and acquired as part of the package a seven-year-old daughter. He still had his pencil-thin RAF moustache. In the wedding photographs it has a seedy, dapper look. My mother suggested occasionally that he should shave it off – she confessed to me once that she couldn't bear it, that eventually it revolted her – but he never did. In his late seventies it's still there, a faded, egg-stained yellow like the rheumy whites of his eyes.

So there we were in Coventry, presumably looking at the ruins of the old cathedral while lamenting the municipal ugliness of the new: and presumably listening to my stepfather pointing out to us how the juxtaposition of the two – the destruction of all that was old and beautiful and the ugliness of all that had replaced it – might be taken as an eloquent Metaphor for Our Times in capital letters. I was about eighteen, but I was a different person then and very full of myself. I thought I knew exactly who I was and what I wanted. It was only later, only very slowly, year by year, that I began to realise that what I thought I knew was all pretence; that rather than being full of myself, I was exactly the opposite and getting worse. And in direct proportion to my growing emptiness, Tony seemed to become fuller, more certain, more immutable. He knew all the rules and understood all the meanings. It was as if he had eaten all the pieces of me that had leached away, as if he were crammed full of self, as if inside his thickening body he held not only himself but the few wispy fragments which had once constituted me. In defence, I erected an exterior which reflected back the expectations of whoever approached it, a kind of cold, glassy mirror.

It was my reflection that Tony saw first: in the mirror hanging on the wall of the Coventry boarding house where we were staying. I was still at an age when the exterior image was paramount. I had a burning desire to be beautiful. Goodness knows why: I can't imagine now why it seemed so important. Now I much prefer the anonymity of ordinariness, but then I wanted simply to be beautiful – a modest enough ambition. There were moments when, at certain angles and with my eyes narrowed – partly to make them look more seductive and partly to blur my vision – I thought I looked a little like Julie Christie, but no one else seemed to notice the resemblance. I was in the hall that smelt of cabbage water waiting for my mother to come downstairs, and practising my Julie Christie look, when the front door opened. I stopped posing, but was still looking in the mirror when I saw the reflection of a dark-haired young man wearing glasses who smiled and said, 'Hello'. And my reflection smiled back at his.

He had just started as a trainee salesman then, working for a firm which had once been the family business, but which had been taken over some years back. My stepfather saw this as another sign of decay: old, established family firms being eaten up by fly, modern business practice. He was deeply sympathetic about it. Tony, who was the perfect exemplar of the fly modern businessman, and who would certainly have sold out for profit had not his uncle already done so, smiled and looked at his fingernails, a mannerism he has, a way of distancing himself. His nails are always perfectly manicured. It seems to me an odd thing for a man to do, to consider his nails, to file them, to push down the cuticles. I never dream of manicuring mine. If they grow, I either bite them or they break. It's another of those things that seem to have been wrongly distributed between us. I should be the one to fuss about dirty chairs, and to buff my nails.

'That boy will go far,' my stepfather said. He warmed to Tony immediately. Everybody did. They talked a great deal about engines together. My mother liked him too. 'What a charming boy he is,' she said, going slightly pink about the neck. Because she was older than he was, and because the reason he came to visit us so often was his quite inexplicable interest in me, she felt it was safe to flirt with him a little. She blushed and laughed a lot when he was there. He filled all sorts of roles in their lives. He was far more satisfactory to them than I was. 'Is Tony coming this weekend?' they would ask wistfully. They spoiled him. He had a very masculine glamour. He confirmed their vision of the world and of themselves. And they were deeply impressed, if not a little surprised, by the fact that he liked me. They looked at me in a different and more approving way because of it.

This is the mystery, of course. Why *did* he like me? We'd only known each other for ten minutes when he asked me to go to the pictures with him. When I said to my mother, 'I'm going out this evening with that boy I met in the hall', she smiled tolerantly and said fine but not to be back too late because Mrs Whatever-her-name-was who ran the boarding house locked the door at half-past eleven.

I forget what film we saw. There were a lot of car chases in it which bored me, but I wasn't allowed to watch much of it. Even before the trailers began, Tony had his arm round my shoulders. He stared fixedly at the screen as if the behaviour of his arm had nothing to do with him, as if he was totally unaware of what it was doing. I was both alarmed and curious but mostly curious. When the big film started he suddenly turned, his face like a huge blackbird swooping down on me, and fastened himself on my lips. His mouth tasted nice, partly of peppermint and partly of something less clean and much richer. It was interesting to explore. He put his hand rather clumsily on my left breast and squeezed it rhythmically. After the first exciting panic of being touched there, in such an unmentionable place, which no one had ever touched before, I decided that I didn't like it at all. I never did manage to convince him that there might be other ways to touch me, subtler, more erotic ways. When the film was over he walked me back to the hotel, stopping every so often to pin me against a wall. I assumed this was passion. I took mental notes so that I could tell my friend Jennifer about it. Looking back, I suppose I behaved in a very passive way. I did whatever Tony wanted. I didn't know how else to behave. And anyway, there seemed no point in doing otherwise. Once, he complained about it. 'Why do you never suggest anything?' he said. 'Why do you never take the initiative?' So I suggested that instead of going to the pictures again we went for a walk. 'A walk?' he said. 'Where? What do you want to go for a walk for? I don't like walking.'

'*I* like walking,' I said.

So we went to the pictures.

Once I suggested that he shouldn't bother coming up for the weekend, to leave it until the following weekend. I think I was getting a little bored with him. I wanted a weekend to myself. His reaction frightened me. He looked as if I'd hit him. 'You don't want me to come?' he said. Then he sulked. Then he lost his temper. He accused me of being frigid, of being a selfish bitch, of not being honest with him. All of which was probably true. It was always very difficult to defend myself in any argument with Tony because I generally agreed with him. Or if I didn't, it was because his accusations were so totally absurd I was left speechless. Anyway, by the end of this conversation we were engaged.

Years later I asked him about all this. 'You remember in Coventry,' I said. 'Why did you want to see me again?'

The question irritated him. 'Because I liked you, I suppose. Why does anybody ever want to see someone again?'

'But *why* did you like me?'

'I don't know. One of those things.'

'So it was sexual attraction, then?' I asked. Well, it certainly wasn't friendship. We didn't spend hours talking to each other, we didn't tell each other the stories of our lives, we didn't laugh together, there was no fascinating, self-defining empathy of thought; we didn't confess any truths about ourselves – probably because we were too young to know any. So what did we do? Obviously we went to the pictures a lot. We spent a lot of time kissing, or in bed in cheap hotel rooms, which after a while I found very boring though I never had the courage to say so.

'Well, yes, partly sexual attraction,' he said, 'but other things too.'

'What other things?'

He was very suspicious. 'Why do you want to know? What's this all about?'

The truth was that I couldn't believe, I simply couldn't believe that he found anything the remotest bit attractive about me. My body had always appalled me: I found it hideous. I suspected (from the evidence of the magazines he kept at the bottom of his wardrobe under his sports bag) that what Tony really felt for it was a kind of contempt and it was this which excited him. I understood that. I felt a kind of contempt for it too. I couldn't bear to look at it naked in a mirror. It was always twice as big as I imagined it to be – except in the places where it ought to have been big – and too different from all the Pirelli calendar images or from the girls lying spreadeagled in those magazines Tony bought and hid. So I don't know – I have never known – what it was he saw in me. I suspect it was my amorphous passivity that interested him. I suspect he understood very early in the relationship that he had all the power, and liked it that way. Well, who wouldn't? He was very young. He only knew about machines. He probably thought women and machines were fundamentally the same. I can hardly blame him if he did. I don't think I offered much evidence to the contrary.

'Oh, for Christ's sake, Maggs,' he said. 'What are you getting at now? I fell in love with you, OK? Why else does anyone get married?'

Oh, lots of reasons. Among which I imagine love probably comes pretty low on the list. I certainly don't remember falling in love with him, although I was very impressed by the idea of him falling in love with me. I married him because that's what one did in those days, and because I was afraid of hurting him. It would be all right, I told myself. My mother liked him. My stepfather liked him. Everybody liked him. I liked him. And I knew my mother would enjoy the fuss of the wedding. No, that's not true. I was the one who enjoyed that. I enjoyed being the centre of attention: I enjoyed people's envy and surprise; I enjoyed being part of a significant ritual in which I was both the heroine and the symbolic sacrifice. But I never really thought much beyond the reception. Beyond that, my imagination failed. It was like the end of a fairy story. Happy ever after was simply a poetical way of saying The End and shutting the book and going off to sleep. Sitting in the car beside Tony in my going-away suit, I remember thinking that this was not at all what I had meant. I wanted to stop and say: This is a mistake, can we please go back. I wanted the wedding, of course I did, but I hadn't bargained for the consequences: I had assumed a different kind of ending, something more literally sacrificial. I remember sitting in the car and looking down at my hands and being surprised that they belonged to me, and that I, the physical I with these odd white hands, was here in this Ford Cortina on the way to Whitby. 'Well, you've done it now,' I remember saying to myself. Outside York it started to rain and the sky grew black. We drove along flat, wet roads. The windscreen wipers slashed monotonously backwards and forwards, clearing spray. I was filled with such intolerable sadness I could hardly breathe.

Tony put his hand on my knee. 'Happy?' he asked. I smiled and nodded because I couldn't speak. And so it went on. And as I grew less and less certain about things, in direct proportion Tony became fatter and more dogmatic, more stuffed full of certainties. Yet for sixteen years we managed to live happily enough together. At least everybody seemed to think so. I certainly thought so.

I lay on the bed, unable to move, paralysed by this sudden access of memory, and made urgent and desperate plans. I felt sick. As soon as Dr Verdoux arrived, I would have to get him to contact Tony. In the meantime, I needed to think up a convincing excuse to explain to Tony why I should have been hitch-hiking south. I practised sentences in my head: rushed, panicky sentences I didn't have the conviction to finish. All I could successfully imagine were the barbed questions, the subtle reproaches, the hurt silences: the endless payment I would have to make.

When Dr Verdoux *did* eventually come, he brought a pile of English newspapers.

'I thought you might like something to read with your breakfast,' he said. Some nurses helped me to sit up, wedging me like a boneless doll between pillows. 'They're a little old,' he said apologetically. 'This one – ' he passed me a copy of the *Daily Mail* – 'this one is the most recent. This is yesterday's.'

The date amazed me. Three weeks had completely disappeared. Dr Verdoux dropped the rest of the papers on my bed. There were a couple of copies of the *Daily Telegraph*, one *Guardian* and a *Sun*. I started with the *Mail*. It was odd to have lost three whole weeks, to have known nothing about the beginning half of these stories, and equally odd to realise that, conversely, nothing much had changed in the world. I had just read a piece about French opposition to some EC plan or other, something like that, and was turning over the page when I caught sight of a small, smudged, grey photograph at the head of an article. I glanced at it without interest. I felt quite sorry for whoever it was supposed to be; they could at least have chosen a more flattering photo, I thought. And then suddenly my throat tightened. I knew that look of blind panic, that pale, rigid corpse propped up against the pleated curtain. I read the caption: 'Mystery of Missing Englishwoman Deepens'. I forced myself to concentrate, to read every word slowly, but my eyes dashed back and forth like hysterical crabs, missing words, missing the sense.

French police are still searching the Limoges area for the body of Mrs Margaret Davison, a 36-year old secretary from Stoke-on-Trent, who disappeared three weeks ago while on holiday in Paris. Her husband, Mr Anthony Davison, 39, a Marketing and Sales Manager, made an appeal last night on

French television for anyone who may have seen his wife to come forward. Mrs Davison's clothing was found in the vicinity of the search area by a local farmer.

I tore rapidly (and literally) through all the other papers. There was nothing in either of the *Telegraphs*, and a brief, four-line item in the *Guardian*. In the centre pages of the *Sun* I found a photograph of Tony, his shoulders hunched, his hands up to his face, shielding it from the camera. I knew it was Tony. I knew at once even before I saw the caption: 'Anthony Davison whose missing wife police believe to be victim of French Sex Killing.'

I sat staring at this for a long time, feeling sick. It was difficult to know what to think. By some ironic miracle, what I most wanted, but thought irretrievable, had been offered back to me. I had ceased to be. I was no one at all. Margaret Davison, thirty-six-year-old housewife and secretary from Hanley, was dead. It said so in the papers. The police were searching for her body. After all, I thought – I was very reasonable about it, even compassionate – after all, if I've been missing, supposed dead for three weeks, then Tony will already have been through the worst. It won't take him that long to get over me. So why disturb him? Stay dead.

It was such a seductive, such a simple idea that I almost allowed myself to be seduced by it. Almost. Instead, I closed the paper and folded it neatly – Tony's hunched shoulders and covered face were too painful – and made the sensible decision to tell the truth. And by the time Dr Verdoux came back, I had nerved myself up to do just that.

'I think I ought to tell you … ' I began, but I was still having trouble getting any complicated combination of words out.

'The Police Judiciaire are outside,' he said. 'They want to speak to you.'

So really, in a way it was very convenient, the police coming, because it gave me a chance to think about how to phrase what I was going to say, and it saved me going through tedious explanations twice. Although, thinking about it rationally, I probably wouldn't even have to go through it once, because they'd recognise me straight away. After three weeks there must be passport photographs of me in every police station in France.

'Do you feel strong enough to talk to them?' he asked.

'Yes,' I said.

There were two policemen: one tallish, slightly balding, wearing a leather jacket, the other small and very dark. The small one stared round a lot as if he were bored, and sucked in his cheeks. He looked like a miniature version of Alain Delon. I sat there with the copy of the *Daily Mail* folded open at my photograph, ready to show it to them as proof of who I really was just in case they needed it.

The tall, balding one introduced himself. I've forgotten his name. And it was clear from the beginning that he hadn't recognised me at all. His first words to me were: 'Marie-Christine Masbou?'

'Before you go any further,' I said, 'I think I ought to explain that I'm not who you think I am.'

No, I didn't. What am I lying for now? The moment I saw the two policemen I knew perfectly well I wasn't going to tell them anything.

'Marie-Christine Masbou?' said the tall one in the leather jacket, and I made not the slightest attempt to contradict him. Why shouldn't I borrow Chris's name for a few days until I felt ready to face things? She didn't need it. I decided to tell them neither who I was, nor who I wasn't. Let them tell me, I thought. Let them decide. And I did have the copy of the *Mail* open on my knee – that bit at least is true. So if they'd wanted to, they could have seen the photograph easily enough; they could have read the article. It was up to them to make the connection. I simply went along with whatever they said. It seemed easiest.

The tall, balding policeman sat down. He understood, he said, that I'd been driving south from Calais. He spoke very good English. Could I tell him where was I going, or was I still having trouble remembering things?

'No,' I said. 'I remember very well. I was driving to Figeac.' I thought the least I could do was answer his questions as truthfully as possible.

'On holiday?' he said. It wasn't really a question. He just wanted me to confirm what he thought he already knew to be a fact, so I said nothing. I felt pleasantly detached, as if all this was happening to someone else.

'What about your family?' he said.

I was alarmed. 'What family?'

He looked up in surprise. We stared at each other blankly for a moment as if he had used a totally inappropriate word. For a second I assumed that by 'family' he meant Tony; and then I realised that of course he meant Chris's family.

'Your family,' he repeated with marginally less confidence, as if he suspected he probably *had* used the wrong word. 'Is there somebody we should notify?'

I shook my head. 'No,' I said. 'No one.'

He was holding out his hand to the small, good-looking one, who handed him a package. 'We did try to make inquiries through the English authorities, but they were unable to come up with next of kin. You have no family in England?'

I made an ambiguous sort of noise and smiled.

From the package he produced two passports.

'If you could just confirm that this is yours.'

He handed me one of the passports, open at the first page. Stuck on the right-hand page was a slightly underexposed photograph of Chris. I knew it was Chris, although it might have been of someone else altogether, someone very young and serious with shoulder-length, undyed, brown hair and a plump face.

'It was taken a long time ago,' I remarked.

'It's not so good,' the balding one said.

'Oh, I think it's very good,' I said truthfully.

He looked confused, or possibly embarrassed. 'No, I mean it's not … ' He was fishing for the right word, so I helped him out.

'Not a good likeness?' I suggested. 'Well, it's quite old.' I looked at the smudged date stamp. I pointed out that I'd been a lot younger when this photo was taken. It was true: I had been. Nine years younger. I'd been twenty-seven and Chris must have been twenty-three. 'People's faces change,' I said.

The other one, the short one, shook his head: '*Les yeux,*' he muttered. '*Les yeux, ils ne changent jamais.*'

'The difficulty is, of course, the height.' The balding one pointed to the place where, beside 'Height/*Taille*', was written 5ft. 4in. 'Five foot four,' he said.

'*Cent soixante-cinq centimètres,*' said the other one.

They looked at the length of me in the bed, with puzzled faces.

I shrugged and smiled at them. It didn't matter to me what they thought. Let them make of it whatever they wanted.

'It's a mistake?' the balding one suggested. 'You are what? *Cent soixante-quinze?*'

'Five foot seven,' I said.

They looked at each other. 'It's some error at the Passport Office?'

'You never had it changed?' the little, dark one asked.

'I didn't think it mattered.'

'And you've never had any trouble with the authorities?'

'No,' I said. 'None.'

They shook their heads in bewildered amazement at the laxness of Passport Control.

'Nobody has ever stopped you?'

'Never.'

The balding one said, 'You must get it changed, *Mademoiselle*. As soon as you get back to England.'

'Yes,' I said, obediently. 'Yes, I will. Immediately.'

The balding one – I think his name was Peyrol, something like that – took the passport away from me and handed me the second passport: a thin, Visitor's Passport. I opened it. I was curious to see whose it was. On the centre page was a very recent photo of Chris. She was instantly recognisable. Her hair was spiky and dyed blonde and her face much thinner, much sharper than in the earlier photo. She was smiling. On the left-hand page I read: Katherine Angela Hughes. Age 30, I read. Distinguishing marks: None.

'This is the young woman you picked up?' asked Peyrol.

'Yes,' I said. 'That's her.' It was the first real lie. And then the small, good-looking one said something which so complicated matters that really I had no choice but to go on lying.

'The money,' he said. 'Tell us about the money.'

'Money?'

His eyes were pin sharp. He was not bored now. He concentrated all his attention on me. 'The money in the car.'

'What money?' I said again, stupidly.

'We found a large quantity of English money hidden in your car,' said Peyrol.

'It wasn't my car. It was a hire car.'

'Hidden in the car you hired.'

'I don't know anything about any money.'

They looked at me as if they didn't believe me. They waited for me to say something more but I had no idea what to tell them so I just repeated myself. 'I don't know anything about it.'

The short dark one snorted and muttered something in rapid French.

Peyrol translated. 'Are you trying to tell us that this is not your money?'

'Of course it's not my money.'

'So this woman you picked up, this Katherine Hughes, you're suggesting she hid £20,000 in banknotes in the boot of your hire car? Carefully wrapped up in the tool-kit?'

Put like that it did sound rather far-fetched. I could see why they were having trouble believing it.

'She must have done,' I said. I was as puzzled as they were. I would have thought international mandates and bankers' drafts were more in Chris's line. On the other hand what did I know about her lifestyle? Perhaps she frequently travelled the continent with £20,000 in banknotes, in which case she'd have to hide it somewhere.

'Where did you pick her up?' Peyrol asked.

'Outside Paris.'

'What time?'

'How much luggage did she have?'

'Did she appear nervous?'

They snapped out questions, one after the other. It was early in the morning, I said. About six. She had one suitcase, I lied. They nodded to each other and said something in French from which I gathered that the second passport had been found in *la valise rouge*.

'That's right,' I said. 'It was red.'

'So two of the suitcases are yours and the red one is hers?'

I nodded in an ambiguous sort of way. I might simply have been flexing the muscles of my neck.

'Where was she going?'

'Toulouse,' I said. 'To see her sister.'

They wanted to know precisely where we'd stopped during the day. I said I couldn't remember. Somewhere between Orleans and Beaugency for breakfast, I said. A village with a square and a Café de Sports. In a burst of creative inspiration I told them we'd visited a supermarket at Beaugency and bought food for a picnic lunch. This was obviously not as inspired as I thought. They looked puzzled. They said there was no sign of any food in the car.

'No,' I said. 'We didn't eat it in the car. And anyway we finished most of it for supper. I threw the rest away.' I was slightly hurt that they appeared to doubt me. I could visualise it all as vividly as if it had really happened. I could see my hand tossing half a baguette and an uneaten piece of cheese into a roadside bin.

'When you stopped at the café did you leave the car unattended?'

'Did you go to the Ladies' room?' the short dark one asked.

'Yes,' I said truthfully. 'I did.'

'And did she come with you?'

'No. She went to the bar and paid the bill.'

'Could she have done that and then gone out to the car while you were still in the Ladies?'

'She could've done, yes.'

'What about the car? Was it locked?'

'I think so. Yes.'

'Did you give her the keys at any time? To get something from the car?'

'No.'

'What about the boot? Could you have left the boot unlocked?'

'I've no idea,' I said, fascinated by how easy it was to answer their questions with a literal if not an actual truth. 'I suppose I could have done. I don't remember.' I lay back against the pillows watching them while they talked feverishly in French together. They were the police, I thought: let them work it out. I just wished they would get on with it because my legs were beginning to hurt again. Painfully, I shifted my weight from one buttock to the other and dislodged the newspaper, which slid on to the floor. Peyrol bent and picked it up. For a moment he held my photograph there in his hand, in front of his eyes: all he had to do was to look down and make the connection. But he didn't. He simply glanced at it briefly, without interest, and handed it back to me.

'You are married?' he asked suddenly, watching me refold the paper.

'No,' I said – the second real lie.

'You should also inform the passport authorities if you have recently married,' he said.

'I certainly would if I had,' I said, 'but I haven't.'

It was as I was moving the glass of water to make room for the newspaper on top of the bedside cabinet that I realised this series of questions had been prompted by his seeing my wedding ring. I'd worn it for sixteen years: I never noticed it any more. 'Oh, you mean this?' I said. 'This is very old.' I slid it over my knuckle as if it meant nothing to me, as if it was just a ring I occasionally wore on any finger it happened to fit. To emphasise this I rammed it painfully over the knuckle of the third finger of my other hand.

After a couple more questions Dr Verdoux came in and made them go. He was convinced they'd tired me. He was angry about it. It was true that my legs and my back hurt, but I was too elated to feel tired. Yes, I know what an unsuitable reaction elation was. I know I ought to have been feeling something else altogether, but then there were a lot of things I ought to have felt and didn't, or ought to have done and hadn't. To begin with I ought to have told them straight out who I was, but I kept assuming – or maybe this is just an excuse – I kept assuming that in a minute they'd realise the two passport photographs were of the same person. It was obvious to me that they were. In a minute, I thought, they'll realise I can't possibly be Chris Masbou. All I did was wait for them to tell me I wasn't. That's all. And I would have done it myself, truly I would, but given the choice – and for the first time ever it seemed as if I *had* been given the choice – I'd really rather prefer *not* to be Margaret Davison, aged thirty-six of Hanley. Looking at it objectively, you have to admit the evidence did seem to be pretty well stacked against it. (Even *I* found it hard to believe, but then I always have.) Whereas the evidence in support of everybody else's assumption that I was Chris Masbou aged thirty-two of Shepherd's Bush was pretty well overwhelming.

In the pale arc of light from the bedside lamp, I tore up the one identifying photograph of Margaret Davison. I stuffed the pieces into the paper bag where I was keeping my discarded tissues and banana skins. All right, then, I said, very sensibly to myself, all right, then, if you don't want to be Margaret Davison and you can't honestly be Chris Masbou, what other option is there? – and I couldn't think of any, not a single one. Except running away again. Running away is frequently the only answer. One way or another, I am always doing it.

It's very difficult, though, running away – physically running away, I mean – when your legs are in plaster. Even somebody as skilled as I am at it, even someone who knows all the tricks, couldn't overcome the fact that it was impossible even to get out of bed without being supported under both arms. Besides, I'd grown to like the white room where I had once floated in limbo without weight and without proper identity, and where the nun came and went as quietly and smoothly as if she were floating too. I was happy there. Every other kind of running away – I practised with my usual dexterity. I dozed and dreamed and tried not to think too hard about anything, particularly not about uncomfortable things like what I was going to do when they'd put me together again.

Once or twice I found myself wondering about Chris; usually after the police had been. They came back several times. They wanted more details about Katherine Hughes. Their English counterparts were having difficulty tracing her. This, of course, came as little surprise to me, but I said nothing. I avoided thinking about the second passport in the red suitcase, and about the money hidden in the boot. They were like biscuit crumbs in a sweaty bed, these thoughts. So I brushed them away and dozed instead.

In the afternoons Dr Verdoux came and sat on my bed and talked to me in a polite, formal way about nothing very much.

I assumed he wanted to practise his English. Sometimes he asked me questions about my work and I smiled a lot and said I worked in an office. A large company, I said. Well, large is a relative term. It simply means bigger than small, which is also relative, and by that criterion I *did* work for a large company. Financial stuff, I said. This was certainly true. He asked once if I played chess. No, I said, I'm afraid not. It occurred to me afterwards that Chris would definitely have played chess. She probably played it very well. One afternoon we got talking about France. Did I often take holidays alone? he asked.

'Yes,' I said.

'In France?'

'All over the place.'

Where was I heading for, he wanted to know, when the accident happened? Without thinking I told him what Chris had told me: that I was on my way to Figeac to stay with relatives. The moment I said it, the moment I heard it coming out of my mouth, I knew it was a mistake.

'You have relatives in Figeac?' he asked. His eyes sharpened in surprise.

I started flannelling. 'Well, no, not close relatives,' I said. 'In fact, I don't really know them at all. They had no idea I was coming. They weren't expecting me.' And even as I said it, I realised that what I was saying must be the truth. If Chris's relatives had been expecting her, then they'd have been alarmed when she'd neither turned up nor contacted them. They'd have been on to the authorities straight away. This relieved me of a problem that until now I hadn't even realised I'd got. It was a comfort to know that, whatever else, I wouldn't be bothered by the sudden appearance of Chris's relatives. 'No,' I said. 'I was just going to pop in on the off-chance.'

'Off-chance' was not a colloquialism Dr Verdoux had met before. As a consequence, we had to discuss a number of 'off' phrases: off-side, off–beat, put off, off-licence. He complained about the inconsistencies of the English preposition. I said

English prepositions were entirely consistent: it was French prepositions that were so arbitrary. The more we discussed grammar, I calculated, the sooner he'd forget about this family of mine in Figeac.

One morning, two nurses came and wheeled me along endless corridors to a room where Dr Verdoux took out all the stitches. I had fifty-four stitches in my face and head alone. Afterwards they made me walk the length of the passage back to the lift on crutches. It was excruciatingly painful. By the time I got to the lift I was shaking and ready to throw up, but they seemed very pleased with me. Everything was healing, they said. After that they made me walk every day. My legs, my stomach, my buttocks ached with exhaustion after these sessions, and sometimes there was a sharp pain in my ribs; but I reasoned that if they were right and I was, as they said, healing nicely, then I needed to get mobile as fast as I could. The idyll was nearly over, and I couldn't see it taking the police much longer to grasp who I was. The sooner I was physically able to get away the better.

When I was beginning to get quite skilled with the crutches, and huge, tight, dry scabs had crusted my face, Sister Marie-Thérèse appeared one morning with two suitcases and a handbag. From her carefully simplified French I managed to deduce that the police had left them so I could check the contents. I sat on the bed searching through Chris's handbag, trying to look as if this were not all completely new to me. In comparison with any of my handbags, it was remarkably clean. There was a purse full of money – quite a lot of money, about 8,000 francs (I counted it) – and another smaller purse holding a pocket mirror, an eyebrow pencil, mascara and a lipstick. There was a cheque book, a cheque guarantee card, a credit card, a driving licence, all the papers relating to the hire of the car, an international driving licence, a postcard, a pen, a hairbrush, a pair of sunglasses and some keys. That was all. No fluff or grit at the bottom, no loose change mixed up with grubby Polos and screwed-up receipts. It seemed very impersonal. I read the postcard. It was unstamped and unaddressed. It said: 'Taken your advice. In Calais. Will phone Uncle Xavier when I reach Figeac. Chris.'

The two suitcases had been badly damaged in the crash. Their spines were crushed, and they had to be secured with string. There was nothing in them except clothes and shoes and a hair dryer – personal things like that.

'*Bon*,' I said to Sister Marie-Thérèse. '*C'est tout.*' I was slightly uncomfortable about this lie: it felt indecent.

She smiled and took the suitcases away. I sat in the chair by the window with Chris's bag on my knee. It seemed a stroke of fortune, this bag, like a posthumous present. I'd have to give Chris her name back, but I could surely keep this. The credit cards, the driving licences and anything that might identify Chris Masbou I'd throw away just before I left. I'd tear them up and flush them down the toilet. The make-up, the glasses and the money I'd keep. Eight thousand francs was enough to keep me going for ages, two or three months, even. The best thing to do, I decided, was to catch a train to the coast. I didn't plan beyond that. I suppose I must have had some vague idea of eventually travelling back to England on Chris's passport, although the police hadn't yet returned it, but I didn't bother to think that bit out too clearly. All I wanted was to spend some time in a cheap hotel all by myself, and walk on the shore, and paddle, and think about nothing but the colour of the water and the illusory point where the sea appears to meet the sky and one thing becomes another. When I was small, I always wanted to be a sailor so that I could sail across the sea to that precise point of mysterious fusion and pass through it, like passing through a mirror and coming out on the other side into a different world. 'A sailor?' my mother said. 'No, darling, I don't think so.'

'A sailor?' said my stepfather, a spoonful of Shredded Wheat suspended just below his milk-dampened, nicotine-yellow moustache. 'What on earth do you want to be a sailor for?'

So I knew from the beginning that it was never really an option.

I worked out a simple plan. In a couple of days, when I could manage for short stretches without the crutches, I'd ask Sister Marie-Thérèse if I could try walking in the garden. This would mean she'd have to find me some clothes. It would also give me a chance to get my bearings. Later, at visiting time, when the hospital was busy, I'd attach myself loosely to a group of visitors and slip out of the gates with them. Then I'd catch a train, and go south until I ran out of land, and pretend that I was quite free, a free spirit, like Chris, and I'd deliberately not think about the future at all.

I was sitting there by the window, working out in detail exactly how long 8,000 francs would last me at the rate of 180 francs a day, when I was distracted by the sound of raised voices in the corridor outside. I heard poor Sister Marie-Thérèse, who sat with me less often now and who had gone to supervise the laundry, twittering like a frightened bird. A man's voice contradicted and overpowered her. The door suddenly burst open as if a great gust of wind had torn it away from its frame, and a small, square man stood there, his arms wide open. I stood up in a panic. 'Marie-Christine,' the man said, and held me so tight I couldn't move. He had a thick neck and a huge, grizzled badger's head, this man who bewilderingly seemed to think I was Marie-Christine. 'Let me look at you,' he said, disengaging me slightly. I was embarrassed by the intensity of his regard. I lowered my eyes. He was deeply affected by whatever he saw, deeply affected – there were tears in his eyes. '*Ma pauvre petite* … ' he said and hugged me to him again. My ribs shrieked with pain. He kissed me three times on alternate cheeks and immediately repeated the whole procedure. There was an odd, pungent smell coming from his hair. He was, he said – speaking in rapid, almost incomprehensible French, which, as soon as he saw I was lost, he changed to rapid and almost equally incomprehensible English – he was, he said, devastated by the news of my accident, enraged by the behaviour of the authorities who had deliberately conspired to keep my family away from me, overwhelmed to find me looking so well. He was, he said, ready to take me home. Now. This minute. The car was waiting outside.

Sister Marie-Thérèse wrung her hands in despair. I felt quite sorry for her. I suggested in French that perhaps she had better fetch Dr Verdoux.

'D'accord,' she said, and she hurried away muttering that she would return.

'Stupid woman,' said the man with the badger's head. His skin was tough and brown. He held me at arm's length again and looked at me critically. I watched the look of puzzlement darken his eyes.

'You don't recognise me do you?' I said. Now the moment had come I was surprisingly calm. I had my cover story ready. I'd worked it out. Well, I'd say, the fact is that everybody was so certain I was Chris Masbou, I naturally assumed they were right; but now everything's beginning to come back to me, I realise I must be somebody else altogether.

'Of course I recognise you,' he said tetchily, before I had time to offer this distinctly shaky loss of memory story. He seemed quite hurt that I should assume otherwise. 'Of course I do. I think, au contraire, it's you who don't recognise me.'

Because I not unnaturally assumed that he must be the uncle whom Chris had mentioned on the postcard, I said so. 'Uncle Xavier?' I suggested.

His face broke into smiles. Lines carved out the skin under his eyes, in his cheeks, in his forehead. 'Such a long time,' he said. 'And you don't come and see us. You forget us. When I saw you last you were so high.' His hand hovered about two feet off the floor. 'You see, it's true. You don't remember. You don't remember your Uncle Xavier.'

I looked at him very coolly: I was, I remember, remarkably cool.

'Oh yes I do,' I said.

He laughed happily. 'I know what you remember. You remember the honey bees?'

'The honey bees?'

'Yes. You remember?' He nodded encouragement to me. It was no good trying to bluff him. It was better to establish from the beginning that I remembered nothing.

'No,' I said. 'What bees?'

He looked disappointed. 'You don't remember the bees?'

'I was very small,' I said.

'So high.'

'I mean I was very young.'

'Eight,' he said. He held me by the shoulders and looked at me as if I were some sort of miracle.

It was such a bizarre situation I had no idea what to do. So I asked him straight out, because I was very curious about it, if I was what he expected. 'Have I grown up the way you thought I would?' I asked. I was thinking how odd it was – the way people simply accept what they assume must be the truth.

'You're taller than I thought,' he said. 'I expect you up to here.' He touched the middle of his forehead.

'But everything else?' I asked. I wanted him to say I was nothing like what he expected.

'You used to have golden hair in curls.'

'Oh, hair. Hair always grows darker.'

'Ah,' said Uncle Xavier, because finally Dr Verdoux had arrived with Sister Marie-Thérèse flapping nervously behind him. '*Bon*.' In rapid French, Uncle Xavier began laying down terms. Dr Verdoux retreated into formal coldness. I sat in the chair by the window and listened; I understood perhaps one word in ten. At one point I thought they were going to come to blows. Uncle Xavier was shorter than Dr Verdoux, but much more powerful. Beside him, Dr Verdoux looked frail and insubstantial. In the end it appeared that some decision had been taken. It appeared that Uncle Xavier had won. He swaggered over to the window.

'You understood?' Dr Verdoux asked. He was very flushed, his face deeply crimson under his ginger hair.

'She understands nothing,' said Uncle Xavier indulgently. 'Alors, she has lost all her French.'

'Your uncle has asked permission to take you home with him,' said Dr Verdoux. He was very ruffled. 'It is, of course, quite impossible. I've told him so. I can't possibly allow it. However, provided you continue to make satisfactory progress, I may permit you to leave on Monday.'

Roughly translated, I assumed this pompous little speech to mean that Uncle Xavier had just given Dr Verdoux an ultimatum to the effect that Monday was the absolute deadline. Whether or not I was officially discharged by then was of no consequence to Uncle Xavier, who was strutting about looking very pleased with himself: he was taking me home anyway.

I shrugged. It was of no consequence to me either. I might even change my plans and let this strutting cockerel of a man drive me on the first part of my journey. It would relieve me of the trouble of having to slip out of the hospital illicitly, and also of an exhausting walk to the station. It would certainly save a chunk of the train fare. I might do that, I thought, or I might do something else altogether. There seemed suddenly to be a wealth of choice. I wasn't used to it. So I sat down on the bed and smiled and waited. There was no hurry.

When Uncle Xavier had gone, leaving an uneasy vacuum behind him, Dr Verdoux collapsed on the chair and rubbed his forehead as if he had a headache.

'Is he always like that?' he asked.

'I don't know.'

I played for a moment with the idea of telling him that the reason I didn't was know because I'd never met the man before. But it was all getting a little too complicated to explain; and, more importantly, I wasn't ready to face the consequences of not being Chris Masbou, not until I was free of the hospital and had reached my cheap hotel by the sea where I could be anyone I chose. I heard myself add: 'I haven't seen him since I was eight.'

Dr Verdoux sighed heavily. 'I'm sorry,' he said. 'I think I've probably landed you in a bit of a quandary.' It was, he said, scratching at some imaginary stain on his trousers, all his doing. He'd made enquiries in Figeac and got his secretary to contact the Masbous.

'Why?' I asked.

Because he couldn't bear, he said, to think of me leaving the hospital with nowhere to go. 'I wanted to help,' he said. 'And when you said you had relations in Figeac … ' His voice trailed off apologetically. 'I didn't realise your uncle would be so … would be such a … ' He looked at me earnestly. 'You don't have to go with him if you don't want to,' he said. 'I can make other arrangements.'

My arrangements were already made, so I smiled kindly at Dr Verdoux and said that on the contrary, I was very grateful to him for contacting my uncle. He was not to worry, I said. I'd be fine.

Uncle Xavier came for me on Monday morning. Until then he sent daily gifts: flowers, a basket of fruit, a couple of bottles of wine. Twice Dr Verdoux, his hands squirming anxiously in his pockets, came to talk to me about whether or not I wouldn't prefer to go back to England. It could be arranged, he said. He himself would arrange it.

'How will you do that?' I said. 'The police haven't returned my passport yet.'

'I'll speak to them,' he said.

The idea of going back to England made my stomach freeze. In England life was real. In England I'd have to get on with it. So I shook my head and said no, thank you very much. No thank you, I said, I think I'd like to finish my holiday in France. The weather, I said, was better in France.

'Are you absolutely sure there's no one in England I can contact for you?' he asked again. And again I shook my head. I liked him. He'd been very kind to me. I thought I'd leave him the bottles of wine Uncle Xavier had given me. It was all I had.

'You've been very kind,' I said and was surprised to see him blush. It didn't suit him. Ginger-haired people, who are the most prone to blushing, should do so as little as possible.

'It's been a very great pleasure,' he said formally.

I was a little confused. I think I may have blushed myself.

I held out my hand to him. 'In case I don't have time to say goodbye tomorrow,' I said. We shook hands. I felt entirely spurious tears spring to my eyes and had to blink and look away in case he noticed and thought they had something to do with him. They didn't. I was moved suddenly to tears by a sense of loss. All change feels like loss. I wanted to stay in the white room where nothing happened. I didn't want to move on. I didn't want to start living again.

In the morning Sister Marie-Thérèse came with my battered suitcases. (No, I mean with *the* battered suitcases. A slip of the pen.) Everything was neatly folded and had been washed and ironed for me. 'Thank you,' I said. I knew she'd done it all herself.

It was odd looking through the folded piles of Chris's clothes and choosing something to wear. Picking out underwear seemed salaciously intrusive. I stood for ages fingering a tiny, delicate-looking bra which, even if the cups fitted, would certainly never do up round my back. In the end I decided I had better do without a bra. Pants, though more intimate, somehow more shocking, were easier: at least they fitted. Chris's clothes seemed to consist largely of T-shirts and shorts. There were some shirts, two jumpers, a couple of summer skirts, two dresses, a pair of jeans, a pair of white cotton trousers and a silky emerald green dress with slits up the sides. Everything, even the T-shirts, even the shorts, looked very expensive. I thought I'd better stick to skirts since the trousers were unlikely to do up, but there was something about the idea of jeans that excited me. Jeans were what I thought Chris Masbou would choose to wear. Or, more to the point, jeans were what Margaret Davison never wore. Tony didn't like women in jeans. He said women's bottoms looked ridiculous in them. I don't know why women's bottoms should look any more ridiculous than men's: it depends on what you consider the norm. I tried to point this out to him once. Simply for the sake of argument I said that I thought it was very ugly the way men's bottoms suddenly jutted out. Men should never wear trousers, I said. But we seemed to be talking a different language. He was dealing in absolute truths which apparently everybody acknowledged to be so, therefore anything I said to the contrary was plainly ridiculous and very childish. We had a lot of conversations like that.

'Wouldn't you prefer to wear a skirt?' Sister Marie-Thérèse said, looking doubtfully at the jeans. 'It's very hot.'

'Just trying them on,' I said. I shook out Chris's jeans, and started to wriggle into them. I assumed – not unnaturally, given the difference in build between us – that they'd be miles too small, but they slid on so easily I didn't have to struggle at all. There was even an extra inch or so on the hips. I looked down at myself in surprise and stuck my thumbs into the loose waistband.

'You've lost weight,' observed Sister Marie-Thérèse.

I had. A lot of weight. More than she realised. I turned round in front of the mirror and squinted at the reflection of my bottom which, as far as I could see, looked quite good. Not only had I lost weight but my hair had grown: I had to use a rubber band to tie it back. My reflection was of someone absurdly frail and very young, hardly a woman at all. The person who looked back at me with her bruised and disconcertingly scabby face bore only the most incidental resemblance to Margaret Davison. This person seemed to take up so much less space than Margaret Davison ever had. Her shoulders seemed narrower, her cheeks thinner. I wondered if I should put some make-up on, but my face was such a mess it seemed pointless. Besides, I was afraid that instinctively I might draw Margaret Davison's face on to this unfamiliar, thin, scabby one, and find that after all I did recognise the person looking back at me.

'It'll heal soon,' Sister Marie-Thérèse said sympathetically, as if she thought I was worrying about the scabs. I don't know why everybody always assumes I'm so vain.

I asked her if she would give the flowers and the remains of the fruit to someone who might like them. I thanked her for all her kindness. '*Je vous remercie de votre bonté*,' I said and it sounded quite good, not schoolgirlish at all. I was picking up new phrases every day now. She kissed me on both cheeks and insisted on carrying my suitcase and my crutches down the stairs. I slung Chris's handbag over my shoulder. I felt very light. My legs, in pale, stone-washed denim, were long and thin and quite foreign to me. I was enchanted by them.

'Shoes,' said Sister Marie-Thérèse, laughing at my absent-mindedness. I stared down at my bare feet.

'Shoes,' I said. 'Yes.'

None of the shoes in the suitcase fitted: of course not, of course they didn't. Feet are very fundamental, very down-to-earth things. They don't change.

'I don't know what's the matter,' I said. 'They're all too small.'

'It must be the heat,' said Sister Marie-Thérèse. I nodded, although it was an absurd remark: the white room was always cool.

She picked out a pair of canvas slip-ons, bright red ones, the sort of thing you might wear on the beach. 'Try these,' she suggested. I pretended they were fine, but before I'd even got to the bottom of the stairs, I'd already given up and was treading down the heel.

Dr Verdoux came to say goodbye. He moved out of the shadows in the cool, dark hallway. He stood under the wooden crucifix that hung above the door.

'*Au revoir, Mademoiselle,*' he said.

I thought for a moment he was going to kiss me in the French manner. I didn't know whether or not to offer my cheek. But then the door burst open, a great gust of heat blew into the dim, quiet hall and there was Uncle Xavier, noisy, voluble, snatching the suitcases from Sister Marie-Thérèse. The drooping, waxen face of Christ stared down appalled at this violation of the formal stillness. I smiled at Dr Verdoux and then, on impulse, leant forward and kissed him. Our heads bumped. He was deeply embarrassed.

'Thank you,' I said. After all, he had saved my life. Someone's life. I should at least thank him for that.

'You must come and see us before you go back to England,' said Sister Marie-Thérèse, passing me my crutches. She dabbed her eyes. It seemed odd that they should have grown fond of me. I couldn't imagine what I'd done or said that they should feel anything for me at all. Perhaps it was enough to allow oneself to be saved.

'Or if things are ... difficult,' said Dr Verdoux enigmatically. 'If you should need any help ... ' He looked down at his feet.

'Thank you,' I said again.

Uncle Xavier's car was parked on the gravel drive. It was a small, battered Renault. I was surprised: I'd expected something grander. He seemed too powerful to drive anything this insignificant. I'd assumed, obviously wrongly, that he was someone of some standing. The Renault and his blue workman's trousers confused me. I didn't know where to place him. Outside, the heat was like a wall: it was like walking slam into an invisible wall and being temporarily stunned. Dr Verdoux and Sister Marie-Thérèse stood on the steps and waved as we drove away. I tried to wind down my window to wave back, but it was broken. I hoped they saw what I was doing, but I suspect it simply appeared that I had already forgotten about them.

The seat belt was broken too.

'I need to buy some shoes,' I said as we drove out of the hospital gates and into the town.

'Tomorrow,' said Uncle Xavier. 'Tomorrow you buy shoes. Today you rest and do as you're told. Today we are going home.'

Home. It was an uncomfortable idea.

My thighs burned against the plastic seat. I was beginning to wish I'd taken Sister Marie-Thérèse's advice and worn a cotton skirt. The jeans were much too hot; but they looked so good, these new thin legs of mine stretching out under the dashboard.

'Is it far?' I asked. I wanted it to be a long way away. I wanted never to get there.

Uncle Xavier wasn't listening. He was distracted by a sudden hold-up in the one-way street. He beeped loudly several times. He leant out of his window, waved his arms and shouted abuse at the drivers ahead. At the road junction where the hold-up originated was a sign which said Figeac 40 kilometres. I had 40 kilometres' worth of limbo left – 40 kilometres before I had to make any decisions.

Next to me, on my right, was a Phildar shop, and beyond that a shoe shop with racks and baskets of shoes spilling out on to the pavement. Uncle Xavier had his fist permanently on the horn now. We inched forward. I could just about read the prices: they were quite expensive. What I needed was a pair of cool, comfortable walking shoes. The honest thing to do now would be to get out of the car, buy my shoes and walk off. But I've never been very good at doing the honest thing, so instead

I shifted my sweating thighs free of the seat and put on Chris's sunglasses.

'You like music?' asked Uncle Xavier. His arms were brown and hard-skinned and there was a strong smell of life about him. He smelt of power.

'Yes,' I said.

He turned on the radio. Some all-purpose singing star, someone like Johnny Halliday, was crooning a sharp-edged, sentimental French pop song. I had finally managed to lower the window and sat with my elbow resting on the frame. I was happy to stay like that for hours, for ever, stuck in the traffic with the music, and the sun burning my arm, and the sky a deep, unnatural blue; but nothing lasts. Inevitably, we reached the junction. Uncle Xavier revved the engine so that it sounded like a sick bi-plane, and roared away. We drove noisily through a wide market square with parking spaces under the trees and smart shops and cafés, then out past the inevitable industrial estate, through some straggling, rather uncertain suburbs quite unlike the endless, identikit estates of any comparable English town. Then suddenly we were in the countryside and on the radio a woman was singing a sad, Gallic song about *l'amour perdu*. The sun pounded on the tin roof. Ahead the road trembled and dissolved in a hazy mirage of damp tar. Uncle Xavier drove straight down the middle. He was not inclined to give way to anyone. On either side, the stone walls were soft with wild vines and grey moss. We passed fields full of walnut trees, of beehives, of tobacco: farmyards cackling with long-necked geese, thick stretches of shimmering green woods.

Eventually we came to a crossroads. The sign said Figeac 29 kilometres. Time was running out. Less than 30 kilometres' worth left.

'Uncle Xavier,' I said after a few minutes. I didn't know what else to call him. 'Uncle Xavier ... '

He turned to look at me. I thought: I'll tell him now. I'll ask him to drop me at the station in Figeac. But just as I was beginning to phrase my next sentence, another small Renault hurtled round the blind corner ahead. Uncle Xavier grasped the wheel. His eyes lit up. He adjusted himself in his seat, leaning forward, his teeth bared. He was clearly not going to give way. Nor, I realised, was the driver of the other car. I closed my eyes. Uncle Xavier gave a kind of triumphant shout, rammed his fist into the horn, and then, at the very last minute, wrenched his steering wheel to the right. The two cars passed with inches to spare. Uncle Xavier laughed out loud and banged his hand on the dashboard in delight. 'Salaud,' he said cheerfully and relaxed back into his seat again. He was glowing with satisfaction. After a moment, when the road was clear again, he remembered I'd been about to say something.

'You were going to say ... ?'

I was going to say that I'm not your niece.

'No, no, no,' he said, patting me on the slim denim knee. 'It's all right. Don't worry.'

I was alarmed. I thought at first he'd read my mind. Or that I'd inadvertently said out loud what I thought I'd said only in my head, I was surprised at quite *how* alarmed I felt. Obviously I hadn't intended to tell him the truth at all. But then what exactly was the truth? I was the last person to know: I was fast losing track. If truth is simply a matter of what the majority believes, then I had nothing to tell him. Or is truth always an absolute, like Tony's absolute truth about women's bottoms or the absolute truth that the world is round? The trouble is, though, that if everybody believes women's bottoms look absurd in trousers, if everybody believes the earth is flat, then doesn't belief itself confer the status of truth, at least until the majority of people are persuaded to believe the opposite?

'No, no. It's all right,' Uncle Xavier said again. 'Don't be frightened. Listen, I am a very good driver. An excellent driver. We used to race every year at Le Mans, your father and I.' He took his eyes off the road to look at me. 'You don't remember your father at all?'

'No.'

As a matter of fact I didn't.

He patted my knee again and squeezed it. 'Too thin,' he said, tutting loudly. 'Still far too thin. I used to make you drink goats' milk. You remember that?'

'No,' I said.

He laughed. 'You remember nothing. What's the matter with your head? It's a … ' He was clearly lost for the English word. 'It's full of holes.'

'A sieve,' I said. 'Head like a sieve.'

In the warm silence of the car I grew sleepy. I closed my eyes.

'You know,' said Uncle Xavier after a while, 'the more I look at you, the more I think how like your mother you are.'

I smiled sleepily.

I must have dozed for a while. When I woke up we were in the outskirts of a town.

'Where's this?' I asked.

'Figeac,' said Uncle Xavier. Without signalling, he suddenly turned right. The road crossed the river and twisted past kitchen showrooms and garages.

'Where are we going?' I asked stupidly.

'Home, of course.'

I should have finished it then. That was my last chance and I should have taken it. I should have told him the truth, apologised and asked him to take me to the station. But I was gripped by a curiously fatalistic passivity. Why do I say 'curiously'? There was nothing curious about it. It's how I've always been. I've always drifted along, allowing things to happen, because to do otherwise seemed to require more energy and conviction than I possessed. And because anyway there always seemed to be far less choice than people pretended there was. So I sat silently in my hot, sticky seat, reluctant to leave its womb-like peace, and waited vaguely for something to turn up and rescue me from a situation I didn't seem to have either the will or the energy to escape from by myself.

Slowly, the landscape changed. We drove through ugly, unsettled villages. We started to climb. The soft hedgerows full of wild flowers gave way to parched, scrubby grass. Soil gave way to stone. Acres of low, stunted oaks and dried-up thistles stretched away on either side of the road. We seemed to be driving on the top of the world. The trunks of the stunted trees were grey with lichen. I had never seen anything so barren. Rock and stone and stone and rock. Skinny sheep with bells round their necks tugged at thin dry grass and thistles. The heat of the sun high up on this barren plain was sickening. Roads crossed and snaked away for miles. Ahead was a windmill. Uncle Xavier stopped.

'Voila – le Causse,' he said, inviting me to admire the view.

'It's incredible,' I said. And then in case that wasn't sufficient, I repeated it. 'Absolutely incredible.'

'There's no country like it,' he said. It seemed a fairly safe statement to make. I'd never seen anything remotely like it, and didn't want to. On either side of us, interminable miles of barrenness disappeared into a distant blue haze.

'On that side,' said Uncle Xavier, 'the river. And on *that* side the river. The Gorges,' he added. He seemed to assume I knew what he was talking about. None of it meant anything to me. I'd never seen so hostile a place.

Uncle Xavier drove on. In the middle of a straggling village where the road was dirty with dried mud and straw, we turned left. There was a faded blue signpost on the corner saying Château de Something or other.

'Nearly home,' said Uncle Xavier, and I was suddenly nervous. My mouth went dry. I started looking more carefully at the houses we passed. The first possibility was a crumbling farmhouse. The shutters were rotting and hanging loose and the back door opened on to a midden heap. But there was a brand new concrete agricultural building in the field next door, so perhaps it was more prosperous than it looked. An old man sat on a chair on the cracked mud of the yard. He waved his stick in greeting, scattering geese and indignant chickens. Or maybe he was brandishing it in anger. It was difficult to tell. Two vicious-looking dogs lay sleeping in the shade of a sickly walnut tree. Uncle Xavier beeped his horn and drove on. I was deeply relieved. Ahead I could see a neat little farm, a stone building sitting in the middle of tidily cultivated strips of tobacco and vines. I was convinced this must be it. But instead of slowing down, Uncle Xavier appeared to speed up. We were going rapidly downhill. Without warning, the road fell away on our right.

'The river,' said Uncle Xavier. 'Down there.' Hundreds of feet below us, a green snake of water wandered between high cliffs.

'*Un grand spectacle, uh?*' said Uncle Xavier. 'You don't remember it?'

'I don't remember any of it,' I said truthfully.

He took a hairpin bend far too fast and on the dangerous side of the road. On the other side of us was a solid wall of rock. I was praying quietly that we wouldn't meet any traffic coming in the other direction. A couple of hundred yards after we'd passed yet another faded '*Site Historique*' sign, Uncle Xavier turned left up a narrow stony track, as if straight into the cliff. Blackberry bushes and stunted saplings grew out of crevices in the rock. Lizards scuttered to safety. Above us the sky burned a dark, heavy blue. The track turned sharply and there, opening out in front of us, was a huge natural amphitheatre in the centre of which, as if carved out of the rock itself, stood a towering, grey-turreted château with pepper-pot roofs.

'*Alors. Nous sommes là,*' said Uncle Xavier.

'This is it?' I said, stunned into stupidity.

He glanced at me quickly. 'Of course this is it,' he said. 'What did you expect?'

'Not this.' I was overwhelmed. The long, slender towers rose out of the rock, and above them great natural columns and fissures had been carved into the stone by time and weather.

'I'd forgotten,' I said – a rapid attempt to repair the damage – 'I'd completely forgotten how magnificent it was.'

He shrugged off my reaction as if I were talking not about the château but about him.

The closer we grew, the huger, the more magnificent it became.

'This is the new car park,' said Uncle Xavier. I was clearly supposed to admire it, so I did, though all I could see was a large gravelled area exposed to the full blast of the sun. 'We made it last year. It'll be better when the trees have grown.' I looked doubtfully at some withered, thirsty saplings. 'We can take fifty to sixty cars,' he added with pride.

'You get that many visitors?' I asked.

'Not yet,' he said. 'Not all at once. But this year, maybe ... '

Ahead of us was a crenellated curtain wall. Uncle Xavier drove through a Gothic archway, past a small gatehouse outside which hung details about visiting the château: '*Visites Guidées, tous les après-midis*'. The gravelled drive passed between parched and neglected lawns and curved so that the main medieval château was now slightly to the right, and ahead was a smaller *gentilhommerie* which had been completely hidden from the outside by the defensive wall: a crumbling but ornately elegant Renaissance wing. Someone had made a half-hearted attempt to plant the flower beds under the windows. By the steps was an abandoned tricycle and some battered plastic toys.

The car drew up sharply in a hiss of gravel, narrowly missing the trike.

'Home,' said Uncle Xavier. I tested myself to see if I was nervous. It was clear to me that I was going through with this, that I was going to let it happen. My mouth was dry and my hands and inner thighs slimy with sweat, but this might just have been the heat. I stood on the gravel at the bottom of the steps looking up at the circular leaded pepper-pot towers burnished into beaten silver by the sun, and I laughed.

'What are you laughing at?' said Uncle Xavier.

He was getting the suitcases out of the boot.

I was laughing at my own private joke. If I'd been asked to describe 'home' I would have felt obliged to give a brief sketch of the semi-detached in Birchwood Road, Hanley; but this – this was what I really meant by home, this was what I meant in my head. It was the culmination of a series of curious signs beginning with the plastic flowers in the rue François Premier which, though entirely meaningless and accidental in themselves, had led – or so it seemed to me as I stood staring up at the silver towers – unerringly to this point. All of which was nonsense, of course, and I knew it. Not just nonsense, either. Worse. It was part of some elaborate excuse I was brewing to justify having let myself go so far. But all the same, that's what I felt, and it made me laugh.

A woman came out through the open front door and stood at the top of the steps.

'Mathilde,' said Uncle Xavier. '*Voilà*. Come and meet Marie-Christine.'

I don't know why but the possibility of there being anyone else to cope with, any other relation, hadn't even entered my head. I was completely thrown. She wore black, this woman. She stared at me for a long time without any expression at all. I stood there in trodden-down canvas shoes and jeans, with my hair secured by a rubber band, and felt foolish.

'*Elle a perdu tout son français*,' said Uncle Xavier, chuckling at my carelessness. He chivvied me up the steps. 'Go in. Go in,' he said.

'You are very welcome,' the woman said. She inclined her head in a sudden sharp way, like a hawk spotting movement in the grass. How reckless of me not even to consider that there might be a wife. 'You must be tired,' she said in elegantly accented English, kissing me formally on both cheeks.

'Yes,' I said. 'I am.'

'Then let me show you upstairs. I've put you in the room where your parents used to sleep. Do you remember it?'

'She remembers nothing,' said Uncle Xavier.

The hall was vast and shabby and as cool as the woman's welcome. She led the way up shallow, uncarpeted stairs.

'Where is everybody?' Uncle Xavier asked. 'Why aren't they here?'

Everybody? Who else was there? How many more?

'I thought Marie-Christine would have enough to cope with this afternoon,' said this woman, whom I assumed Chris would think of as *Tante* Mathilde. In French, she added, 'I sent Françoise into Figeac to the bank. And Celeste has taken the children swimming.'

She opened a heavy carved door. '*Voilà*,' she said. The room was enormous, and papered in a design of overwhelming blue cabbage roses.

'It's beautiful,' I said. It was. Two tall leaded windows looked out over a private garden. There were a couple of sun-loungers on the grass. A sleepy grey cat lay spreadeagled under one of them. 'It's a beautiful room,' I said.

'You would like tea?' *Tante* Mathilde asked.

'I'd prefer something cold.'

She nodded. 'The bathroom is the last door along the passage.' She looked at me critically. 'Would you like to rest before dinner, or would you prefer to have your drink in the garden?'

'She must rest,' said Uncle Xavier. 'You must rest. Every day. And eat. And grow fat. We make you better.'

'In that case,' said *Tante* Mathilde, 'I'll fetch some Vichy water to your room. Or would you rather something else?'

'Vichy water will be fine.'

She continued to look at me, her eyes unnervingly and icily dispassionate.

Uncle Xavier had put the suitcases down on the small padded chest at the end of the bed. 'No, no, no,' he said. 'Stay and talk to Marie-Christine. I'll fetch the Vichy.' He smiled at me. 'Look at her eyes,' he said to Tante Mathilde. 'She has her mother's eyes.'

Tante Mathilde shot him a look as sharp as if he were a vole she had just spotted in a distant field. '*Au contraire*,' she said. 'I was just thinking how little she resembles either of her parents.'

'You don't see the resemblance to her mother?' Uncle Xavier looked at her in amazement.

'Not in the least,' said *Tante* Mathilde. 'The colouring is quite different. The features ... everything.' Dismissively, she added in French: 'Her mother was a very pretty woman. And very silly.'

I thought of my mother with her mouse-coloured, tightly permed hair and her worried, permanently exhausted face, and was hurt. How dare this woman call her silly.

'*Il faut que je vous dis que je n'ai pas complètement oublié mon français*,' I said indignantly and probably inaccurately. And then I remembered that I had nothing to feel indignant about. It was not *my* mother they were discussing.

Tante Mathilde smiled distantly as if it were hardly worth trying to grasp what I had said. She murmured something about the kitchen, and walked away.

Uncle Xavier cleared his throat. 'Take no notice,' he said. 'My sister feels things very deeply.'

His *sister*?

'She is angry with me because I drive all the way to fetch you by myself.' He held out his arms. I could see the tears in the corners of his eyes. He hugged me very tight and kissed me on alternate cheeks. 'Welcome home, Marie-Christine,' he said.

· THE MIDDLE ·

When Uncle Xavier had gone, I lay across the bed, my feet dangling over the edge, and stared for a while at the blue cabbage roses. I was too exhausted after the journey to think about anything more rigorous than how frequently the pattern recurred, and whether or not it precisely matched at the corners. My mind was vacant. Odd words and fragments of meaningless pictures floated about behind my eyes. My eyelids started to prick, and after a while the meaninglessness drifted into its own slithery logic, so I gave in to it and let my eyes close. Unconsciousness is so easy, so seductively simple. I do it so well.

The sound of children's voices finally woke me. The small clock on the mantelpiece said twenty-five to seven. I had no idea whether or not it was right. I was hot and crumpled. My mouth was dry. My ill-fitting canvas shoes – Chris's canvas shoes – had fallen on to the floor, and I seemed to have completely lost the rubber band. I searched the bed, but it had gone. From outside, in the garden, I heard a woman call petulantly: 'T'arrêtes-toi, Brigham.'

Brigham? What an extraordinary name. I thought perhaps she was talking to an animal, to a dog, and got up to look. I stood in the shadow of the curtain and looked down. On the brown grass below, two young women lay on the sun-loungers. The petulant one had bronze hair, and wore sunglasses.

'Brigham!' she shouted irritably, looking up from a magazine. A couple of feet away from her, on the gravel path, a small boy was flicking up the stones with a plastic spade. He stopped for a moment and stared at her with grave insolence as if waiting to see what she would do to stop him. *'Je t'ai dit: t'arrêtes!'* She pronounced his name in an Anglicised way, with the stress on the first syllable.

There were two other children in the garden: a boy of about seven who was cycling round and round the lawn, and a smaller girl with wet hair, who was wearing nothing but a pair of knickers and who was stolidly trundling behind him on the plastic trike.

The other woman was turned away from me and shading her face with her hand. I stood at the window observing them for a while. Brigham returned to his original pursuit of flicking up gravel. After a couple of desultory flicks he grew bolder. He scooped up a whole spadeful of stones and sent them showering over the lawn. One hit the stolid little girl on the cheek. She screamed and threw herself face downwards on the grass. The bronze-haired woman flung away her magazine, grabbed Brigham by the arm and smacked him hard across the legs.

I let the curtain drop and moved away from the window. What shall I do now? I wondered. I had no idea. To waste time, I drank a little of the Vichy water someone had left on the bedside table while I slept, and considered whether or not to unpack. There's something very final about the act of unpacking: it signifies an intention to stay. I was still deliberately not thinking that far ahead: or, indeed, thinking at all if I could help it. So I emptied the smaller of the two suitcases on to the bed and fidgeted with the contents a little, unfolding things, shaking them out. Then, still without thinking about it much, I started hanging clothes up in the wardrobe. You can't possibly expect to get away with this, I told myself. But I *had* got away with it. So far, I had. People were falling over themselves to tell me who I was. And anyway, I thought evasively, I wasn't going to stay long; just a couple of days; just until I felt strong enough to take up the burden of Margaret Davison again.

I watched my reflection in the triple mirror on the dressing table as I came and went from bed to wardrobe, back and forth across the stained floorboards, wading knee deep through the shadows: a thin, narrow-faced woman shaking out Chris Masbou's T-shirts, and arranging the shoes that didn't and never would fit in the carved drawer below the hanging space. I watched the woman slip on a cream silk dressing gown with a rip under the armpit and a stain down the front. I watched her pick up a pale green sponge bag. Out of the mirror's range, I connected with myself again. I stood with my fingers on the handle of the bedroom door, and panicked. Suppose I met someone on the landing between this room and the bathroom. But it was all right. Apart from a grey cat who came to meet me with all the indiscriminate affection of the self-obsessed, the passage was empty.

The cat followed me into the bathroom, weaving her way between my legs. I sat on the lavatory, an ancient contraption with a mahogany seat and a design of flowers round the bowl, and we stared at each other, the cat and I, for a long time as if we thought we recognised each other. Later, while I washed, it perched on the edge of the bath, apparently as intrigued by my herringbone body as I was. My breasts drooped softly over the bones, two empty triangular pouches. My hip bones jutted out as if ready to burst through the skin. For the first time in my life, my stomach was concave, and the loose skin, bruised yellow and purple, fell in a soft, wrinkled purse above my pubic hair. And yet, ugly as it was – and it was, very ugly – I liked it. I liked the feeling of being pared down to the bone. The cat purred, perhaps mistaking me – understandably – for a half-eaten fish. I thought it might follow me back to my room. I would have welcomed it. But it had lost interest in me. It stayed on the edge of the bath staring fixedly at the spot where I had been as if all the time it had really been looking at something else, something far more interesting and intriguingly insubstantial.

I put on the least creased of Chris's skirts and a white T-shirt. The shoe problem was partly solved by the discovery of a pair of Indian sandals, the sort that consist of a sole and a V-shaped thong. My heel slopped over the edge, but apart from making a terrible clattering noise on the stairs, they were manageable.

Downstairs, the hall was empty and full of early evening sun. I hovered there for a long time, uncertain where else to go. I looked through a pile of brochures on the table. '*Le Château de Rougearc,*' I read, '*est situé sur le D21, au bas d'une falaise.*' I skimmed through a long paragraph about the history of *le château,* and then, because I couldn't think of what else I might legitimately do, started on a section which began, '*Après ce bref exposé de l'histoire de Rougearc, il nous reste encore à pénétrer à l'intérieur du château qui présente aussi beaucoup d'intérêt.*' But exactly what there was of interest defeated me because the words strayed far beyond the childish limits of my vocabulary. So I abandoned that and started looking through a leather-bound visitors' book as if it were the most interesting thing I had ever seen. It was surprising how many English people came. Rod and Jackie Woodward from Croydon. The Lynch family from Ashford, Middlesex: 'A very educational and enjoyable tour. Many thanks.' Bob and Pearl Swift from Cleveland. 'A welcome break from saddle sores,' Bob – or maybe Pearl – had written in the comments column. Who on earth did they think was interested in their saddle sores? I was amazed by what people wrote. After a bit I became so engrossed by the inane remarks of Eileen and Hugh Potter from Carlisle, or Toby and Jenny Pleat from Berks – 'Wonderful Gothic vaulting. A treat' – that I was miles away, laughing to myself. I heard nothing.

'You're lost?' *Tante* Mathilde asked. She moved silently from the shadows. I jumped. I felt as if I'd been caught reading her private correspondence. She was carrying two dusty bottles of wine: I assumed she must have emerged from a cellar.

'I was just looking at the visitors' book.'

She nodded. 'You'll find it interesting. We have a great many foreign visitors. Your cousins are in the garden,' she said. '*Venez.*'

I followed her through a large dining room full of old furniture and silver. All but a narrow passageway was roped off. This was clearly part of the tour. At the far end, between two threadbare tapestries, was a door marked '*Privé.*' I followed *Tante* Mathilde through into a passage. Coats hung on a whitewashed stone wall. Shelving collapsed gently under the weight of flower vases and the sort of things no one knows where else to put. On the floor were two Butagaz cylinders and a pile of shoes and toys and old magazines. The passage was flooded with sun.

'You won't, of course, remember your cousins,' said *Tante* Mathilde.

At the end of the passage, a door led out to the private garden. The woman in sunglasses was still stretched out on the sun-lounger, but the other one was now kneeling on the grass, trying to put the wheel back on the plastic tricycle. They both looked up.

'Let me introduce you,' said *Tante* Mathilde. 'Marie-Christine, your cousin, Françoise.' The woman who had been crouching, and who was the nearer to us, stood up. Her hair was mouse coloured and pulled back with a hair slide. She wore pale-rimmed glasses which seemed to be too big for her face.

'*Ma cousine,*' she said and kissed me on both cheeks. I was rather nervous of her glasses in case I knocked them off. She was too. She kept poking at them and adjusting them. Her skin smelt clean and childish. She smiled shyly at me. Neither of us knew what to say.

The woman with elegantly cut metallic hair had risen from the lounger.

'Marie-Christine,' she said.

The alarming thing was that as she approached I saw how remarkably like Chris she was, the same small-boned build, the same sharp face, the same nose, the same jawline, the same short hair and long neck. For a moment the similarity unnerved me. But it was only a surface likeness, a physical thing. What in Chris had been a masculine self–assurance, a careless confidence, presented itself in this woman as a self-aware, very feminine chic. 'Such a terrible accident,' she said, kissing me gingerly, a matter of cheeks brushing, like colliding with a perfumed butterfly. She looked at my scabby face. 'A terrible accident,' she repeated. She spoke English as if she'd learned it in America.

'My younger daughter, Celeste,' *Tante* Mathilde was saying. 'And these are my grandchildren – '

The children had come like curious animals to see what I was.

Celeste introduced them. Richard, Zoë and the gravel-flicker, Brigham. They stared at me with the same absorbed and entirely false interest that the cat had shown. I didn't know whether to shake hands or kiss them or what.

'Kiss your cousin,' said *Tante* Mathilde in French. None of them wanted to be kissed: they fidgeted and tensed their heads. The moment it was over they ran off back to their bicycles and their solitary games with stones.

'*Attention*, Zoë,' said Celeste mechanically.

'Of course,' said *Tante* Mathilde, 'you used to play together, you three girls.'

'I'm afraid I've got an appalling memory,' I mumbled nervously. 'I don't remember anything.'

The three women stood there like three points of the compass observing the fourth. I could see each of them trying to connect me with their memory of an eight-year-old girl who had played on this lawn. *Tante* Mathilde's head was slightly tilted as if what she saw displeased her. Celeste was looking at my crumpled skirt and ill-fitting sandals. I wondered what I'd do if one of them said: 'Hang on a minute – you're not Marie-Christine. You're nothing like her.' That's what I was expecting. I suppose in one form or another I'm always expecting it, and to tell the truth it would be far easier and less frightening to be unmasked now, when there was another mask still in place underneath, than when, as usual, there was nothing there at all. So I waited, and stared at the dry spikes of grass round my feet, but none of the three women said anything. I said nothing either. I'd already discovered that I no longer suffered from the anxious necessity that people should like me. Why should I? It was, after all, not me they were judging. So the lengthening silence didn't worry me at all. Eventually, Françoise broke it by making polite and nervous enquiries about my journey.

'Maman, j'ai faim,' shouted the elder boy as he swerved in a big circle round us.

'Take the children inside, Françoise, and wash their hands,' said Tante Mathilde.

We ate, not in the elaborate dining room but in the kitchen, a cool, vaulted, stone-walled room which seemed to be part of the older building. We were already halfway through a plate of crudités, when Uncle Xavier appeared; he smelt of animals and hot grass. He reached for my hand as he sat, held it very tightly for a moment and smiled at me, his leathery face warm with pleasure. His teeth were strong and very even. He launched at once into a long conversation with Tante Mathilde, who was sitting at the other end of the trestle table. They appeared to be talking either about deer or goats: I couldn't work out which because I couldn't remember what chèvre meant, but on balance, and from the faint smell on Uncle Xavier's skin, I guessed it must be a conversation about goats.

'You keep goats?' I asked.

'Goats,' he said, reverting to English for my benefit. 'Sheep. Chickens. Bees. Geese. We make cheese, honey, pâté ... '

'Your uncle runs the farm,' said *Tante* Mathilde, 'and we organise the guided tours.'

Celeste yawned. She pressed clover-coloured fingertips against her mouth. 'I don't see why people can't go round by themselves,' she complained. 'They do in England.'

'England,' said *Tante* Mathilde dismissively. 'In England they do all kinds of things.' She switched suddenly to French. 'They're not interested in fine art, the English. Or architecture. Or history. It's all football and politics with them. Besides, if we let people wander round by themselves, they'd only steal things.' But she made this sound rather like a French virtue, as if only the French had the good taste to know what was worth stealing.

I pretended not to understand.

Uncle Xavier raised his glass.

'We should drink a toast,' he said. 'To Marie-Christine. To her recovery.'

Glasses were raised. I smiled at them. I suddenly had a picture of Chris and me sitting together in the restaurant smiling at one another like conspirators over the wine. 'Look where I am now, Chris. Isn't this odd?' I said to her in my head.

Celeste put down her fork. 'And how long do you expect to stay?' she asked.

'As long as she chooses,' said Uncle Xavier. 'This is her home.'

Celeste tightened her lips. Skilfully shaded brown and gold eyelids came down like shutters. She pushed her plate away.

'A couple of days,' I said. I was amazed to hear myself add, 'Maybe a week?'

'No, no, no,' said Uncle Xavier. 'Longer than that. You need time to heal.'

Brigham was making a lot of noise with his knife and fork, trying to catch fragments of grated carrot.

'*Tais-toi*, Brigham,' Celeste said irritably.

Françoise leant over and helped him.

'Brigham,' I said. 'What an unusual name.'

The eyelids lifted. She looked at me. 'It's American. My husband is an American. In the army.'

'Really?' I said politely. 'Is he stationed near here?'

'He's in the States,' said Celeste. Stifling another yawn as if the whole subject was infinitely tedious to her, she added, 'We're separated.'

'Oh,' I said. 'Oh, I see.'

Tante Mathilde tapped her upper lip and said, 'Françoise, something on your lip. A piece of lettuce.'

Françoise blushed and dabbed her mouth with her napkin.

'That's better,' said *Tante* Mathilde

'Do you know America well?' Celeste asked.

'I've never been,' I said, without thinking.

It was a mistake.

Her eyes widened in surprise. 'You've never been? But I thought … '

I could have kicked myself. People who deal in commodities must fly to the States as regularly as I popped into Asda.

'Oh, well, yes, the usual places, yes,' I said hurriedly. 'New York, and um … ' Where else was there? 'Los Angeles. But beyond that … '

'I used to live in New York once,' she said. 'We had an apartment on Upper Forty-Fourth. Do you know it?'

'Vaguely,' I said. I wished someone would change the subject.

'You know the delicatessen on the corner of Forty-Fourth and – ?'

'Let me help you,' I said to Françoise, who was collecting the plates, but Uncle Xavier caught my hand and pulled me down again.

'Sit,' he said as if I were a dog. I sat. He beamed at me. 'You're on holiday,' he said. 'Let Françoise do it.' He squeezed my hand. 'You don't work. You rest. We look after you.'

Celeste chattered on about the quality of charcuterie at this New York delicatessen I was supposed to know about. I was grateful when Françoise returned to the table with a dish of richly smelling pork. She handed it first to me.

'And what about you?' I asked, as I helped myself.

'Me?' There were two small marks on her bottom lip where her top teeth constantly cut into the flesh.

'What do *you* do?'

'Nothing.' She pushed nervously at her glasses. 'Well, I do the cooking. And the guided tours. Would you like me to show you round tomorrow? You've probably forgotten.'

'She's forgotten everything,' said Uncle Xavier. 'Everything. Head like a sieve.' He laughed and filled my glass. It was a standing joke with him now, my inability to remember. If a memory should ever surface – which of course it couldn't, so he was quite safe – I think he'd have been disappointed.

'What do you mean "nothing"?' Celeste said. 'We never stop all day. The same old boring things.' She assumed what I took to be a parody of a tour guide's voice: '*Remarquez aussi des meubles Renaissance ...* '

'No, I meant in comparison with Marie-Christine,' said Françoise. 'Nothing in comparison with what she does.'

'Ah, but Marie-Christine was always clever,' said Uncle Xavier. 'Always reading books.'

'Always in trouble,' said *Tante* Mathilde. Uncle Xavier made noises of dissent. She ignored them. 'But, of course,' she said, 'in England children are allowed to run wild.'

'It's worse in America,' said Celeste, looking at her own children with distaste, although they'd hardly spoken during the meal. 'In England they just ignore them: in America they spoil them to death.' I thought as far as ignoring went, she was doing a pretty good job with hers. She sat smoking while Françoise cut Zoe's meat into manageable pieces.

'Of course Hervé was always the clever one,' Uncle Xavier was saying. 'You have your father's brains, Marie-Christine. I was the dunce. The stupid farm boy, me.' He tapped his grizzled head. 'Empty,' he said, and laughed.

That was an interesting and useful piece of information – so Chris's father was called Hervé.

'Some more haricots, Marie-Christine?' said Françoise.

'Chris,' I said. It seemed such a mouthful, Marie-Christine. 'Everybody calls me Chris.'

'Not here,' said *Tante* Mathilde. 'Here you are Marie-Christine.' Dismissing any other possibility, she turned to Celeste and began a conversation in French which was too rapid and complex for me to follow – something to do with some brochures Françoise had collected from the printer's. I was beginning to feel tired. I gave up trying.

We drank coffee, still sitting at the kitchen table, while the children were sent up to bed. Outside it had grown dark without my noticing. The conversation about the brochures had long ago dried up. A heavy silence fell. Celeste yawned delicately from time to time and smoked, crushing her lipstick-stained cigarettes into the ashtray before they were properly finished. Françoise fidgeted with a piece of bread and smiled at me shyly. *Tante* Mathilde sipped coffee from a tiny cup, which she held, like the silence, in the bowl of her hands. Uncle Xavier reached across from time to time and touched my hand as if he needed to make sure I was still a physical reality – which indeed was *all* I was. A small voice in my head – so far away as to be almost inaudible – said: 'You ought to tell them. They have the right to know Marie-Christine is dead.' But a closer, more comforting voice, a voice warmed by wine, a wise-sounding voice said: 'Don't be ridiculous. Why burden them with unnecessary pain?' and I listened to this voice, because it sounded as if it was telling a greater truth than the other one. I had only to look at Uncle Xavier's face to know how much he wanted his niece to be sitting there beside him; and I made a good enough niece for him: he seemed to like me. He might not have liked the real thing half so much. I looked at him with affection.

'You're tired,' he said, watching me closely.

'Yes, I am,' I said. I felt ridiculously happy to hear him tell me these intimate little details about myself.

I lay on the bed in the darkness. Both windows were wide open. Outside the sky was thick with stars, incalculable millions of them blurring into a luminous softness. My body stretched out long and pale on the cover. I was too exhausted to sleep. My brain buzzed. To try and numb myself, I'd taken two of the painkillers Dr Verdoux had given me that morning, but they hadn't worked. I kept seeing the photo of Tony, the one in the *Sun*, the one with his shoulders hunched and his hands shielding his face – the bereaved and grieving husband. Was he grieving? He claimed frequently that without me he'd be lost, but I took this to be a piece of subtle blackmail: a kind of warning. I used to ask him sometimes if he loved me.

'Do you love me?' I said, curious to know what it was other than habit on his part and fear on mine that kept us locked together in the semi-detached on Birchwood Road.

'Yes, of course I do,' he said.

I needed regular reassurance. If he really did love me, I reasoned, then perhaps that explained what I was doing there. Perhaps that was sufficient excuse, because it conferred on me such a huge responsibility that naturally I had to stay and get on with hoovering the carpets and cooking the meals. So his answer was like a pin fixing me firmly in place. I was very grateful to him for it. Sometimes I had to ask so frequently that he got irritated. Well, understandably. 'For God's sake,' he said, 'you know I do. I tell you often enough.' And he did. It was true. He often said it spontaneously without any prompting. But I *needed* him to tell me. I needed him to pin me down and make sense of things.

Had he cried at the news of my supposed death? He's not a man who cries easily. I've only seen him do it twice in sixteen years, and both times were my fault. Twice I watched him racked with unbearable and unpractised sobs. I was appalled. I was so terrified by his depth of feeling that I felt ill. I put out my hand to touch him, to make some sort of contact, but he shrugged away from me. I had no idea how to comfort him. I didn't understand how he could cry so painfully and yet still reject the one source of comfort on offer. I suppose his logic was that since I was the cause of his pain, I could hardly effect the cure. And yet it seemed to me that, for precisely the same reason, I was the only one who could conceivably heal it. So there was nothing to do but to go through the usual rituals: to negotiate for forgiveness, to endure the consequent subtle punishments. Poor Tony: his emotions are so much more complex than mine. Mine are very simple. Sometimes I think I only have one. Sometimes I think the only emotion I have ever felt is fear. It's a very wide-ranging emotion, of course: it covers everything from mild anxiety to frozen terror, but in the end it all boils down to the same thing. Even happiness is only the temporary relaxation of fear.

The problem was that it was almost impossible to imagine him without me. I still half suspected that in reality I was lying on the double bed in our room at Birchwood Road waiting for him to finish in the bathroom. It certainly seemed more probable than the alternative: that I was masquerading as someone else in a turreted château in France waiting for the tyranny of consciousness to lose its grip.

Once upon a time – I use this opening because it's a comfortable way for stories to begin, and this is a story – once upon a time I was in a computer shop in Stoke on an errand for Tony: some piece of software he wanted. It was an irritatingly hot day, one of those days when your skin doesn't fit properly, when your flesh feels pale and damp and hideous, when anything is enough to set your teeth on edge. I could hardly bear to be inside my own body. God knows how far I walked trying to find this particular shop. The pavements were blocked by phalanxes of slow-moving, fat-legged girls with stained armpits, and gangs of young men in shirt sleeves, eating chips and swigging canned lager.

When eventually I found this computer shop I was looking for, a young boy, thin and white like an etiolated seedling, told me that the piece of software I wanted was no longer in stock. They had, he said in a scarcely broken voice, sold out yesterday. He looked a little frightened when he told me this: I don't know why. I don't know what he thought I might do. I couldn't move: I couldn't speak. I thought I might pass out from an excess of irritation. The pale, etiolated boy kept glancing nervously at me. I stood there in the middle of the shop like a pillar, suddenly – and inconveniently – overwhelmed by the monstrous and tyrannical fact of my own being. This is perhaps an odd thing to strike one in the middle of a computer shop in Stoke, but these seminal moments of revelation have to happen somewhere, however improbable. So I stood on the stained carpet thinking of all the millions of years when I hadn't been, and of how nice that was: and of all the millions of years to come when I wouldn't be again, and was knocked almost senseless by it: by the horror of it, by the horror of being forced – as a result of this meaningless accident of consciousness – into a continual state of apprehension, a continual stream of physical feeling, of emotional feeling, a constant barrage of wittering, shapeless thought.

'It's intolerable,' I said. 'It's quite intolerable.' I must have said it out loud, because people turned to look at me, and the etiolated seedling's eyes were darting about in a panic-stricken way.

After a moment, a man in a shiny suit came and said he was the manager, Madam, and did I have a complaint.

'Yes,' I said. 'I do. I do have a complaint.'

He apologised a great deal – although the accident of consciousness was hardly his fault – and said meaningless things about his difficulties with the suppliers and how he would phone me as soon as the software was in stock, and I just kept saying, 'It's intolerable. It's quite monstrous,' because that was all I could think of. The manager grew more and more upset. 'Well I'm sorry, madam, but you have to understand that we have our problems as well,' he said huffily, his neck going a mottled purple. He accused me of being unreasonable.

'I know that,' I said. I walked out of the shop and into the heat, into the smell of chips and petrol fumes and curry sauce. I was suddenly very thirsty. That's the trouble about thinking, about trying seriously to come to grips with things. You can only go so far before this tyranny of physical consciousness gets in the way. In the end, aching feet and thirst always take precedence. Descartes got it completely wrong. The reason you know you exist is because the pain in your gut is intolerable, or your bladder's about to burst, or you bang your elbow, or you're just plain thirsty.

I was. I was so thirsty when I stumbled out of that shop that I couldn't swallow, so I went into the first café I came to. I sat at a table and ordered mineral water with ice. It was a café run by Greeks. There was a cracked, crudely coloured painting of the Acropolis on the wall. After a while the place got quite crowded. On my table was a puddle of spilt coffee and I kept putting my glass down in it and then idly making a design of wet, overlapping circles on a dry bit of the formica surface. A man came and sat opposite me. He had a cup of coffee and some kind of pastry. He looked foreign. He said his name was Elefteris. He was very dark skinned. He wore a checked shirt with the sleeves rolled up.

'What's your name?' he asked.

'Marina James,' I told him.

No, stop that. That's the end of that story. I am not going on with that one. I only tell it to myself sometimes to remind myself of when it was that this revelation occurred, and how anxiously from then on I chased oblivion.

The sun woke me. I must have slept for hours – a blank, empty sleep. I was amazed to wake up feeling so clean, so unburdened by the usual worrying wisps of dreams. I lay, still naked, in a puddle of sun. Never in my life had I had a dreamless night before. It was an astonishing feeling. The sun burned through my pale, ragged flesh. I lifted my legs up in the air and examined the puckered needlework along the scars. Then I got up. No, I didn't. I didn't just get up. I jumped. I jumped out of bed. I didn't know you could do that. I'd often jumped *into* bed before, but never out of it. Energy hummed and buzzed out of my skin. This was another feeling I was quite unfamiliar with. It was probably something to do with not dreaming. Usually dreams leave me exhausted, with a slightly sick feeling of apprehension. Usually I have to lie in bed for a good half-hour fighting an overwhelming sense of dread, and carefully assembling the masks and the reflecting surfaces before I can begin.

One of the things I used to hate when I was Margaret Davison was staying with strangers. I used to worry for ages about arriving downstairs hours before anyone else had got up, or so late that everyone else had had breakfast ages ago. I used to hover about in a panic, trying to find the precise and perfect moment to go downstairs. Tony never worried about things like that. 'What does it matter?' he used to say. Well, it mattered to me, because getting it wrong seemed to be indicative of a whole range of things that I'd always got wrong and always would get wrong. Even the simplest things that other people never thought about at all, I found appallingly difficult.

'But it's so simple,' he used to say, his lips thinning with affectionate exasperation. He said it all the time. It didn't matter what we were talking about: how to use the spit on the cooker, how to convert kilometres into miles, how not to get paint on the carpet. 'It's basically a matter of following a few elementary rules. You can't go wrong.'

I could. The fact is I never really understood these elementary rules of his.

As I clattered downstairs, my size-six feet hanging over the heel of my size-five sandals, I found myself moving closer to Tony's position. He was right. (Well, of course he was. When wasn't he?) What the hell *did* it matter? I must have driven him mad.

I took the stairs at a kind of skip. I was humming. I stuck my fingertips in the hip pockets of Chris's jeans and even swaggered a little. I walked across the hall and through to the kitchen, swinging my new legs further than Margaret Davison's legs had ever dared stretch, striding along the dusty passages as if I had every right to be there.

Françoise was sitting alone in the kitchen drinking coffee from a bowl. Her glasses were on the table. She had that pink, alarmingly naked look people who wear glasses have when they face the world without them. She blinked as if her eyes hurt.

'Good morning,' I said. She jumped. 'Everybody else already up?'

'The children are,' she said. 'I've just run them to school. And Uncle Xavier was up hours ago.' Her English wasn't as confidently fluent as Celeste's nor as precise as *Tante* Mathilde's, but it was streets ahead of my French. We spoke English automatically – a consequence of my ignorance and her instinctive courtesy. 'Would you like some coffee?' she asked.

I poured a cupful and helped myself to a piece of bread. Françoise wiped her glasses on her skirt and put them on again. I saw my reflection doubled in her lenses.

'You're not at all what I imagined,' she said. 'I thought you'd be very stylish and superior.' She smiled shyly as if she'd offered me a compliment. I was, in fact, offended. Give or take a scar or two and ragged hair, I thought that my new legs, my jeans and my borrowed name had given me sufficient confidence to lay claim to a little of Chris's style. 'Really?' I said, confused by my misapprehensions.

She was sliding a small pat of butter into a glass dish. 'I do remember you a bit,' she said. 'I remember going swimming once. And a picnic.'

I was still smarting over her unintentional insult. I needed to look in a mirror. I needed to see if Margaret Davison was so obviously still there.

'I'll just take this up to *Maman*,' she said, picking up the tray. I stood up to open the door. The gesture flustered her. She was already standing on one leg so she could balance the tray on her other knee while she opened the door for herself. The butter dish slid off on to the floor and crashed. Coffee swilled about the tray.

'I'm sorry,' I said. 'I'm so sorry.'

'No, I am,' she insisted. 'It was my fault.'

I picked up the butter, removed a couple of shards of china, flicked some specks of dirt and fluff off it and put it on a spare saucer.

'You can't do that,' she said, her eyes wide with alarm.

'Why not?' I said.

'It's been on the floor.' Her mouth made a damp pink circle of horror.

'You know that,' I said, 'and I know that, but nobody else does.'

She pressed her lips together as if she were afraid of laughing. Behind her glasses, her eyes crinkled.

Recklessly, I added, 'People only ever see what they expect to see.' I made a pattern on the butter with a fork. 'There you are.'

Hovering in the doorway, she said: 'Marie-Christine ... I don't know whether you'd be interested ... but later on I've got to go into town for *Maman* ... '

'Oh, good,' I said. 'I need to buy some shoes.'

She seemed almost to tremble with pleasure. 'In about half an hour then?' she said.

When she'd gone, I ate another piece of bread. I stared round the kitchen, learning where everything was. I was just thinking of doing some washing up, when Celeste appeared, dressed in a kimono. She had that pale yellow look that very tanned people have when they're tired.

'Oh God,' she said, yawning. She sat down.

'Good morning,' I said.

'Is the coffee hot?'

There was barely half a cupful left. I told her so. 'I wouldn't mind another cup myself,' I said. I didn't really want one but I was interested to see which one of us would give in first and do it. She did.

'Did you sleep well?' she asked politely as she filled the filter jug.

'Extraordinarily well. Yes. And you?'

She yawned, and ran her hand through her hair implying that she'd slept hardly at all. 'Has Françoise taken up *Maman's* tray?' she asked.

I said that yes, she had. She'd also, I said, taken the children to school. Celeste raised an eyebrow. It was a skill I greatly coveted. It elegantly implied more than any other piece of body language I could think of.

'How do you do that?' I asked. 'That's so clever.'

'Was that a criticism?' she said, 'You think why doesn't *she* take her children to school. Why let her sister do it?' She lit a cigarette, and said coldly. 'You haven't got any children, have you?'

'No,' I said. Sometimes Tony and I talked about it. Sometimes we wondered if it might not be an idea to see someone, a specialist, but we never did. I don't know why.

'Well, I don't think you're in any position to criticise then,' she said.

While the coffee dripped into the jug, Celeste told me a great deal more than I wanted to know about her soldier husband, who, apparently, was an insensitive brute with limited intelligence and clumsy fingers. He chewed gum and understood nothing whatever about her needs. Worst of all, he refused to give her any money: her financial situation was quite desperate. Why else would she stay in such a dump? Given half a chance she'd be off to Paris like a shot.

I was rather bored with this. 'Would you like some bread?' I asked in the hope that if her mouth were otherwise occupied she might shut up, but she had absent-mindedly lit another cigarette.

'If only I could find a job,' she yawned.

It would have to be a very good job, I thought, to support not only her and her children but also her nicotine habit. 'What kind of thing do you do?' I asked.

'Wander round showing stupid tourists the same thing six times a day.'

'No, I mean what kind of job are you thinking of?'

'Oh … ' She sipped her coffee, closing her eyes, as if the first mouthful was a wonderful relief to her. 'This and that. Anything. A little boutique, maybe. Or a flower shop. I don't know.' She opened her eyes again and looked at me as if expecting some comment, but I was thinking my own thoughts. After a moment she said with genuine horror, 'How can you bear it? All those scabs on your face. I think I'd die. Will you be permanently scarred?'

Her ingenuous vanity was rather touching. 'I don't know,' I said. I didn't really care. The more my face was covered in scabs and scars, the less I could see anyone I recognised there.

'Aren't you scared?' she asked, staring at me in appalled fascination.

'Not really.'

She stood up hurriedly as if it offended her to be in the same room with someone so physically disfigured, and dumped her coffee bowl on the draining board. 'Well,' she said – a small in-joke between two cosmopolitans – 'have a nice day.'

*

Nice is hardly the word. It was – from beginning to end – a day of perfect happiness.

I remember once at primary school being told to write an essay entitled 'My Happiest Day' and finding it almost impossible, because even at ten I was beginning to grasp that happiness was only a temporary state. It seldom lasted as long as a whole day, and was anyway always tempered by physical imperatives, so that in the middle of perfect happiness a tooth starts to ache or a mosquito bite starts to itch. Happiest moments I could have coped with easily. Happiest hours were possible. But happiest days seemed to be stretching credibility too far. I sat, staring at the paper, paralysed by the impossibility of the task I'd been set. It was like being asked to spin golden thread out of straw. But now I could do it easily, because once upon a time I had one whole day which was pure happiness from beginning to end.

What did I do on this day of perfect happiness? Well, first of all Françoise and I drove into Figeac. It was still early: lines and angles, which by midday would be razor sharp and slice the eye, were still softly smudged. The road wound downwards through grey and orange rocks. I couldn't imagine why yesterday I'd found this landscape so hostile.

Figeac was full of cars and crowds. I waited in the bank for Françoise to pay in the weekend's takings from the 'Visites Guidées', and then we went to buy some fish. In the market we bumped into several people, to whom I was introduced as her cousin, Marie-Christine from London. My cheeks were kissed, my hands held and shaken.

'It'll be all round the village now,' said Françoise when we stopped for a drink at a pavement café because my legs were aching. 'Everyone'll want to see you.'

I sat slouched in a white plastic chair with my legs sprawled out in front of me and watched people pass. It felt like the first day of a holiday, except it was better because the first day of a holiday was always shadowed by familiar anxieties: the imperative to enjoy oneself; the worry that Tony wouldn't. I stretched my legs out further on the pavement and drank my glass of beer. Beer, I felt, was probably what Chris would have drunk.

Afterwards we wandered off to find a shoe shop, where suddenly I became very reckless. I tried on pair after pair: sandals, court shoes, flat shoes, every kind of shoe you could think of. The floor was littered with them. In the end I bought four pairs, including some red high heels for Françoise, who kept saying she couldn't possibly; she'd never dare wear them; what would *Maman* say; how could she possibly accept such an expensive gift?

'Oh, I've got plenty of money,' I said rashly. I'd already spent over a thousand of my 8,000 francs.

Her gratitude was out of all proportion. I told her so, and made things worse. I had a sudden memory of Chris insisting on paying the bill at the Relais Routier in the same slightly irritable way that I was now brushing away Françoise's protestations about the shoes.

So then we drove back. As we passed the house with the walnut tree and the midden heap outside the back door, I said, 'Nearly home.' The pleasure of turning the corner and seeing ahead the turrets against the rock was as sharp as salt on the tongue.

By this time I was very hungry. Françoise cooked the fish she'd bought in Figeac for lunch. Celeste arrived in the kitchen, sniffed, and said, 'Oh God, not fish.' She was wearing a lime-green dress with a bronze belt, the colour of her hair. She sat pushing bits of food about her plate and ate nothing except a few leaves of salad. She looked as if she was sulking about something but when I asked if anything was the matter she looked surprised and said no, she was just bored.

'You have an excellent appetite, Marie-Christine,' *Tante* Mathilde observed, as I helped myself to more potatoes. The remark sounded more like a criticism than a compliment.

'I like food,' I said.

'Really? You never used to.' She turned the full force of her hawkish scrutiny on my face. 'You never ate anything when you were small. I was always surprised your mother was so calm about it. But then she had a very poor understanding of how to bring up children. I told her she should consult a doctor. You used to refuse everything – meat, vegetables, cheese – you wouldn't touch them. And now look: here you are with an excellent appetite, and Celeste, who was such a pretty, plump little girl, and no trouble at all, picks at her food as if it were poisoned.'

'I'm not hungry,' said Celeste sulkily. 'Don't fuss.'

'I am,' I said, helping myself to another fillet of fish. 'Ravenously hungry.'

After lunch, Tante Mathilde walked down to the gatehouse carrying a small tin cash-box. Already cars were parked in the sparse shade of the walls, and visitors were finishing their picnics under parasols in the car park.

'Would you like to see round the château?' Françoise asked. 'You wouldn't find it too tiring to follow the tour? All the steps?'

A gaggle of tourists were drifting up the drive towards us. Most of them were in shorts. The men had cameras hanging from their necks. There was a strong smell of suntan oil.

'*Mesdames, messieurs, bonjour,*' said Françoise, when she'd checked all the tickets, and the group had coalesced. 'Is there anyone from England?' she asked.

There was: a pair of elderly women whom I typecast immediately as teachers, and a young sandy-haired couple with a toddler. There was also one Canadian, a dark boy who was backpacking. Any Germans? Françoise asked. None. 'Any Dutch?'

She was very good, Françoise, surprisingly good. There was nothing theatrical about her approach: she was never anything more than a quietly unobtrusive voice drawing one's attention to this or to that, answering questions in both French and

English with grave politeness, leaving people time to look at the things she saw interested them, interspersing the drier stuff with a few stories which she told so badly, blushing and pushing at her glasses, that people were instinctively in sympathy with her, and smiled kindly if they suspected there might conceivably have been a joke hidden somewhere in the story. She told us how the original château had been built to defend the Causse from the marauding English. The English in the party laughed at this. She told us that the later wing of the château had been built in the reign of François Premier. That made *me* laugh.

'I'm sorry,' I said to the blank, puzzled faces that turned to stare. 'I just had a sudden thought.'

'Oh, you're English,' said one of the elderly women. 'Eileen, she's English. How lovely. Are you working here, or on holiday, or what?'

'Yes,' I said, and left them to decide.

We were invited to look at examples of '*style gothique*' and to admire the vaulting. I drifted along at the back of the party, half listening, half lost in my own deep absorption of stone and wood. I had twenty-four years to make up, I had a childhood familiarity to establish. The spiral staircases up to the tiny circular tower rooms – where princesses must once have spun their golden threads and waited for something to happen – were worn almost to glass. The tapestries were threadbare and mould speckled. Moths had ravaged the dusty upholstery. The gilt was chipped. But this was all exactly how it should be. I touched and breathed and smelt and folded myself into it.

The tour ended in the kitchens of the original medieval château. Françoise began looking at her watch and trying to herd people through into the smallest kitchen where, to get back out into the courtyard, they had to pass between two tables covered with things to buy: postcards, jars of honey, pots of honeycomb, goats' cheeses, fresh eggs, jars of *confits*.

'You don't want to go all the way round again, do you?' said Françoise, when the last straggling members of that group had been shepherded out, and across the courtyard the next group of tourists were waiting for their turn.

I didn't mind what I did. Happiness is like that.

'Why don't you sit in the sun for a little?' she suggested. 'You ought to rest.'

I did as I was told. I lay on one of the sun-beds in the garden and let the warmth soak into my skin and soothe the pains in my legs and lower back. I'd climbed too many staircases. I'd walked too far. I ought to rest, I knew I ought, but resting bored me. I was too full of energy to lie about doing nothing. I turned over on to my stomach and became absorbed in trying to rescue a scarlet beetle which had fallen helplessly on to its back, and which for some reason was determined not to be saved. Every time I got him back on his feet he tumbled over backwards again. Energy seemed to be fizzing out of my fingertips. I think it was probably this excess of energy that kept overbalancing the red beetle. My legs jiggled. My fingers tapped and fidgeted. I didn't want to lie down in the sun. I wanted to do something. I wanted to walk. Why not? I could go where I wanted. I was quite free. I had never been more free in my life. So I wandered through the house, through the hall and out into the courtyard. The last stragglers from the 2.30 tour were drifting towards the car park. I followed them. I passed through the gatehouse where *Tante* Mathilde was sitting at a small table under an umbrella.

'Just going for a walk,' I said.

I thought she might stop me, but she just nodded coolly and said what a good idea, there are some nice walks, be careful not to overdo it.

I stood for a moment deciding which way to take, and chose to go in the opposite direction from the tourists, who were heading back to their cars and the road. A rocky track wound under the defensive wall. My new sandals slithered over the loose stones. Thistles scratched my ankles. But I kept on walking until the track grew thin and the château was far behind me. On one side the rock cliff rose sheer above the path, on the other it fell away into a scrubby thicket of trees clinging on to the sparse soil with starved roots. Brilliant yellow butterflies fluttered ahead. There were constant scutterings. Lizards darted into holes. Birds panicked and exploded out of the bushes halfway up the rock to swoop down and fly low ahead of me, their bellies brushing the blades of dry grass. White delta-shaped butterflies drifted round my head like scraps of paper caught by the wind; tiny blue ones flitted from thistle to thistle. Wherever I trod, insects shot away from under my feet in all directions like firecrackers: crickets, grasshoppers, unidentifiable transparent creatures trembling on the ends of leaf blades, whirring beetles. In the bushes, cicadas cackled like mad birds. The place seethed and hummed with life.

After a while, the grass grew greener and thicker till there were small brilliant mats of it between the stones; the rock walls on my left were darkly streaked with damp. Wet ferns dripped softly from orange fissures. Ahead I could hear the sound of running water. Round the next corner, the path ended suddenly. A vertical cliff face rose maybe a hundred or so feet above the path, and from somewhere near the top a thin silver thread of water trickled down a smear of brilliant green, and splashed at the bottom into a hollow rock basin. I stood on one of the fallen boulders at the edge, kicked off my sandals and dipped my foot in. The water was ice cold and perfectly clear. Below the surface the stones and pebbles at the shallow edges were cream and orange and blue: a curious and beautiful combination of colours. I knelt and fished in the water for one of the blue ones. It dried rapidly in the sun. In my hand, it was hardly blue at all: it was a mottled greyish-brown colour. But as soon as I dropped it into the pool again, it became as vividly blue as a bird's egg. Which was the illusion? I wondered. I suppose it depends on which is the stone's natural element: air or water. The orange pebbles had the same property: in one reality they were dull looking things, veined with some kind of rust-coloured mineral deposit, in the other they glowed like jewels. I let my arm trail in the water for a bit to see if it had the same effect. It did. It refracted, and my skin turned the colour of wild honey; my fingers drifted and rippled like ragged weed. I think water must be my natural element: the one mirror through which it is possible to pass, the one mirror that neither repels nor cracks. It was impossible to resist. I pulled off all my clothes and lowered myself in. For a second or so, the cold took my breath away. In the middle was a deep place between huge cream boulders where the water came almost to my armpits. Above the surface my skin was red with sunburn and mottled with old bruises; below it was the colour of honey. I tried a couple of strokes, but there was no room to swim properly, so I lay on my back and floated, and let the ice water cool one half of me and the sun warm the other. I squinted up at the brilliant, darkly blue sky. Above me a bird of prey – it was a goshawk but I didn't know that then. I was still very ignorant about these things: they don't have many birds of prey in Hanley – above me a bird of prey hovered and made strange, urgent, worried noises.

I could have stayed there for hours. Maybe I did. I never bothered to look at the time. I only got out because I heard sheep bells and thought maybe I was closer to civilisation than I'd realised. I shook myself like a dog, and let my clothes soak up whatever damp was left on my skin. From my pool, the water overflowed and dribbled away between small boulders, down through a thicket of young oak trees. Someone had trodden a narrow, perilous path down the side of the stream. I followed it, hanging on to the fragile trees to keep my balance, slipping sometimes, scrambling to keep my footing. Once I fell, and slid several feet on my behind. Once the path disappeared altogether and I had to climb down the almost vertical bed of the stream. At the bottom of the cliff the trees cleared. I emerged into a field full of the skinny sheep that looked more like goats and there, a small figure on the other side, was Uncle Xavier. He saw me and waved.

'Where've you come from?' he called.

I pointed. 'Up there.'

He was shocked. He came across to me. 'From up there?' he said. He shook his head. 'It's too dangerous. You'll break your legs. You're not recovered from one accident yet. Look at you. You're covered in scratches.' He reached over and removed some dried leaves and bits of twig from my hair. 'Why is your hair wet?'

'I've been swimming,' I said.

'Up there?'

I nodded.

'What a liar you are,' he said, laughing fondly.

'I have,' I said, indignantly. 'Honestly I have.'

'Oh, yes. Yes. Swimming, yes. But all those lies about forgetting everything. You didn't forget at all, did you? Straight to the pool.' He took a grubby piece of cloth out of his pocket and dabbed the blood from the scratches on my palm. 'I keep telling Celeste," Why don't you let the children swim in the rock pool? Marie-Christine was never out of it when she was their age." But she always takes them down to the river.' He spat on the cloth and wiped some dirt from the scratches. 'Where are you going now?' he said.

'Nowhere.'

'Would you like to come and see the farm?'

I wandered through the field with him. We closed the gates on the grazing sheep and walked over more fields until we came to a muddy pond and a cluster of farm buildings. There were two stone barns with vines curling and twisting under the roofs, but Uncle Xavier was less impressed by these than by the new, prefabricated, cement-floored dairy where the cheeses were made. The smell there was sharp and rich. It made me cough.

Uncle Xavier laughed. 'You don't like it? It's a good strong smell, uh? The smell of goat.'

We admired the new technology. We sampled some of the cheeses: they tasted exactly like they smelt. Then we went out again into the blazing afternoon. Wood pigeons burbled sleepily in the trees. My skin pricked with the heat. Everything moved slowly as if too heavy, too exhausted with the weight of the afternoon to make any effort. The ducks drifted silently on the pond. Lost in thought, the chickens scratched abstractedly in the dust.

'So – shall we go and see the bees?' said Uncle Xavier, shooing away some curious geese.

We walked across several more fields, and came to a small apple orchard. In rows between the trees stood the beehives.

Uncle Xavier slid off the front shutter of a hive. Inside was a maelstrom of activity. Bees clung to the shutter, crawling about in a blind panic at this arbitrary exposure to sudden fierce light. Uncle Xavier brushed a bee gently away from his arm. 'See,' he said. 'They know me. They do as they're told, these bees. Because they know they can't get through this.' He pinched the tough brown skin of his arms. 'You still like honeycomb?' he asked, sliding the shutter back into place.

'I love it,' I said, because I wanted to be everything he expected his niece to be. I wanted to be a good niece for this man whose kindness warmed me as powerfully as if he himself were a small fizzing fragment of the sun.

'What a wicked child you were, stealing my honeycomb,' he chuckled. Waving his arm to disperse some bees near my face, he said, 'And so, tell me the truth – are you still wicked?'

It was difficult to know how to answer that. 'Fairly wicked,' I said.

He smiled broadly at me. 'I think so, too. A little wickedness is good for the soul. A person must not burden himself with too much common sense.'

'No,' I said. 'I'm not known for my common sense.'

He laughed. He closed the gate behind us, and stood for a moment with his back to me, so that with delicate consideration he was not looking at me when he asked, 'Are you in trouble now, Marie-Christine?'

Without warning, my stomach lurched and span. Even in the burning heat of late afternoon I was suddenly cold. One reality had sickeningly and vividly obtruded on the other. All day I had been Marie-Christine Masbou, and she had fitted me as perfectly as her clothes. All day I'd been so comfortable inside my own skin that for the first time in my life it seemed to belong to me. But what was it, all this? Nothing but a sham. In the other reality, the reality of absolute truth, I was not Chris Masbou and knew nothing about her. For the first time I realised in my gut, instead of just distantly in my head, that of course she was in trouble. She could well be in very serious trouble: trouble of a sort I couldn't even begin to imagine. Why else would she need two passports and a boot stuffed full of money?

'I can't talk about it,' I said.

He turned back to face me, his face deeply furrowed like an anxious, gentle lion. 'A man?' he asked.

It seemed the most acceptable thing to confess to, so I nodded.

He sighed. 'You should be married,' he said. 'Thirty-two and no man, no home, no babies.'

'There are other things,' I said.

'As well, yes. As well, but not instead.'

'I have my work,' I said.

'Work is fine,' said Uncle Xavier. 'But it's not enough. A woman needs more.'

'So does a man.'

He laughed. 'True,' he said. 'So does a man. A man maybe more. I want you to be happy, Marie-Christine.' It was a very trite remark, but he said it so simply, with so much feeling, that my eyes pricked with tears. Why he should care about me at all was incomprehensible. He hadn't seen me since I was eight.

'I'm happiest on my own,' I said truthfully.

'Ah, but that's because you haven't met the right man yet,' said Uncle Xavier. He shook his head and sighed. 'Thirty-two. You must have had enough opportunities.'

'Not really,' I said.

'Don't be absurd. What about that red-headed boy in the hospital? That doctor? He was already halfway in love with you.'

'Dr Verdoux?' I said in amazement.

'Oh yes,' he said. 'I could see it.'

'In love with *me*?'

'It was a good thing I got you away. He certainly wasn't the right one.'

We walked in silence for a bit, across a couple of fields, while I digested this idea and reconsidered my conversations with Dr Verdoux in a new and rather puzzling light.

'Anyway, I don't believe in love,' I said eventually. I thought this was probably true for both of us, for Chris Masbou and for Margaret Davison. 'Not in that kind of love, anyway.'

Uncle Xavier stopped to stare at me in astonishment. 'You've never been in love?' he said. 'Not once? Not ever?'

I thought about it carefully for a moment. 'No,' I said, truthfully. 'Never.'

Tutting and shaking his head he went off to call in a small herd of goats at the far side of the field. He picked up a stick and used it to keep them in a group. 'You're not afraid of goats are you?' he asked, because I was hanging back, still busy thinking. 'No, no. My Marie-Christine is not afraid of any-thing, uh? Bees, goats, rock pools, nothing. My Marie-Christine is afraid of nothing – except maybe of love.'

'I didn't say I was frightened of it,' I said, picking up a stick as well. 'I just said I didn't believe in it.'

The goats skipped ahead, jangling their bells and making haughty, bleating noises when they bumped into each other. We steered them down the path towards the farm buildings, although they obviously knew the way better than I did.

'I think it's something men make up,' I said. Although I didn't really think that at all: or rather it was an idea which had just popped into my head and I was testing it.

'Men!' said Uncle Xavier as if I had in some way impugned his honour. 'What do you mean, men? It's got nothing to do with men. It's women.'

I laughed. 'So you don't believe in it either.'

He shook his head and complained I had tied him up in knots. You could prove anything with words, he said. It meant nothing.

In the courtyard we parted. He said he was off to have a shower. I washed my hair and lay in a cool bath, picking scabs off my legs. Underneath, the skin was pink and unnaturally smooth. Then I went down and sat in the garden and talked to Céleste – a rather sticky conversation about London, a city I've only visited twice. She wanted to talk shops.

'Yes, you must know,' Céleste insisted. 'It's just off Bond Street. Your office must be somewhere near there. You must know what it's called.'

'Things change so fast,' I said vaguely.

'So where do you buy your clothes?' she asked. 'I love the cut of that shirt.'

I tried to remember what the label said. Not that it meant anything to me. 'Here and there,' I mumbled.

'In America?' Her face was sharp with fascinated envy. 'Do you like Ralph Lauren?'

I made an ambiguous gesture with my hand to indicate that I could take him or leave him. We went through a long list of designers – at least I assume they were designers – few of whom meant anything to me. I devised a system. I decided to react enthusiastically to anyone whose name sounded Italian.

'You're so right,' Céleste said. 'The Italians have such style.'

I struggled not to yawn. So much walking had tired me. I was glad when it was time to eat. Outside the sun drifted lower in the sky. The baked earth cooled. The late evening scent of thirsty flowers and sadness seeped in through the open windows. It grew dark and cool. But Uncle Xavier was still radiating warmth. He filled our glasses. He talked, he laughed, he strutted about the room re-enacting a triumphant encounter he had had that morning with an old enemy. When we'd finished eating and were still sitting around too full of wine and sun, too exhausted by hard work (or in my case happiness) to move, he produced a couple of large leather books, which he laid beside me.

'Photographs,' he said. 'Look.'

So I looked. I lifted my hand to open the first one, but Uncle Xavier couldn't bear not to show me everything personally: he turned the pages for me, flipping them over impatiently when there was nothing he thought of interest. '*Voilà*,' he said, catching a loose studio portrait as it fell. 'Look. This is us when we were children. The three eldest. Before Gaston was born.'

I stared at a sepia-coloured photo with crimped edges. Three small children stared back at me.

'That's your father,' said Uncle Xavier, pointing to the po-faced boy in the middle.

I turned it over. On the back it read: 'Mathilde 8, Hervé 6, Xavier 3'.

'And here,' he said, pointing to the album, 'here's your father a bit later.'

It was a photograph of a schoolboy with trousers almost up to his armpits, who, in the style of the times, looked as if he were pushing forty. He had a closed, conventional-looking face. It meant nothing to me. Underneath was written, 'Hervé – 1949'. I wasn't that interested. I preferred the photograph on the opposite page.

'Is that you?' I asked. I knew it was, because it said 'Xavier – *juin* 1958' underneath. But the point of this exercise was not, apparently, to look at photographs of him.

'No, no, don't look at that,' he scolded, turning the page.

I was sorry. I wanted to look at him properly.

'You were very handsome,' I said. 'Much better-looking than my father.'

This was true in either reality.

I could feel his pleasure. I could feel him preen himself.

'This is the one,' he said. 'This is your mother. You've seen this one? This is when they got engaged.'

I saw a pretty, rather frightened-looking young woman with pale, fuzzy hair and a 1950s twin-set. She looked completely bewildered, like someone who had lost all control of events. Beside her stood an older Hervé with his hands in his pockets and a relaxed smile.

'He doesn't look a bit like you,' I said.

'No, Hervé was different from the rest of us,' said *Tante* Mathilde. 'Gaston and Xavier are very alike to look at, but Hervé was different. Taller. Not so broad.'

Gaston was a name I remembered. He was the uncle whom Chris had mentioned, the one she saw from time to time. He was probably the one person who'd know immediately that I was a fraud. It was important to find out where he was.

'Uncle Gaston ... ?' I began. 'Is he ... ? Where is he at the moment?'

'At sea,' said Uncle Xavier.

'At sea?' I tried not to sound too surprised. Or too relieved.

'This is another one of your mother.' Uncle Xavier had turned over the page. 'This is in England.'

It was a wedding photograph.

'How old was she then?' I asked.

'Very young,' said Uncle Xavier.

'Nineteen,' said *Tante* Mathilde. 'Too young. She was still a child.'

'I was nineteen when I got married,' said Celeste defensively.

'That was different,' said *Tante* Mathilde.

And then there was the first photograph of me: a small baby held in the fluffy-haired woman's arms. The woman was smiling but her face looked harder: her mouth was slightly pinched as if she were in pain. There followed photographs of 'Marie-Christine 2 *ans*', (a fat toddler grinning stupidly at the camera and reaching out for it); 'Marie-Christine 3 *ans*' (longer legged, with blonde curls and a mutinous expression); 'Marie-Christine 5 *ans*' (the hair turning straighter and mousier, and a front tooth missing); 'Marie-Christine 7 *ans*', (a huge gappy smile, shorts, scabby knees); 'Marie-Christine 8 *ans*' (the hair longer and darker, almost the colour it was now, the smile suddenly self-conscious, the hands twisted behind the back). That presumably was the last summer in France.

'How awful I was then,' I said, with a dangerous feeling of excitement. 'Look at me.' I said, challenging them to see it wasn't me at all.

Uncle Xavier tried to turn over, but I stopped him. There was another photograph on that page I wanted to see. It was a picnic. It had a *Déjeuner sur l'Herbe* flavour about it. In the foreground *Tante* Mathilde, looking very little different, sat on a rug by an open basket. Beside her sat another woman, a sad-faced, sallow-skinned woman with beautiful eyes which stared straight at the camera.

'Who's that?' I asked.

'My wife,' said Uncle Xavier. 'Your Aunt Geneviève. Do you remember her?'

'No,' I said.

'No, she was ill for a long time.'

'Cancer,' said *Tante* Mathilde. 'She died three years ago.'

Two fat little girls in identical dresses with bows in their hair sat near her, their legs stuck straight out in front of them, their faces solemn.

'Celeste and Françoise?' I asked *Tante* Mathilde.

She nodded.

In front of them a young man, a youth, lay on his stomach. His discarded shirt lay in a crumpled heap beside him. Astride him sat the girl I was coming to think of as 'I'. And in the background, unaware that a photograph was being taken – nobody except Uncle Xavier's sad-eyed wife seemed to be aware of that – sat Uncle Xavier and my mother. His whole attention is concentrated on her as if she is saying something so personal, so intimate, that he has to strain to hear. She sits hugging her knees, her head bent, her hair (the fuzzy perm had grown out) falling down over her eyes in a soft, pale curtain.

I looked up at him in surprise. He met my eyes, and rapidly turned over the page.

'Ah, look,' he said briskly. 'Hervé again.'

Hervé and Xavier stood together beside a low sports car. Hervé had his hand on the bonnet as if he were patting it.

Tante Mathilde came to stand behind me. She put on her glasses. 'That was taken a couple of weeks before the crash,' she said.

What crash?

On the next page my eye was caught by a photo of a much younger Uncle Xavier. He had a beard and wore a white T-shirt open at the neck. He was holding a cigarette in a very casual gesture. But underneath was written: 'Gaston – Vacances 1967.'

'Uncle Gaston,' I said, as if I recognised it.

'He was still a cadet there,' said *Tante* Mathilde. 'He always wanted to be a sailor. From when he was so high.'

'Oh, so did I,' I said. 'That's what I wanted.'

Celeste, who was yawning and fiddling with her glass, raised an eyebrow. Françoise's pale mouth fell open; a string of saliva stretched from her top teeth to her bottom lip. Uncle Xavier laughed.

'To be a sailor?' said *Tante* Mathilde, as if I'd confessed in public that my one ambition in life was to be a four-tricks-an-hour tart.

'You see,' said Uncle Xavier. 'It runs in the family.' But the three women looked at me as if I'd made a particularly inappropriate and tasteless joke.

Later, when we drifted up to bed, *Tante* Mathilde followed me upstairs.

'Have you everything you want?' she asked.

'Yes, thank you. Everything.'

Outside my door she hovered for a moment.

'Good night,' I said.

She was the most perfectly complete person: there was nothing out of place, no creases, no wisp of hair escaping, no unnecessary gesture. The space she occupied was like a small, square fortress. No part of her leaked out into the space beyond. The thing she called 'I' was rigidly contained.

'You realise, of course,' she said, 'that your Uncle Xavier had a – ' she made a humming noise and shrugged while she considered what word to choose – 'a ... what shall I say? ... a sentimental attachment to your mother.'

'Yes,' I said. 'I gathered that.'

'It was never anything more,' she said firmly as if she thought I might try and contradict her. 'Never. *Une amitié sentimentale.* That's all.'

'Yes,' I said. There was a long pause. Assuming that the conversation was now over I said good night to her again.

'At any rate on his side,' she went on. 'On hers ... ' She shrugged. 'He's a good man, my brother, but not a clever one. He's always been susceptible to pretty women. He never grasped what she was.'

'And what was she?' I asked.

Tante Mathilde gave me an odd little smile. 'My dear,' she said, 'you lived with her for over twenty years. You must know what she was.' She shook her head. 'Poor Xavier. He's so very fond of you.'

'I'm very fond of him,' I said. I felt as if I were walking on ice: one unconsidered or over-hasty move and my feet would go shooting out from under me.

'I find that difficult to believe,' she remarked coldly. 'If you're as fond of him as you claim, then why have you never bothered to visit us?'

There was no answer to that. Why hadn't I visited them? I had no idea.

'It was, I suppose, understandable while your mother was still alive – I can quite see she wouldn't have wanted you to come and stay with us. But since her death ...' She let the sentence fade away into eloquently disdainful reproach.

I considered whether I could reasonably claim pressure of work and decided I couldn't. It sounded a very feeble excuse. On the other hand, what other excuse was there? It was incomprehensible to me that Chris had never bothered to visit her father's family. Even more bafflingly incomprehensible was the fact that she'd spent long childhood summers at Rougearc, and yet apparently, after her father's death, hadn't wanted to go back. I couldn't think of anything else to do but apologise, so I did – on Chris's behalf. 'I'm sorry,' I said.

Tante Mathilde caught my eye and held it for so long that in the end I grew nervous. It was like being impaled on a fierce hook. I was forced to look away.

'It takes an accident, does it,' she said, 'before you deign to allow yourself to accept our hospitality?'

I mumbled another apology.

'So where were you going?' she demanded. I could see that the idea of my being in France without letting them know was particularly offensive to her. I found it rather offensive as well. I wondered if I should lie, as presumably Chris had lied to me, and say that I was, in fact, on my way to see them, but it sounded too glib now.

'Business,' I said, avoiding her eye.

She nodded. 'Well, at least we both know where we stand.'

'Yes,' I said, watching her walk away into the shadows of the ill lit landing. It was a meaningless response: I hadn't got the faintest idea where I stood.

But nothing, not even a cold, accusatory conversation on a landing, could disturb the perfection of my happiness. I went into my room – *my* room – and spent a long time hanging out of the window, listening to the rhythmic pulsing of the crickets, breathing in the soft darkness and the rich, heavy perfumes bleeding from the throats of exhausted flowers. I didn't want that day to end. Ever. I wanted it to go on and on and on. Although, of course, it did end, because days always do. Even happiest days. Everything does.

I'm using the word 'I' an awful lot, which is odd because it's the one word whose meaning completely escapes me. Well, no, that's not true. I know what it means: it's a piece of shorthand to describe this scabby bruised body, and the thing that's trapped inside it. But that's where the difficulty starts. That thing, that trapped thing, what is it?

I used to think of it, this business of 'I', as a life sentence. I used to be weighed down by the burden of it. The trapped thing always seemed too fragile to bear so much weight. So I ran away. I ran down long tunnels in my own head, till I was so far away that no one could ever catch me. I tried all the ways I knew: I lied, I cooked, I hoovered, I invented myths to comfort myself. I invented myths to provide meanings. But it was none of it any use. I was still 'I'. I would always be 'I', the dreamer of the nightmares, the one whose gritty eye blinked open once in a computer shop, and who from then on could never properly close that eye again. 'I' was the hot, chip-smelling streets of Stoke, the windy subways in Paris, the shabby hotel room, the graffiti, the danger in the eyes of the man with the gold medallion who offered me money. 'I' was all of this.

And now, here I was, relieved of these burdens. 'I' was dead. I was not that 'I' any longer. I was another 'I', a stranger, a light, unburdened stranger whose past was nothing more than a fairy tale, whose pain I didn't have to bear. I was a clean slate. Nothing could hurt me now. Not even the old 'I'. I looked at her objectively. I visualised her as a small, soft, disgusting thing like a slug. I was amazed by her vulnerability: I watched her flinch as if I'd sprinkled her with salt. I thought coldly: imagine being so afraid of such meaningless things.

Which, I suppose, was why I was so happy – because for a whole day I forgot to be afraid.

When I woke up it was raining. I could hear it: heavy rain. A damp mist softened the rock, and turned the trees grey. It was another day altogether.

On the table in the hall someone had laid out the post. I stopped on my way to the kitchen to investigate. In both realities, it seemed, I was shamelessly curious. Uncle Xavier had four letters, all official looking. Celeste had two. I picked up the single letter in the pile by itself. It was addressed to Miss C. Masbou.

I stood holding it for a long time. My stomach stirred queasily. I don't know why I didn't put the envelope down straight away. It was nothing to do with me. Nothing. I didn't want to be burdened by the real fragments of another past. I was not stopping that long.

Tante Mathilde was coming downstairs. 'You've found your letter?' she said.

Clearly I had found my letter. I stood there holding it as if the envelope were steeped in poison.

'Delivered by hand,' she said.

I looked down at the envelope. There was no stamp, no postmark.

'A friend?' she suggested curiously.

'I suppose it must be.' More in hope than any real expectation I added, 'It could be from Dr Verdoux.'

'Ah, the doctor,' she said, as if she knew all about him. 'Yes, of course.' After a while, she added, 'Aren't you going to open it?'

I could think of no excuse not to. I wished she would go away so I could do it in private, but she was busy sweeping dead petals from the table into her hand. I started to tear open the envelope and did it so clumsily that I ripped the paper inside. There was just one sheet, raggedly torn out of a notebook.

'Is it from your doctor friend?' she asked. 'If you should want to invite him one evening to take dinner with us ... ' Her eyes rested on the scrappy piece of paper. It was clearly not a letter from a doctor.

'No,' I said.

She waited politely for me to say more.

'A friend from England,' I improvised. 'She's on holiday. Locally.'

'How nice.' She removed a lupin, stripped it of some dead flower heads at the bottom. I had no idea whether or not she believed me.

'Yes,' I said. 'A friend.'

'Well, if you should need a car, one of them is usually available in the afternoon. Either the Renault or the Citroën. You may have a bit of trouble with reverse on the Renault. It's a little temperamental. Celeste prefers to drive the Citroën ... '

'Thank you,' I said.

She inclined her head. 'Have you breakfasted?'

'No,' I said, stuffing the note into my pocket.

Later, alone in my room, I unscrewed the piece of paper and read it again. It was written in pencil. It said: 'Chris, 3.00 p.m., Café de la Place, Billac. Be there. You owe me. Mal.' I tore it into little pieces and flushed them down the lavatory.

The rain went on all morning: a soft, rushing, unrelenting sound. I wandered up and down passages, unable to settle. I drifted in and out of strange rooms, picking things up and putting them down, moving chess pieces, looking at books, fiddling. Wherever I went the noise was still there, the gentle, heavy noise of summer rain. I got it confused with what was going on in my head. I convinced myself that the drumming rain and the unremitting panic in my head were the same thing.

Think, I told myself. Think.

The only thing I could think was that it was time to run away again.

But I didn't want to run away. Not yet. I wanted yesterday again. I wanted uncomplicated happiness again. I wanted to be the Marie-Christine Masbou of yesterday who was so much loved by her Uncle Xavier, whose past existed painlessly in memories and photographs, whose consciousness floated as lightly in air as in water. I wanted to stay here in the castle with the pepper-pot towers.

Think, I told myself, as I stood staring through the window at the hissing gravel. And there seemed to be two alternatives. One: I could ignore the note. I was tempted by this evasion. But it was dangerously flawed. If I didn't keep the appointment, then this Mal person would either write again, or, worse still, turn up at the château to find out what had happened. Two (the unthinkable alternative): I could keep the appointment. But that was obviously out of the question.

Through the streaming window I caught the shadowy, incomplete reflection of a woman's face. She floated up towards me, her face trickling and distorted. She was smiling, this drowned woman. She was thinking how stupid she was. Or maybe how stupid I was. I smiled back at her, leant closer to the glass until our mouths were almost touching and then obliterated her with a fog of breath. I laughed out loud because it was all so simple. It would be the easiest thing in the world to keep this appointment. The person who'd written the note, the person who was expecting to see Chris Masbou, didn't know me from Adam, so I could quite safely go to this café in Billac. I could say: 'Excuse me, but are you expecting to meet Marie-Christine Masbou here?' And when they said, 'Yes,' I could say, 'Well, I'm a friend of hers. She asked me to come and tell you how sorry she was she couldn't make it, but she's still very shaky after the accident. She's not seeing anyone.' Or better still, I could say she'd left that day for Marseilles. And maybe we could talk a little, so I could find out exactly who this Mal was, and if there was any element of danger, the slightest hint of it, then there was no question, I'd have to pick up my strange, insubstantial plan of heading towards the sea and staying there until everything ran out.

At lunch I asked where Billac was. *Tante* Mathilde drew me a small map.

'What on earth do you want to go to Billac for?' asked Celeste. 'It's a dump. One church, one café and a *pissoir*. Go to St Julien. It's nearer. It's on the river. There's a beach there and a caravan site.'

'I'm meeting a friend,' I said. 'Does anyone need the Renault this afternoon?'

No one did. Celeste looked mutinous. She was on tour duty. 'I wish *I* was meeting a friend this afternoon,' she said. 'Is he nice?'

'It's a she,' I lied.

I had the map *Tante* Mathilde had drawn on the seat beside me. I drove very slowly.

The rain had stopped. Small impromptu streams ran across the road. The sun appeared from nowhere, a huge red eye, and grew rapidly hotter. At a crossroads I stopped. I looked at myself in the mirror and put on Chris's sunglasses. I rehearsed my speech. I said to myself: you are not nervous. I reminded myself that nothing mattered. After all, I said with arguable logic, what can anything matter if you're dead? I drove off again down the road signposted to Billac.

In the dirt square outside the church, some old men were beginning a game of boules. I parked the Renault under a tree out of their way. Across the road was the Café de la Place. Two gnarled and mossy old men were sitting at a table outside, drinking beer. I sat at the table next to them.

'*Messieurs*,' I said politely. They nodded. I angled my chair so I could peer in through the window. Apart from the woman behind the bar who was reading the paper, and a large dog sprawled on the floor, the place was empty. I checked the time.

It was ten to three. After a while the woman shuffled out to serve me. The dog followed her and collapsed heavily at my feet. I was uncomfortably nervous. I patted the dog, sipped my orange juice and waited. A battered-looking van loudly spewing exhaust fumes and American country music screeched into the square. Three ageing French cowboys in leather jackets and studded boots swaggered across the road into the café, where two of them started an animated conversation with the woman and the third fed money into the fruit machine.

I finished my orange juice. It was two minutes to three. I wished I'd brought something to read. Or at least paced the drink better. I shifted about in my seat. The two men beside me stood up, shook hands and walked off in different directions. There are few places more deserted than a French village in the middle of the afternoon. No one passed. No one drove through. Eventually the middle-aged cowboys returned to their van and drove away as loudly as they'd come. The sound of a ropy engine and Grand Ol' Opry faded slowly into silence and dust as if this were a film I was watching. The whole thing had the atmospheric unreality of a film: a scarred woman waiting for a stranger on a hot afternoon in a deserted foreign village. The bar owner came out to wipe down the tables. I ordered another orange juice. It was ten-past three. This drink I will pace better, I thought. I was sipping it very slowly when a car with GB number plates drove into the square and parked under the tree next to the Renault. I tried to look normal and inconspicuous. I bent down to stroke the dog so that my face was hidden. A young family tumbled out of the car and came towards me. It seemed unlikely that this was anything to do with Chris. The children wanted ice-creams. They were hot and fratchety, and whined a lot. Relief was rapidly superseded by panic: suppose they recognised me from photographs in the English newspapers? I kept my head down and didn't dare look up again until they were well out of the café and crossing the road back to their car. From the corner of my eye, I watched them drive away.

Over the road, in the dirt square, I caught a sudden movement that was nothing to do with the boules game. A man
had slipped from nowhere into the camouflaging shadow of
a tree. I knew it was him: I knew at once. He must have been
waiting in one of the parked cars. He must have been there
before I arrived. He was young – late twenties, early thirties
– and good looking in a bland, beige, long-haired sort of way.
He wore an expensive white shirt and cotton trousers. He
didn't move: he just stood there, under the tree, watching the
café. I pretended to look casually in the direction of the
crossroads, but I watched him all the time. He was getting
irritated. In a minute he's going to give up, I thought. He
looked at his watch. Surreptitiously I looked at mine: 3.25.
He'll wait till half-past, I guessed, and then he'll go. I was
right. He stood with his hands in his pockets, idly scuffing at
the dust, then suddenly he kicked the tree trunk with his
heel, and walked away into the deep shadow towards a car
parked close under the church wall.

My lungs collapsed in relief. It was an entirely spurious and
temporary relief, because the problem hadn't been solved, only
postponed. I left 20 francs on the table and ran back across the
road. I think I meant to stop him getting into his car and driving
away, but I was too late. He was already pulling out on to the
village street. I could, I suppose, have stopped him then, but I
lost my nerve. Helplessly, I watched him drive off in the
direction signposted to St Julien. The obvious thing to do was
to follow him, but it seemed so ridiculous. People only did
things like that in films. On the other hand, if I didn't follow
him, if I didn't speak to him, the likelihood was that he'd turn
up at the château looking for Chris.

I ran back to the Renault, started up the engine and drove
out of the square. My head began to ache. There was an edgy,
thin, anxious feeling in the air. I wound down all the windows to try to suck in some cool air, but it rushed past the car
and I sat there in my airless vacuum with my head caught in

a band of steel. Just outside the village, at a road junction, I caught up with his blue BMW. I assumed it was his, although I hadn't had sufficient wits to make a note of the registration number. After the junction, the road zigzagged narrowly down to the river, and although I kept losing him, from time to time I caught a glimpse through the trees of the blue car on the bend below. I was right behind him when we approached the main road into St Julien. And then, stupidly, I lost him. He pulled out in front of a lorry. By the time I'd managed to pull out as well, there were two lorries, several cars and a tractor between us. I overtook the tractor and one of the lorries, but it was too late: he was already miles ahead. He could have been halfway to Figeac by the time I reached the village. I cruised slowly round the square looking for a blue car in case he'd decided to stop, but it was market day and there were blue cars everywhere: cars lined the streets bumper to bumper and filled every space. My head was throbbing with pain now. The sun was lancing through the car roof on to the back of my neck and I was sticky with sweat and frustration. I wanted to kick something very hard. Apart from that I had no idea what to do. What could I do? Nothing.

So I drove home.

Françoise was still on gate duty. 'Did you have a nice afternoon?' she called as I drove through.

'It was all right.'

'Is your friend staying here long?'

'I don't know. Excuse me. I've got a headache.'

She was all solicitousness. She insisted on finding *Tante* Mathilde, who pushed my hair back so she could feel my forehead. 'You've been overdoing it,' she said. 'You must rest.'

Together they helped me up to my room and turfed the cat off the bed. They turned down the covers and closed the curtains. I wished they would go away. Just fuck off, leave me alone to think. I clenched my teeth together so I wouldn't inadvertently say it out loud. I swallowed it whole like a snake swallowing an egg. *Tante* Mathilde found my painkillers and offered me cool drinks. Should they send for a doctor? she asked. Did I feel nauseous? No. Just leave me alone. Fuck off.

Finally, when my nerves were stretched to vibration point, they decided to leave. They tiptoed over the floorboards in exaggerated slow motion; they took half a lifetime to close the door. My one happy day seemed like a child's story now, one of those tales designed to reassure children that, contrary to all the evidence, life is quite safe. Here is a nice little structure for you, the story says, a method of getting from one day to the next. We call it reality. Keep your eye fixed firmly on that, ask no questions, and you'll be all right.

Once upon a time – here is a different sort of story: here is my favourite beginning again – once upon a time there were three sisters. But what comes next? I don't know. One of them was dead, I know that much. And one of them was lying on a bed with a pounding headache worrying about what to do, because as a consequence of her fear-induced passivity her disguise was about to be exposed by a man called Mal. And where was the third sister? You can't have a story with only two of them. It doesn't work. Without the third sister how can there ever be a proper ending?

Despite the pain in my head, I honestly tried to get to grips with things. I did try. And I came to the conclusion that the safest and most obvious thing was to stop being Chris Masbou at once. There was, after all, no imperative to be Chris. It had suited me well enough for a couple of days but it was beginning to wear very thin now: it was not a safe thing to be. I didn't *have* to be

Chris. I didn't have to be Margaret Davison either. At least I didn't think I did. I could be whoever I wanted. I could be nameless if that's what I chose. Names define. And on the whole, I'd prefer not to be defined.

So I slid off the bed and pulled out the stronger of the two suitcases. All I needed was a change of clothes and some washing things. Travel light, I said to myself. Jettison all unnecessary luggage. That was the secret. That was the essence of my one happy day: twenty-four hours without any luggage at all. It was the only way to live – like a blank sheet of paper, without a name, without a past, without any connections. It would be easy enough, I thought, to get a temporary, illegal hotel job on the coast somewhere. I could make beds. I could sweep floors. I'd live in a cheap room with peeling shutters, and stare at the sea, and no one, least of all me, would ever know who I was.

I closed the case and pulled the strap tight. I thought about writing a note, but the pen in Chris's bag didn't work. I was just shaking it, when there was a knock at the door.

'Marie-Christine?' It was Uncle Xavier.

'Come in,' I said, automatically.

He stood in the doorway in torn blue dungarees and a striped shirt and said, 'There's a phone call for you.'

I didn't take it in at first. I was very confused. I assumed, stupidly, that it must be Tony. I couldn't think who else it could be. It never occurred to me that anyone would phone Chris. I'd taken it for granted that she lived in some convenient vacuum. I'd also assumed – another serious misconception – that once inside these walls I was somehow magically beyond the normal commerce of the real world.

'Someone called Mal,' said Uncle Xavier.

'Mal?' I repeated, my mouth as dry as old glue.

'He says he's a friend of yours.'

'Yes,' I said. 'Yes. Tell him – ' I was thinking very fast – 'tell him I'm ill. Tell him I can't speak to anyone.'

Uncle Xavier looked at me closely. 'So this is the man you're running away from, is it?' he asked. 'The one you told me about?'

'Yes.' I pounced on the conveniently established explanation. 'And I really don't want to talk to him. Please.'

Uncle Xavier frowned. 'I'll deal with him,' he said.

I paced about the room, biting my nails. Ten minutes later he came back. 'This is not the man for you,' he announced. 'He has a weak voice. Who is he? I don't like the way he speaks. What are you doing with your suitcase?'

'Nothing,' I said hurriedly.

'You should be lying down. Is your head still bad?'

'No,' I said. 'No, it's a lot better.'

'Good,' he said, 'because I want you to come out to dinner with me tonight. But if you don't feel up to it … '

I said yes at once, before he'd even finished speaking. Yes, I said, I did feel up to it. My headache was completely gone, I said. As a matter of fact it had gone. It had miraculously disappeared the moment Uncle Xavier had relieved me of the problem of Mal. Yes, I said, dinner, what a lovely idea. After all, I told myself, it didn't make any difference whether I left now or in the morning, did it? One more night couldn't do any harm. And it might not even be necessary to leave then, not if Uncle Xavier had convinced Mal I wasn't well enough to be seen. Anyway, I didn't have to decide now. I didn't have to make any decisions now, none at all, except possibly what to wear. This took an unusual amount of time. I tried on Chris's emerald-green dress. It had slits up both sides. It seemed far too young for someone of thirty-six who'd always been on the plump side. I had no idea whether or not I looked ridiculous in it. In the end I decided what the hell if I did. It probably looked passable on someone who was only thirty-two and distinctly skinny, so I kept it on. I was still afraid of make-up, but I washed and brushed my hair and sprayed myself enthusiastically with Chris's perfume.

'You look beautiful,' said Uncle Xavier as I came down the stairs into the hall.

I laughed.

He was offended. 'What are you laughing for? You don't like compliments? Are you one of these women who don't know how to accept a compliment?'

'I'd prefer you to tell me the truth,' I said.

He sulked all the way down the drive. His sulking wasn't at all like Tony's: it didn't freeze me out. It didn't frighten me. There was nothing childishly dependent about it. It was a comical sort of absent-minded huff which lasted only until he had something else he wanted to say to me. I understood that in his eyes, for reasons that had nothing to do with absolute truth and a lot to do with the fact that he had once loved Chris's mother, I *was* beautiful and there was no point in arguing about it.

'Where are we going?' I asked.

To the Hôtel des Falaises in St Julien, he said, where the food was good. None of your finicky Parisian Michelin nonsense, he said. Real food.

We sat at a table by the window overlooking the market square. At one end of the dark, old-fashioned dining room was a heavy oak dresser covered in wine bottles. Hunting trophies hung on the walls. From where I sat I could see out of the window, past the tables on the pavement and across the tree-shaded square to the lights of the garage on the other side.

'So,' said Uncle Xavier, putting on a pair of half-moon glasses to examine the menu, 'tell me who you are.'

I looked up alarmed. I expected to see him staring accusingly at me over the top of his glasses, but he was running his finger down the list of entrées. It was clearly intended as a general rather than as a specific question.

I shrugged. 'I don't know,' I said.

'This work of yours, which is so important to you. What is it?' he said and then answered his own question. 'Nothing. Shifting hypothetical money from one country to another and back again. Gambling with other people's resources. Does it satisfy you, this work? Does it make you rich? Does it make you happy?'

I was considering how to answer this, but Uncle Xavier saved me the trouble by answering for me again.

'No,' he said. 'No, I don't think so. It's not right for you, this life. You are not this kind of person at all.'

His shrewdness amused me. 'Yes, I am,' I said.

'No,' he contradicted me. 'You're not.'

He cut short any further argument by insisting that we decide what to eat. 'Do you like mussels?' he asked. 'Serge!' he called to the patron. 'Serge, this is my niece, Marie-Christine.' He was so unashamedly excited to introduce me to his friend, Serge (and to Serge's wife, the wife's mother, the waitress and the assistant chef) that I could understand how Chris's mother had fallen in love with him. Women must constantly be falling in love with him. Under the artificial light, his grizzled hair sparked with bronze. His tough, badgery face was warm with expansive pleasure. He looked, in his best white shirt, and his corduroy trousers, like an ageing Greek hero who had popped up in the wrong century or possibly a shipping tycoon in the right one.

'As a matter of fact,' he said, when Serge (his wife, the waitress, the assistant chef and the wife's mother) had taken our order and all the necessary gossip had been swapped, 'since we're talking about your work, I'd be grateful if you'd take a look at some of our investments. The mortgages, trust funds ... things like that.'

I said nothing.

'I can't discuss these things with Mathilde. She deals with the day-to-day accounts, she's excellent with those, but she's too sharp. I don't want her to know how bad things are.'

'Are they bad?' I asked.

'I'm a farmer, Marie-Christine. That's all I know. The farm. The animals. I'm not a financial expert like you.'

I smiled vaguely and fidgeted in my seat.

'You're not comfortable?' he said solicitously.

'I'm fine,' I squirmed.

In a painfully unconvincing way, and probably using all the wrong words, I explained to him that I worked in the very specialised and speculative field of commodities. I was not, I said, the right person to advise him. He smiled at me tolerantly. I could see he thought I was being unnecessarily modest. 'Money is money,' he said. He had a point, although I doubted whether my limited experience in an accountant's office would be of much help to him. Fortunately some food arrived and Uncle Xavier forgot about investments.

'I like to see a woman eat,' he observed as I wolfed my way through half a melon. He filled my wineglass. 'You're far too thin,' he said. 'You should forget about this work you do. And about weak men you have to run away from. Neither of them makes you happy. You should stay here. This is your home.'

I shook my head. 'It isn't,' I said gently. 'I wish it were. But it isn't. I have to leave soon.'

'Why?' he demanded. 'Where are you going? Where do you have to go so urgently you can't even spare time to grow strong again?' A thought struck him. 'You have some kind of appointment? Where were you heading for when you had the accident?'

I pretended to finish a non-existent mouthful in order to give myself time to think. I chewed this imaginary piece of melon with as much energy and stamina as if it were a lump of gristle. 'I don't know,' I said truthfully. 'I was just running away.'

'From this man?'

'Yes.'

'Why didn't you come straight to us?' he demanded.

Fishing a little I said, 'Well, I couldn't, could I? Because I wasn't sure ... I wasn't entirely sure what kind of welcome I'd get.'

He was very shocked. 'You doubted your welcome? How can you say that?'

'Well ... ' I said lamely, 'after all this time ... '

There was a long silence. Uncle Xavier appeared to be engrossed in reading the label on the wine bottle. Finally he said, 'After your father died ... there was a very big scandal.' He looked up at me. 'You understand? A big scandal in the family. When your father discovered ... ' he broke off. 'He was a brilliant driver, your father. There was no other car involved. You understand what I'm telling you? It was not an accident.' He poured me another glass of wine. 'Your mother was very bitter, very hurt. She went back to England. It was my fault. She expected more from me than I could give her. I had a wife already. A good wife. But the past, Marie-Christine, the mess we made of the past ... this is nothing to do with you. It doesn't touch you.'

I chewed hard on another mouthful of non-existent melon, because I couldn't trust my voice to say anything.

'Tell me about the farm,' I said, when finally I felt safe enough to swallow. It seemed a good diversionary subject to keep us away from dangerous ground. Besides, I was interested. Uncle Xavier was interested too. He talked at length and I listened. I loved the stories he told about neighbouring farmers and land squabbles. I felt no responsibility for him at all. I was required neither to entertain him nor to soothe his ego. I didn't have to boost his confidence, or comfort him, or bear his reproaches, or do any of the hundred and one subtle things I was used to doing. The memory of them exhausted me. Why had I always felt obliged to provide these services? How was it that Tony and I had silently and mutually arranged things in this way between us? It was a self-perpetuating pattern that neither of us seemed able – or perhaps willing – to unravel. Uncle Xavier, on the other hand, required nothing of me, nothing at all, except that I should eat and enjoy the wine and be happy. That was as complicated as it got.

We talked goats and geese and wild boar and boundary disputes all through the main course and the cheese. Outside it had grown dark and a string of battered and uneven fairy lights had been switched on to illuminate the outside tables.

'That's pretty,' I said.

Beyond the lights, I watched a man climb out of a car he had just parked in the square. He looked familiar. He walked over towards the hotel and sat at the table on the other side of the glass from where we were sitting. I could see him quite clearly. He was wearing a white shirt and cotton slacks. I was ninety-five per cent certain it was the same man.

'You don't like the cheese?' Uncle Xavier asked, picking up instinctively on my unease.

'It's delicious,' I said.

'Good. Because that – ' he pointed to the lump I was eating – 'that comes from Rougearc. From our goats.'

I was watching the man out of the corner of my eye as Uncle Xavier discussed cheeses. He was as close as if he was sitting next to me, which I suppose he was: nothing but the window divided us. So this was Mal. I watched him order a drink. He wasn't at all the sort of person I imagined Chris would know. He was too bland. He had longish hair, which he flicked back a lot with his hand, and a rather attractive, slightly androgynous profile.

We moved on to dessert. For some reason Uncle Xavier had it fixed in his mind that I had a sweet tooth. I tried to deny it, but he insisted on ordering a rich chocolate *bavarois* for me, the sort of thing I never ate because of bulging waistlines. 'Yes, yes,' he insisted, 'don't be silly,' waving his arm to dismiss my objections. 'Don't argue. You'll like it.' He was right. I did like it. I ate it in small, dark, melting mouthfuls, while I considered what I was going to do about the man on the other side of the glass.

At one point his gaze wandered into the dining room. I looked away. When I let my eyes slide back again, he was staring at me with a look of slight puzzlement. This time *he* was the one who looked away. He stood up. I was afraid he was going back to his car, but he wasn't. He came in through the main door of the hotel. Either he was looking for someone to pay, or for the Gents. Or – a third possibility – he was staying here.

I excused myself. 'I won't be a moment. The Ladies' room,' I muttered. I dropped my napkin on the table and hurried through the glass doors into the hotel reception area. The man with the flopping hair and the white shirt was by the desk, taking a key off the hook.

'Mal?' I said.

He turned. Full face, he was far less attractive than in profile. He stared at me with pale, cold, blank eyes. Then something clicked: he snapped his fingers.

'I knew I'd seen you before,' he said. 'You were in the café, weren't you? This afternoon. In Billac.'

I nodded.

'I *knew* I recognised you.' But after this triumph of recognition, suspicion set in again. 'Where did you get that dress?' he asked suddenly. And then, more suspiciously still, 'What is this? How do you know my name?'

There was no point in wrapping things up. 'I'm sorry, this is very difficult,' I said, trying to keep my voice down, so no one else would hear, 'but there was a car crash. On the N20. About two months ago. Chris Masbou was killed.'

He was very tense. He absorbed the news of Chris's death without his expression noticeably changing, as if it were a relatively unimportant detail. 'So who are you?' he said.

'It's difficult to explain.'

'You must have a name,' he insisted.

'Yes,' I said, 'but after the accident – I was in the car with her, and everybody assumed that I was Chris. And I ... well, when I gained consciousness again, I just went along with it.'

He looked, as well he might, completely baffled.

'It's only temporary,' I said hurriedly. It was hopeless trying to explain this in the few minutes it would take to go to the Ladies. 'Could we meet again tomorrow?' I said. 'I'll explain it all properly then.'

He looked at me warily as if he suspected I was laying some kind of trap for him. 'So who are you?' he demanded.

'Nobody, really. Nobody at all. I just hitched a lift with Chris.'

After a moment he said, 'What happened to the money?'

I was tempted to prevaricate and ask him what money, but things were already too complicated. 'The police have got it,' I said.

'Shit!' He banged his forehead hard with the heel of his hand. 'Oh, shit!'

'Look, someone's waiting for me. Can we meet tomorrow?'

'Ten o'clock,' he said coldly. 'Here. I'll wait for you.' He managed to fill the promise to wait with an eloquently unnerving and sulphurous whiff of threat.

When I got back to the table, Uncle Xavier had ordered coffee, and two cognacs. 'Do you drink this stuff?' he asked.

I didn't. Or rather, Margaret Davison didn't. But I was very grateful for it. I held the bowl of the glass in my cupped hands to stop them shaking. By the time I was calm enough to drink the coffee without spilling it, it was cold.

We drove home in silence. I was very sad. I sat beside Uncle Xavier working out what to do next. I'd meet Mal at ten, and after that there was really no choice any more: after that I'd have to catch the bus for Figeac and a train south. It was the note that was worrying me. Obviously, I'd have to leave a note. I couldn't just disappear without an explanation. I tried possible versions: 'Dear Uncle Xavier' – except I couldn't honestly call him that any more. 'Dear Monsieur Masbou, your niece is dead and I am an impostor. Thank you for your hospitality. Many apologies. Margaret Davison.'

You see my difficulty?

'What are you thinking?' asked Uncle Xavier as we turned off the river road and up into the hills.

'Nothing,' I said.

Actually, I was thinking that what I'd done to him was unforgivable. The trouble was, that putting it right was going to be equally unforgivable.

'Thank you for a lovely evening,' I said as we drove through the gatehouse. As we parted at the bottom of the hall stairs, I kissed him impulsively on the cheek. 'Thank you,' I said again.

I sat for a long time staring at the freckled mirror on the dressing table, and angling the wings so that I could see the multiplying images of myself disappearing into infinity on both sides. I found it hard to meet my own eyes.

When I went downstairs the following morning, Uncle Xavier had already been up and out for two hours. I was glad. I'd chickened out of writing the note. I'd managed to convince myself that it would be kinder to send a brief postcard from the village. I drank some coffee and found a carrier bag, into which I pushed a change of clothes and my washing things. I told Celeste I was going for a walk. 'Will you be back for lunch?' she called, but I pretended I hadn't heard.

It was much further to the village than I'd thought, and unbearably hot. It was stupid of me to assume I was sufficiently recovered to walk that far. By the time I arrived at the hotel it was nearly eleven. My head was swimming and I felt sick. My legs were gelatinous lumps of pain.

He was waiting for me at one of the pavement tables. As I limped across the road, he stood up politely.

'Christ,' he said. 'Are you all right? You look terrible.' He seemed genuinely alarmed. He ordered me a brandy and a carafe of water in heavily south-London-accented French. He suggested I put my feet up on a spare chair. It was hard for me to connect him with the man I'd seen yesterday. He was making an effort to be charming. He expressed concern about the car accident and seemed genuinely upset now about Chris's death. 'Dead?' he kept saying, and shaking his head in apparent bewilderment. He apologised if he'd appeared cold-blooded about it. 'I couldn't take it in yesterday,' he said. 'It was the shock. Poor Chris.'

'Did you know her well?' I asked. I was very puzzled by him. I was puzzled by the terse nature of the note he'd sent, and by the fact that he'd stayed hidden, waiting to see whether Chris would keep the appointment. I couldn't work out what his relationship with her was. And he knew about the money as well. It occurred to me suddenly – a revolutionary idea – that maybe Chris had been running away from this man. The trouble was I couldn't imagine Chris running away from anybody, let alone somebody as colourlessly fashionable as Mal.

'Yeah,' he said. 'Pretty well. Listen, I can't talk to you when I don't even know who you are.'

'Marina James,' I lied. It sounded as false as ever.

'Nice name, Marina. Unusual. And that accent? What's that? Brummy? Somewhere up that way?'

I was slightly offended. I didn't think I had any kind of accent. I was also alarmed. Even with sunglasses and a scarred face I was still recognisable. I didn't want him pinning me down to Stoke. 'Yes,' I lied. 'Birmingham.' I told him that I was on my way to Toulouse when I'd met Chris and hitched a lift from her. I explained about the crash and the general assumption that I was Chris Masbou. It had suited me for a time, I explained, to go along with whatever people in authority said. With certain small edits and evasions, which I hoped would prevent him from making any connection between me and the 'Mysterious Disappearance of Stoke-on-Trent Secretary' stories that had been in the English papers a couple of months ago, I told him the whole story.

I waited for his reaction: I expected appalled condemnation. I closed my eyes. For a moment, he was quiet. Then he said, 'That's brilliant. That's fucking brilliant. Chris would have loved it.' He laughed and slapped his hand on the table. He leaned back in his chair. 'Listen,' he said. 'Let me explain things to you. That money in the car – the fact is Chris and me, we were partners. Business partners. Financial stuff, yeah? Buying. Selling. You know what I mean?'

'I thought she was a commodity broker,' I said.

'Yeah. Oh, yeah. That's right. In fact, if you want to know the truth, she worked for me.'

'But I thought you said you were partners?'

'Well, yeah, we were. Well, in a manner of speaking we were, yeah. But the fact is, she worked for me. It's my business. And the money she had on her, that was my money.'

In the shade of the parasol, I sipped the water and let the pain slowly drain out of my legs. It was difficult to concentrate on what Mal was telling me, but I got the gist of it. 'The fact is,' he said – he used that phrase a lot – 'the fact is we had a bit of a row, Chris and me. Differences of approach. That kind of stuff. It all got nasty. Next thing I know she's disappeared with twenty thousand quid of my money. Which is theft in anybody's book, right?'

I said that I supposed it was, yes.

'I was going to tell the police, but I thought no, hang on a bit, let's see if we can't sort this out between ourselves. So I did a spot of detective work and tracked her down. Or at any rate, tracked *you* down. Which is more or less the same thing.' He laughed.

'I'm not stopping,' I said. 'I'm going south. Now. Today.'

'What a pity,' he said, smiling at me. 'Because when the police have done all their checks, they're going to return the money to you, aren't they?'

'No,' I said. 'No, they won't do that. I told them it wasn't mine.'

He looked at me in disbelief. 'You did what?' he said. 'Oh, shit!' He kicked the table leg. 'What did you do that for?'

'Because it *isn't* mine,' I said.

The charm leached rapidly away, leaving a sediment of irritated preoccupation. 'Shit,' he muttered.

'Well,' I said lamely, 'now you know.' I stood up. 'I'm sorry if I've caused you any inconvenience. About the money. And I'm really sorry about Chris.'

He mumbled something in reply. I didn't catch what.

'You could always go to the police and tell them it's yours,' I suggested. 'Only I'd be grateful if you'd wait until tomorrow. If you could just give me time to get away.'

He looked at me briefly. 'Yeah,' he said. 'Yeah, that's what I'll do.' But I could see from his eyes that he wouldn't. I could see he was lying.

I walked away from him across the square and sat on the steps that led up to the church. It was cool there in the shadow of the huddled roofs, cooler than waiting for the bus at the stop outside the garage. I sat resting my cheek against cool stone, and thought about Chris. I had a lot of revision to do. I had to reinvent her in my head. She was obviously not the person I'd thought she was. This left me feeling uncomfortably rootless. I believed about half of Mal's story: I could see it was as carefully edited and as full of evasions as the story I'd told him. One thing was very clear to me: I definitely couldn't go back to Rougearc now. If I stayed, then I'd have to assume, along with Chris's name, responsibility for whatever it was she and Mal were up to, whatever 'business' they were in together. I would have to take the consequences of something that far transgressed the suburban conventions of Margaret Davison's dull and law-abiding life.

I am lying again. Can you tell? Or, if not lying, certainly not telling the whole truth. No one, least of all me, is going to deny that Margaret Davison's life was dull and law-abiding, but the question is: why was it so? And the answer is that it was so because that's what she chose. She chose suburban, law-abiding dullness. She is not as passive as she pretends. She knew what she was doing when she married Tony. Poor, frightened Margaret Davison. She married him because she was afraid that without the anchor of his unquestioning certainties she might drift out of control. She deliberately cut herself off at the knees to prevent herself from doing those things she suspected herself to be capable of doing: shapeless, unimaginably dangerous things, things that slithered round the edges of her dreams, things into which, without the limitations imposed on her by Tony's presence in her life, it would be seductively easy to slide.

Once upon a time – you know the beginning of this story already. This is the story that begins on a hot, uncomfortable day in a computer shop in Stoke, and ends in the Acropolis café with the chipped mural on the wall and a man who said his name was Elefteris.

Remember this? Let me tell you the rest.

The man called Elefteris talked a little about the heat and then he leaned across the table and said in an odd voice, 'It's a beautiful name, Marina. It suits you.'

No one had ever said that to me before.

'A beautiful name,' he added, 'for a beautiful woman.'

I laughed. It was such an obvious and absurd chat-up line.

'What do you mean?' I said.

He brushed away my attempt to be truthful as a piece of false feminine modesty. He took my hand. He shouted something in Greek to the men behind the counter. They laughed. One of them nodded and pointed upstairs.

'You come upstairs with me?' he said. 'Please. You come?'

First of all I didn't understand him. He must have thought I was very stupid.

'Upstairs,' he said.

It was such a sordid, such an unthinkable thing to do that I thought it might almost be sufficient punishment for the day. So I shrugged and stood up and followed him through multicoloured strips of plastic and up some uncarpeted stairs with plastic bottles of bleach and catering tins of black olives piled on the treads. At the top was a narrow landing. Elefteris opened a door and I followed him into a small storage room full of broken furniture. A dismantled bicycle was propped against the wall. There were several sacks of potatoes and a galvanised iron bucket with a mop sticking out of it. The glass in the window was cracked. In one corner was a damp-stained mattress. I sat down on the edge of it. It felt lumpy, as if it was full of straw. It was a long way down: less like sitting than falling.

I suppose he must have been surprised at how easy it had been to get me there. He pulled his shirt over his head without undoing any buttons. His chest was very brown and smooth. There was an awful smell in the room, a smell of rot and old clothes. I remember the smell.

He knelt down and took off my shoes, first one and then the other, very gently, and kissed my feet, the left one then the right one, such an odd, gentle gesture. I was horrified. I was horrified by his gentleness, I hadn't expected it. Gentleness had no place in my scheme of punishment, my instinct to subdue the tyranny of consciousness by some act of ritual humiliation. But his gentleness, his acceptance of my pale, sweaty, malodorous feet frightened me. I wanted self-obliteration and he was offering something quite different. He was nuzzling my knees. I stared down at his head between my thighs and panicked. I had no idea what I was doing in that room. I had no idea who this man was or what I wanted from him. I lay on the mattress too heavy with self-loathing to move. And then I panicked. I don't remember at what stage I panicked. I don't want to remember. I pulled myself stickily away from him. I fought off his urgent attempts to re-establish my body underneath his. I ran. I remember thundering down the wooden stairs with that filthy smell of rot in my mouth and knocking over a tin of olives, which went crashing down beside me and bruised my foot. I tripped over it and staggered down the last few steps. My shoe flew off and landed several feet ahead of me in the passage, but I didn't dare stop to pick it up. There was no way out except through the café, which suddenly fell silent. I hobbled past the counter out into the street. Countless cold eyes stared at me. I ran a long way in the heat and the crowds before the panic and the horror began to subside a little.

How much of that is true? Sometimes I think none of it. It's just a story I tell myself, a way of explaining things. Did I ever go up the stairs to a junk room above the Acropolis Café with a man called Elefteris? Surely not. It's impossible. I would never have dreamed of doing anything so dangerous. But you see that's obviously a lie, because I *have* dreamed of it. And if it wasn't so, then where did I pick up all those details like the catering tins of olives on the stairs? No, it's a story. Reality ends at the moment when the man with the cup of coffee came and sat at my table and tried to pick me up. The rest I formulated for a purpose. This, I told myself, is what might happen were I not so rigidly Margaret Davison. This is why I allowed myself to go on being Margaret Davison, why I hid behind her timid constraints for so long. And another reason I know it's only a story is because although it happens in Stoke, there's a suspiciously mythic quality about some of the details. The business of the lost shoe, for example – that's clearly a piece of plagiaristic storytelling. No, I made it all up. Of course I did. I must have.

I sat on the stone steps up to the church for hours. I had a lot of thinking to do, a lot of adjustments to make. When eventually I remembered about the bus, it was too late: it had gone. According to the woman at the garage there were only two buses in the afternoon and the last one had left dead on time, ten minutes ago. So I wandered down to the river, worrying about what to do next. It would be cheapest, I decided, to stay the night at the other hotel – not the Hôtel des Falaises where Mal was staying, but the dead-windowed one on the edge of town – and catch the first bus to Figeac in the morning. I sat on the bank watching the tourists from the camp site splashing about on the other side. I was very tired. My eyes kept closing. I stretched out on the grass and drifted into an odd hallucinatory kind of doze.

Something touched my cheek. I woke. Uncle Xavier was sitting beside me with a blade of grass in his hand.

'Good,' he said. 'At last. Time to go home.'

I was so confused to find myself lying on the grass by the river, and so pleased to see him, so comforted by the idea of home, that I temporarily forgot I was supposed to be running away and allowed him to help me up.

'How did you get to St Julien?' he scolded. 'You walked all this way?'

I nodded.

'What did you do that for? You could have taken one of the cars. Don't frighten me again, huh? You don't come back for lunch – no phone call – you could have been dead. Don't ever do this to me again.'

I smiled weakly, and allowed him to steer me towards the square, although the temporary state of forgetfulness had long worn off by now.

'How did you know where to find me?' I asked.

He shrugged. 'You think I'm stupid? You think I don't see you last night? Of course I saw you. Talking to this man. And I think: so this is the one. This is the one with the weak voice, the one on the telephone she's running away from.'

'I had to see him,' I said.

He glanced at the carrier bag I was holding, but said nothing.

The late afternoon sun blinded us as we drove home. I closed my eyes; every muscle spontaneously relaxed. I felt myself giving up. There was no point in trying to leave, I told myself. This was where, when I didn't turn up, someone came to find me. Just a couple more days – I wasn't greedy. Two more days couldn't possibly hurt anyone.

Two days slid into three, three into five, five into seven. Nothing happened. There was no further contact from Mal, and no word from the police. I began to feel safe. I began to forget what I was doing. I lost touch with the enormity of it. I answered automatically to the name Marie-Christine. It grew harder to remember quite who Margaret Davison was. There were things I had completely forgotten about her. I couldn't remember her body at all. I had an entirely new one now. In the bath the last scabs softened and fell away. Underneath I was amazingly pink and smooth in patches, as if I were a snake who'd shed its skin. I liked this new body. Margaret Davison had never liked hers. She'd preferred the light off, so she wouldn't have to see it. She always avoided looking in mirrors. This new body of mine was still thin, but less alarmingly so. There was a little substance on the bone now. I liked the way the hip bones stuck out. I liked the rather silly breasts stuck lopsidedly on the ribs. I liked the rakish scarring. I was comfortable with it. To tell the truth, I was very comfortable, full stop. I slept well. I ate. I swam in the pool under the waterfall. It grew hotter. Day after day, the sun rose early and by midday burned like a furnace. The earth cracked. The budding fruit failed to fatten. The flowers crumpled into flaccid heaps.

There was no corner of Rougearc I didn't know now. I knew the damp-stained stone, the arrow slits, the portraits, the turret rooms with the view of the river slithering hundreds of feet below in the valley. I knew the outhouses. I knew the chickens. I knew the orangery where abandoned pieces of old farm machinery and a broken governess cart were kept. There was a huge glass box in there as well, an enormous display case, like a vast block of ice in which a moment of death had been frozen. A stuffed *sanglier*, its mouth open in terror was crashing through some artificial undergrowth. Attached to its neck was the lean and terrifying figure of a stuffed hound. Its bared yellow teeth had the boar in a savage death grip. It disturbed me. I thought how strange it was that once upon a time this dog had been fiercely and violently alive. The blood had pulsed through its arteries. It had sniffed the air. It had answered to its name. It did what it was trained to do. The boar had no name at all. It answered to nothing but its own boarish instincts. It didn't even know it was a boar. It simply was. And now it wasn't, and hadn't been for nearly a century. The nameless boar and the hound whose name was long forgotten were both dead, and to whom did it matter? To them? To me? Sometimes, when I had nothing else to do, I sat in the lopsided governess cart and worried about this business of names, and what precisely it is that they define.

A couple of times I went into Figeac with Françoise. I knew

it was a dangerous thing to do because one of the English tourists there might identify me, but as one day slipped into another and my sense of being Marie-Christine strengthened, I forgot about possible danger. Everyone who knew the family always accepted me immediately as Marie-Christine. They had no reason not to.

One morning, there were a couple more letters for me on the table in the hall. One was from a London bank. It stated that as requested they had, as from the 24th of the month, transferred all my funds, amounting to a sum of £9,327.95, to the Banque Nationale, which would be contacting me in due course. This was a very interesting and useful piece of news.

The other letter was from someone called Alec Ferguson. Dear Miss Masbou, he wrote. It was a very short letter on ordinary writing paper from an address in Peterborough. He had, he said, passed on Chris's forwarding address to a young man who claimed to be a relative. Was that all right? He was a little worried now that he might have done the wrong thing, but the young man had been very plausible.

I assumed this plausible young man must be Mal. I screwed the letter up and threw it away.

The money in the bank knocked me off balance a little. Coincidentally – or perhaps not – the Banque Nationale in Figeac happened to be the one the family used. They wanted a specimen signature. The only official means of identification I had were Chris's driving licence and English credit card, the signatures on which bore very little resemblance to the one I produced for them, but nobody seemed to mind. Everyone in the bank knew who I was. They knew Françoise: they knew I was her cousin, she had told them so. The bank manager was a personal friend of Uncle Xavier's. So my identity was never in question. If they noticed how little the signatures resembled each other, they presumably put the discrepancy down to the consequences of the accident. The manager insisted I fill in an application form for a new credit card. I was a little worried about this because I wasn't sure if I'd remembered Chris's date of birth accurately from the information on her passport, but I must have done because nobody questioned that either.

One evening we were sitting in the kitchen having dinner when the phone rang. I was eating an artichoke. My skin was hot with fresh sunburn and I was feeling very safe and sleepy. Uncle Xavier got up to answer it. 'It's for you,' he said.

'Me?'

Which me? Who?

He held out the receiver. 'Someone phoning from England.'

I stood up very slowly, trying to give myself time to think. I took the receiver from him. 'Hello?' I said carefully.

There was a pause. 'Hello?' said a woman's voice on the other end of the line.

I cleared my throat.

'Hello?' she repeated. 'Is that Chris?'

There was no pretending it was a wrong number or that she'd got the wrong person. Everyone at the table, even the children, had stopped talking. 'Let me take this on another phone,' I said.

'No, no, listen,' said the woman on the other end. 'This is Sue. I've only got a minute. Is that you?'

'Yes,' I said.

'You sound very odd.'

'It's a bad line.'

'No, I mean your voice sounds odd. Have you got a cold, or something?'

'Yes,' I said.

'You don't sound a bit like you.'

There was really no answer to that. I caught Uncle Xavier's eye. He smiled at me.

'Listen,' she said, this woman Sue, whoever she was, 'I got

your address off your ex-landlord ... ' Mr Alec Ferguson from Peterborough presumably, who appeared to be inconveniently liberal with my address.

' ... so I rang up International Directory Enquiries. How are you?'

'Fine,' I said, monosyllabically.

'Except for the cold.' She laughed. 'It sounds awful. Poor old you. It's made your voice sound really weird. So, listen, I was thinking about you today because me and Denise, we were talking about you at dinner time and Denise said: "Give her a ring. Tell her what she's missed." We've had massive scandals here. You've no idea. Apparently someone in management went and leaked information about the takeover bid for Mawsons. Well, sold it probably, Mr Taylor says. He says somebody'll have made a thumping great killing out of it. He's livid. They had the police in and everything. You've missed all the fun.'

'Goodness,' I said, lamely.

'It's been like the telly. So listen, how's the holiday? It is still a holiday, is it?'

'Fine.'

'And what's this château place you're staying at? It sounds dead posh. Is that a hotel or a camping site or what?'

'A camping site.'

'I bet you're lovely and tanned. When are you coming back? When the money runs out?'

'Yes.'

'You lucky sod. Well, actually, Chris, to be honest, that's partly why I rang. We're getting a bit pissed off with Middlemass and Dunn, me and Denise. Well, with Peterborough really. And we were thinking why not do it Chris's way and try temping for a bit. So I was just wondering, as soon as you know when you're coming back, could you let us know and we'll fix up a date for lunch or something. Have a chat about it. We were thinking of trying London. Only Denise is worried about her pension and her stamp and things. Oh yeah ... '

Clearly she hadn't finished yet. I shifted position. 'I know what else. I've still got that posh designer thing of yours I borrowed off you for my sister's wedding. Do you want me to hang on to it or what?'

'Yes,' I said.

'You don't mind if I wear it again sometimes, do you? Like Saturday nights?'

'Fine,' I said.

'I'll get it cleaned,' she said hurriedly. Then she laughed. 'You sound really weird. Like you're doing a silly accent or something. It must be all that vino. Anyway, listen, Chris, lovely talking to you again.'

'And you,' I said politely.

'Catch up with you as soon as you get back. Don't forget to give us a ring, eh?'

She said goodbye and take care of yourself several more times than I felt was necessary. I sat down heavily in my chair.

'A friend?' Uncle Xavier asked.

'Yes,' I said. Boldly I added, 'My secretary.'

I was afraid they might have noticed how oddly monosyllabic and gruff my side of the conversation had been, but they'd lapsed into a quiet conversation of their own in French. Something about a hospital appointment. I was very grateful for it, and glad that they went on talking after I'd sat down. It gave me the chance to cut off and think.

How many Chris's were there, for God's sake? Chris the independent, free-living partner in a firm of commodity brokers? Chris who worked in some kind of uneven relationship with Mal and who'd absconded with what he claimed was his money? Chris the temp with her mates, Sue and Denise, at somewhere called Middlemass and Dunn in Peterborough? I could make no sense of it. I had to make further rapid revisions in my head. The Chris I thought I had such a clear grasp of, the Chris I aspired to be, was constantly changing. Except that the bottom line, the real truth, to judge at least from this evidence, was that she was nothing more or less than an ordinary secretary. Like me.

I found this very hard to take. Very hard. I didn't want her to be like me. I wanted her to be powerful and strong and to know everything. I wanted her to be exactly what I'd originally thought she was.

Around the table buzzed a heated conversation in French.

'Yes, you will,' I heard *Tante* Mathilde say firmly. 'You'll go if I have to drive you there myself. I want to speak to the doctor. I don't trust you to do it.'

I thought for a moment they must be talking about me: the word hospital – the word doctor. I thought perhaps they meant Dr Verdoux. But it seemed they were talking about another hospital altogether. And about Uncle Xavier.

'It's a waste of time,' he said.

'Why are you going to hospital?' I asked him, alarmed suddenly by something other than my own problems.

He shrugged. 'Nothing. Just a check-up.'

Tante Mathilde said something in French which I didn't catch, something fierce.

'Don't fuss,' said Uncle Xavier. 'Will you all stop fussing? I'm sick of women fussing. Look at me. Do I look ill?'

He refused to talk about it any more. He changed the subject.

Later, sick with apprehension, I asked Françoise what the matter was. Was he ill? I asked, afraid to hear the answer.

A coronary, she said. Last February. He'd collapsed suddenly with pains in his chest. She saw from my eyes how necessary it was to reassure me. No, really, I was not to worry, she said hurriedly. He'd recovered very quickly: he was very strong. This was just a routine check-up.

I couldn't bear to listen. I ran upstairs so I wouldn't have to talk to anyone until I'd adjusted to this. I lay in a hot bath to warm myself: I'd gone cold with fear. Don't think about it, I told myself. Stop it. It was obvious how well he was now: he sparked with energy. And it was so generous and so powerful a force, this energy of his, that its overspill was like the sun, healing my scabs, strengthening me, warming the bruised bones. He couldn't possibly be ill. It was a contradiction in terms. It was inconceivable. I couldn't allow it.

In the morning Françoise drove Uncle Xavier and *Tante* Mathilde to the hospital. Uncle Xavier wore a short-sleeved shirt and a tie. He kept trying to free his neck from the restriction of the collar. *Tante* Mathilde, her hair drawn tightly back, wore a navy-blue dress with small white spots on it. It was the first time I'd seen her in anything but black. I could see she believed – and rightly – that if she wasn't there to make sure he kept his appointment, Uncle Xavier would spend the morning drinking vintage Cahors in a café.

The bleached sun was exhausted by midday. It drained everything of subtlety. I took some books Uncle Xavier had found for me, English books, out into the private garden and lay under a parasol trying to read. The books were all American thrillers. People called Chuck and Todd who spoke incomprehensible slang chased each other in cars. At regular intervals they shot at each other with automatics and then indulged in bleak sex in a hotel room with a doll or a chick, a species that bore only a marginal resemblance to the human female. I understood about one word in three. I was flipping through one called *Slaughter on the Subway*, or something like that, when Celeste shouted through the kitchen window, 'Marie-Christine, there's someone to see you.'

I forgot I wasn't Marie-Christine. I dropped the books and rolled off the sun-lounger. It was only as I opened the door to the kitchen that I remembered the dangerous nature of the game I was playing.

It was Mal. He was leaning against the dresser looking arrogantly relaxed.

'Hi,' he said as I came in. 'I've just introduced myself to your cousin. She's been looking after me.'

I could see that she had. She'd given him a drink. She sat at the table smoking with a self-consciously studied elegance. Occasionally she ran her hand deliberately through her hair so that it fell back into place with a delicate ghost of perfume. She crossed and uncrossed her legs. She looked at him through narrowed eyes as if what he was saying was so fascinating that she might easily be seduced by his wit alone.

'I've just been explaining to Celeste,' Mal said, 'that you and I work together.'

I smiled thinly. I suggested that he might like to see round the château.

'Yeah, OK,' he said. 'Why not? That'd be good.'

Celeste stood up. 'I didn't know you were interested,' she said, 'or I'd have suggested it before.'

'Actually, Celeste,' I said, 'Mal and I have things we need to discuss.'

'Business,' said Mal, smiling at her. He was very clever. He managed to exude charm in Celeste's direction and at the same time send me messages of arrogant confidence. 'You know how it is,' he said.

Celeste exhaled a cloud of smoke to screen her disappointment.

'Come back for a drink, then, when you've finished,' she suggested.

'Wow,' said Mal, as we crossed the courtyard. 'She's a dead ringer for Chris, isn't she?'

'What are you doing here?' I said curtly. He had no right to obtrude on this reality. He belonged to another one.

'What are *you* doing here?' he countered. He was irritatingly well dressed. He stuck his hands casually in his pockets. He was enjoying this. 'You said you were leaving.'

'I changed my mind.'

'Obviously.'

'It's a temporary thing,' I said. 'I just put it off a few days. I'll be going soon.'

'That's a shame. Saturday week they've got a big fête on down in the village. Fireworks, it says on the posters. And a dance in the square. A band. All sorts.'

'Yes, I know,' I said. I did know. Uncle Xavier was on the committee.

'Shame to miss it,' he remarked, as if we were having a normal conversation about nothing very much.

'What do you want?' I asked him bluntly.

'Well, I'd quite like to have a look round now I'm here,' he said.

I took him into the main banqueting hall. He wandered round staring at pieces of china and the lacquered cabinets. 'Very nice,' he murmured. 'Very nice indeed.'

I refused to let him off the hook. 'I had a phone call yesterday,' I said. 'From someone called Sue, who says she works with Chris.'

'Sue?' said Mal vaguely. 'What's through here?'

He wandered into the library. 'Wow,' he said, staring up at the painted ceiling. 'I like that.'

'Chris is a secretary, isn't she?' I persisted. 'She doesn't work for you at all.'

'Oh yes she does,' said Mal. 'She works for me all right. Put it like this: she uses her talents – her secretarial talents – to our mutual advantage.' He slid a book off the shelf. 'Christ,' he said. 'You've fallen on your feet all right here. I'd no idea Chris was related to all this. She never said anything.'

'Perhaps she didn't want you to know,' I said coldly.

He laughed.

'There's a fortune sitting on these shelves,' he said. 'Tell you what, I could contact an antiquarian book expert, find out what was worth putting into circulation, and then you could slip a couple of books out to me from time to time. No one would notice.'

I said nothing. He put the book away.

'So let's get this straight, shall we?' he said. 'Who exactly are you?'

'Who exactly are *you?*'

He laughed. 'Marina James, eh?' he said. He leant against the shelving and stared at me. It was an uncomfortably direct stare. I looked away. 'Funny,' he said, 'I'm sure I've seen you somewhere before. Something familiar about the face.'

I froze.

He smiled kindly at me. 'Still,' he said, 'we don't have to worry about things like that, do we? Details. Not yet, anyway. So what are you going to show me now?'

I took him through to the next room on the tour: an anteroom full of worm-eaten display cases where the collection of firearms and antique weaponry was kept. 'Oh, very interesting,' he said. 'I like this kind of thing. Now those –' he pointed to a pair of pistols with chased silver butts – 'those are worth a couple of grand of anybody's money. At least.' He squatted to take a closer look at a nineteenth-century revolver. 'So tell me, Marina,' he said, 'have the police been yet? About the money?'

'No,' I said.

'Pity.' He stood up. 'Mind you, when you say "no", you could be lying, couldn't you? I should imagine you're a very good liar. Well, you'd have to be, wouldn't you, to do what you're doing? And I admire that. No, honestly. I admire it. The problem is, an accomplished and talented liar like yourself, you could tell me anything, couldn't you? How am I to know what the truth is? For all I know the police could have called round here yesterday and returned the money.'

'They didn't.'

'All right, the day before then. "Here you are, Miss Masbou." I bet that's what they said, isn't it? Not very bright, the police. They can't see what's under their own nose sometimes. "Here you are, Miss Masbou. Here's your money back. Best to put it straight in the bank, eh?" '

He drifted out of the ante-room into an unfurnished room with a huge fireplace where Françoise always paused to point out the vaulting. I scuttled after him.

'Yeah,' he said, standing in the grate to peer up the chimney. 'That's what I'd do. I'd put it straight in the bank. Into the account you've just opened. Well, I expect that's what you opened it for, isn't it?'

A thin, intangible menace hung in the air like a thread of smoke.

'How do you know I've opened an account?' I asked, following him up the circular stone stairs.

'This is a very interesting place,' he said. 'I must come and do the official tour one day. You should be doing the full spiel for me. I feel deprived.'

'How do you know?' I repeated.

'How do I know what?'

He was beginning to annoy me. 'Look,' I said. 'I told you. The police haven't been. They haven't returned the money. And they won't, because I've told them it isn't mine. They think it belonged to a woman called Katherine Hughes. That was the name on the visitor's passport Chris was using.'

'Yeah, that's your story,' he said, stopping at a glazed arrow slit on the circular staircase. 'But I don't happen to believe it. I don't believe you told them the money wasn't yours. Why would you do that, a skilled con artist like yourself? I mean look at that.' He peered down at the courtyard below. From this height you could see the defensive walls punctuated by small towers, the gatehouse, the corner of the Renaissance wing, the woods, the cliffs, the farmland falling away into the valley. 'Just look at it all,' he said. 'Fucking brilliant. If this isn't one of the best scams ever.' He laughed as if the whole thing delighted him. 'Makes anything I've ever come up with look fucking amateur.' He moved away from the arrow slit. 'Well,' he said, 'I think I've probably seen enough now. Give my regards to that poor, bored, sex-starved woman who thinks you're her cousin.'

He started down the steps. I followed him. In the courtyard he said amiably, 'Do you know, Marina, I really enjoyed that. I think I'll definitely come again.'

'I won't be here,' I said.

'Yeah, I've heard that one before,' he said. 'But you're not going anywhere, are you? Not until you've got what you're waiting for.'

'If you mean the money,' I interrupted, 'that's not what I'm here for. And if you want it so badly, then go and tell the police it's yours.'

'Oh, that'd go down very well, wouldn't it? "Excuse me, officer, I think you've got twenty grand my ex-girlfriend nicked off me, but I can't actually prove it's mine, not unless I land myself up to the neck in shit." ' Mal shrugged. 'Not the brightest idea in the world. So – I'll leave it to you, shall I? They'll hand it over eventually. And I'll be watching you very closely, Marina James.' He laughed. 'No, sorry, it won't do. It really won't. You want to choose something more convincing. Like –' he pretended to fish for a likely alternative – 'like Margaret, say.' He grinned amiably at me. 'So, don't forget – twenty grand. And no tricks.'

I watched him walk away across the courtyard. My legs were shaking. When he'd disappeared through the gatehouse, I ran back to the house. Celeste was hovering in the hall. 'Oh God,' she said. 'He's gorgeous. Who is he? Tell me all about him. You must invite him for dinner.'

'He's a little shit,' I said, running up the stairs.

'But I thought he was a friend of yours,' she called after me. 'Do you want any lunch?'

'No,' I shouted back.

I slammed my bedroom door and collapsed on the bed. I was sick of this man. He was ruining everything. I was sick of trying to work out the complications of Chris's past. They were both liars, both Chris and Mal. Liars and shits, both of them. And he knew who I was. He must know. He hadn't dropped the name Margaret by accident. I had a short and murderous fantasy about getting rid of him. I'm very good at murderous fantasies. I used to have them a lot. So I spent a satisfactory half-hour disposing of Mal. I dealt with him very efficiently – a hammer to the skull – and tipped his body into the river. This made me feel a lot better.

Outside there was a burning wind. It bent the scraggy trees and blew small tornadoes of dust and dead leaves against the window. The day grew heavier and hotter. I wanted to be cool. I wanted to wash things away. I wanted a cold, clean place where I could make cold, clean decisions. I slid off the bed and went out. I passed Celeste in the hall talking to the lady from the village who'd come up for the afternoon to take the gate money.

'Just going for a swim,' I said.

I strode off, my hair flapping limply in the wind. Along the rocky path, the birds were silent and unmoving as if stunned by the heat. The cicadas fell into long silences. A couple of ragged, thirsty butterflies hung in motionless exhaustion on the thistle heads.

Then I heard splashing. I heard someone whistling. I thought maybe Uncle Xavier was back from the hospital and had come to cool off in the rock pool; and for a moment, as I turned the corner, I thought the man I saw, the man standing there on a boulder with his back to me, quite naked, *was* Uncle Xavier. His short, powerful legs were thick with hair so that he looked almost like a satyr there in my rock pool, half man, half beast. But it wasn't Uncle Xavier at all. It was someone different. He was pouring water from his cupped hands over his head. It splashed on to his shoulders. He was very dark-skinned. He flung his head back and shook it like a grizzled lion come to cool himself at a watering hole in the heat of the day.

I stood under the overhanging cliff watching him, this trespasser. He turned. I was taken completely off guard. We stood staring at each other. He didn't cover himself. He just stood there. I panicked. I turned and ran, powered by total outrage.

How dare he? Who was he? Uncle Xavier, Uncle Xavier, where are you? There's a man trespassing on our land, a man in my rock pool. Do something. Get rid of him. Make him go away. But by the time I got to the end of the path, stumbling over the stones, I'd remembered that Uncle Xavier wasn't there. And I urgently wanted to see the man again, to have another look, to check that he was real.

'What's the rush?' Celeste asked, as I ran past her in the courtyard. 'Where are you going?' But I was far too breathless to answer her, even if I'd had an answer.

I ran across the lawn. There was a rough path up the rock face behind the kitchen wall which led up to the top of the cliff where brambles and broom and juniper bushes grew. I scrambled and slithered on the stones. By the time I reached the top, I was winded by a stitch and the usual pains in the legs, but I kept on going because I was afraid that if I didn't hurry the man would be gone. Branches whipped back into my face and tore at the skin on my arms. Scratches on my leg dribbled blood, but I crashed on. At the far edge, where the cliff overhung the spring and the limestone was crumbling away, I threw myself down on my stomach and peered over.

He was still there. I didn't know whether this was a relief or a greater outrage. He was standing on one of the boulders, staring down at his own reflection in the water. Then he stretched upwards with a grunting noise. The dark hairs on his chest gathered into a wet V on his belly, then flared out again into the paler, bronzed bush of pubic hair. He bent his knees and slipped down into the water where it was deepest. A spray of drops shimmered in an arc above him, and I knew then exactly what it was I felt. Not outrage. Lust. I lay on my back in the rough grass, closed my eyes and let myself drift into a fantasy that involved a couple of gentle fingers and a lot of spit. And I did such things to the man who came to the water-hole that finally the sun exploded in my head and burst through my body, leaving it to twitch and jerk all alone at the top of the cliff. But these are private things. These are things between him and me. I don't want to write them down.

Once upon a time – I'm going to try this one again – once upon a time there were two sisters. There should, of course, have been three, but there weren't. I don't know why. And they were remarkably alike, these two sisters. Both of them were secretaries and they were both running away. One was full of surprises and the other was constantly being surprised. They lived in the middle of a deep, dark, tangled forest as sisters do. If anyone tried to come too close, if anyone tried to hack a path through the briars, they dreamed their murderous dreams.

But the truth is that in all the stories I know, someone does finally hack his way through, one way or another. And in whatever form he comes, he invariably turns out to be a prince. I don't know whether or not it's possible to avoid him. It's an inevitable part of the story. It has to happen.

When I opened my eyes again and rolled over, the golden man had gone. I wasn't surprised. I'd already begun to suspect that after all he was nothing more than the disordered invention of a feverish afternoon.

Celeste was lying on a sun-lounger on the grass when I scrabbled back down the cliff path.

'Where've you been?' she demanded. 'Come and talk to me for ten minutes before I start work. I'm bored.'

'Sorry. Off for a swim,' I said.

'*Another* one?' Her voice was delicately incredulous.

'I need to cool down,' I explained.

It was quite late when I trailed home, my hair dried to a straw-like tangle, my face and arms scarlet with fresh sunburn.

'Ah, *mon Dieu!*' said Celeste, who was collecting the cash-box from the gatehouse. 'What have you been doing to yourself?' She stared disapprovingly at the long scratches on my legs. 'I've never met anyone as careless as you are. Don't you mind what you look like?'

'I'm on holiday,' I interrupted curtly. But to tell the truth I was impressed by her insight. I *was* careless of myself. I always had been.

Upstairs in my room, I examined myself critically in the spotted mirror in which multiplying reflections floated and sank. I saw a brown, tight-skinned woman. Her scarred skin was slightly freckled although that could have been the flaking silver on the mirror's surface. Poor, old, fat, stupid, passive Margaret Davison was still there somewhere, I could still just about make her image float up to the surface if I thought hard enough, but it was tough to keep her there. She was very insubstantial – a bloated, drowned woman, who sank back again among the weeds where she most wanted to be. The moment she was gone, the scarred woman came into focus again. I was beginning to recognise her. I was getting to know her quite well.

I washed my hair and had a bath. I cleaned my permanently dirty fingernails. I dried my hair with Chris's dryer, and then pinned it up and watched the shorter pieces fall down again round my neck. It was time to stop punishing my body for the crime of forcing Margaret Davison to be, because she wasn't. Not any more. The trouble is, though, that the habits of a lifetime are hard to break. I'd only got as far as filing the third nail before the boredom and distastefulness of the process wore me down. Whichever way you look at it, there are few things more boring than doing your nails.

I put on Chris's silky dress, the one that showed a lot of leg, and a pair of heels. I sprayed myself with some very expensive perfume, which, among a number of other extravagant things, I'd bought with my new credit card. I even thought about putting some make-up on. 'Look at me,' I said. Oddly enough, I think it was Tony I was talking to. I wanted him to see me in my elegant dress with my thin, scarred face and my three manicured nails. I wanted him to see me in my vast, shabbily beautiful bedroom in the Renaissance wing of a French château. 'You see!' I said triumphantly, as if I had at last proved something to him.

It was ages since I'd worn high heels. I stumbled over the loose runner of carpet outside my door. I had to hold on to the banister and come downstairs in a careful, self-conscious way. Celeste saw me first. 'My God,' she said. 'What have you done to yourself?' I smiled coldly at her, and went through to the kitchen. Uncle Xavier was opening a bottle of wine. *Tante* Mathilde was putting bread on the table. Françoise was at the stove stirring something. And there was someone else in there, apart from the children: a man who, at a distance, you might easily for a moment or two mistake for Uncle Xavier; a man on whose short, square body I had, in the deranged heat of the afternoon, built an erotic fantasy so powerful that the moment I saw him again certain muscles jerked in response.

'Marie-Christine,' crowed Uncle Xavier, his face lighting up to see me. 'Look!' He was bursting with excitement. 'Look who's here.'

What was I to do? I felt my face and neck burn brilliant red. The sweat gathered damply in the palms of my hands. I forgot how to swallow.

Smiling in a rather odd way, *Tante* Mathilde said, 'Don't you recognise him?'

Of course I recognised him. I recognised him at once. My whole body recognised him.

Uncle Xavier laughed at such an absurd idea. 'Not recognise him? Her own uncle? Of course she does.'

My *uncle*? It was one of those moments that last so long you begin to wonder why other people haven't noticed the unnatural elongation of time as well. Well, obviously, he was my uncle. Who else could he be? He was maybe ten years younger than Xavier but the resemblance was unmistakable. The moment stretched out further and further. I had an age in which to consider every possible option and to reject them all. I had time to think how ridiculously unprepared I was for the one thing I thought I'd been preparing for all my life. Any second now, someone was finally going to say it. Someone was finally going to look me in the eye and say it. I was suddenly shaking with excitement. I wanted it to happen. I was ready for it. I waited, nerves taut, poised like an athlete under starter's orders. But nothing happened. Time dragged on. Finally, the man – Uncle Gaston – held out his hand to me. Like an automaton, I took it. Then his face loomed towards mine, and we were kissing, right cheek, left cheek, right cheek.

'We've already met,' he said, holding me by the shoulders and leaning back a little to look at me. He was shorter than I was by about an inch, but then I was wearing high heels.

'I thought you were at sea,' I said, in a ridiculously high voice. I was very aware of *Tante* Mathilde watching us.

'We docked on Monday,' he said.

I couldn't remember how to move, how to breathe, how to do anything. I didn't understand any of this. He was surely the one person who knew without any doubt whatsoever that I was not Marie–Christine. Why didn't he say so?

We sat down. Over the conversation, which was centred on Uncle Gaston – his trip, the political situation in North Africa, problems with the Algerian crew – I sat pushing pieces of to-mato salad about. Under the painful tightness of my ribs, my lungs gasped and trembled.

Tante Mathilde hardly took her eyes off me. 'You've lost your appetite?' she enquired.

I rapidly ate a piece of tomato. It lodged halfway down my gullet like a stone.

Uncle Xavier looked at me anxiously. 'What's the matter?' he said. 'Are you ill?'

I shook my head. 'Too much sun.'

'You should wear a hat,' *Tante* Mathilde said.

'I've told her,' said Celeste. 'She'll ruin her complexion.'

'What complexion?' I said in a strained attempt to sound natural. 'Nothing left to ruin.'

Uncle Xavier leant over and took my arm. 'Look. Look at this,' he said, tutting at me. And he held out my arm across the table so Gaston could see the bloodstained scratches. 'Scars, scabs, scratches, bruises.'

And still he said nothing, my Uncle Gaston. He wore a blue shirt with the top button undone. I found myself staring at the triangle of coppery hairs sprouting from just under the collar-bone.

'How's Sandrine?' *Tante* Mathilde was asking.

'Very well,' said Uncle Gaston. 'Very busy. She's in Rome at the moment.'

I can't imagine now how I ever got through that meal. It went on and on, course after course, and the longer it went on, the less I understood what was happening. They talked endlessly about the farm, about subsidies and parasite infections. They discussed village gossip. They complained about the drought. They asked polite questions about Uncle Gaston's wife who ran some kind of business. I said nothing.

'You're very quiet, Marie-Christine,' said Uncle Xavier, taking my hand and squeezing it.

'How did you get on at the hospital?' I asked him. This was what I most wanted to know, and what I was most scared of knowing.

He made a colourful noise of contempt. 'Waste of time,' he

said. 'Do I look ill?' He opened his arms expansively and offered himself to the whole table for judgement. 'Do I look as if I need a hospital? They're all fools, these doctors. They know nothing.'

Gaston – it was impossible to think of him as 'Uncle' Gaston after the intimate and exquisite things that I had done to him in the long grass on the clifftop – Gaston looked me straight in the eye.

'Good to see you again, Chris,' he said. His English was as fluent as Celeste's. 'It's been a long time. Nearly a year.'

I stared back at him in a glazed way. Reality spiralled dizzily into meaninglessness. What was happening *now*?

'I can't remember,' I heard myself say.

'You were just back from one of your trips.'

'Really?' I said coldly. 'Was I? I'd forgotten.'

'And we had a meal at that Italian restaurant. What was it called?'

I could see what he was up to. He was deliberately throwing the ball straight at me in the hope of catching me off-balance. He sucked in his cheeks and tapped his fingers on the edge of the table, pretending to try and remember. But I wasn't going to let a man, even a man who made my legs melt, play this kind of game with me. 'Rossini's,' I said. It was the first Italian name that came into my head.

He laughed out loud.

'Rossini's,' he said. 'That's right. Rossini's.'

'Off the Edgware Road,' I said, improvising icily.

'Very good fish at Rossini's,' he said. 'And so, tell me, how's the world of coffee futures, Chris?'

'Much the same as ever,' I said. If he wanted to play games, fine. I could play games too.

'You look very well on it.'

'Rubbish,' said Uncle Xavier. 'It's sun and food and rest. That's what makes her look so well.'

'I gather from Xavier you had a very lucky escape,' Gaston said.

'We didn't recognise her when she first arrived,' Celeste said.

'I did,' said Françoise loyally.

Uncle Xavier laughed. 'Of course we recognised her. Don't be absurd.'

Celeste slapped Brigham's hand. 'If you want bread, ask for it,' she snapped. He started to cry. They were very bored, the children. Zoe was almost asleep, leaning against Françoise's arm.

'Take the children up, Celeste,' said *Tante* Mathilde.

Françoise started to move. 'I'll do it,' she said.

Before I could stop myself, I said, 'Sit down. You haven't finished.'

'No, really,' said Françoise, blushing and stubborn. 'It's all right. Really.'

'Sit down and finish your cheese.'

Celeste said, 'I do wish you wouldn't interfere, Marie-Christine.'

'They're your children,' I said. 'You put them to bed.'

Uncle Xavier barked with laughter. I thought: I've gone too far. I was feeling dangerously over-confident. Celeste, her face closed, her neck rigid, pushed back her chair. 'Hurry up and kiss *Grandmaman* good night,' she said.

The two boys obediently lifted their faces to be kissed, and then made the tour of the table. I lifted up the sleeping Zoe and handed her to Celeste. We avoided each other's eyes.

When they'd gone, Françoise said in a half whisper, 'I honestly don't mind. I like putting them to bed.'

'Nonsense,' said *Tante* Mathilde. 'Marie-Christine is absolutely right.' She pronounced my name in an odd and deliberate way as if in inverted commas. 'Finish your cheese.'

Françoise sat down.

Uncle Xavier was still chuckling. 'You see,' he said to Gaston. 'This one has a tongue like a razor blade.'

Later, when we were clearing the table, *Tante* Mathilde asked Gaston how long he was staying,

'Well,' he said, 'I'm on shore leave till Thursday night, and there doesn't seem much point in going all the way back to Paris just for five and a half days, so – '

'What a pity,' I said. I still had no idea what was happening, but I was balancing on a tightrope of buzzing confidence as if I'd drunk too much. 'What a shame,' I said. 'So we'll both miss the fête next Saturday.'

'What are you talking about?' Uncle Xavier demanded. 'You won't miss anything. You're not going anywhere until you're completely healed.'

Gaston caught my eye. Reaching across to move the cheeseboard off the table, I accidentally brushed against him. Our bare arms touched. I jumped away as if I had been electrocuted.

It embarrasses me to write about love. I know so little about it: I am such a novice. Truthfully, I have no idea at all what it is, how it happens, whether or not it's a self-induced illusion, or maybe just a mutual fantasy built on a foundation of self-obsession. I don't understand the first thing about it.

Certainly I had all the classic symptoms from the very start. I couldn't eat. I couldn't sleep. I lay awake tossing and turning as if there were a pea under the mattress. It was suffocatingly hot, but I'd slept through worse. I was sleeping very well these days. My dreamless nights were light and fresh. I woke every morning with a clear head and an excess of energy.

Ah yes, you say, but at any moment this man could have denounced you. True. I had no idea why he didn't. But the physical symptoms I'd attributed to my initial panic – the trembling under the ribs, the sweaty hands, the inability to swallow – all these might just as easily, and more truthfully, be symptoms of something else altogether.

I tried to remember if I'd ever felt like this about Tony. Had I lain awake for hours, my head, my eyes, my skin, my gut so full of him that there was room for nothing else? But surely this – what I am describing now – this is lust. This is nothing to do with love. Love has to have time to grow. You can't love someone you don't know.

Except, I *did* know him. I'd been expecting him all my life. Forests, bloodstains, lost shoes, the long sleep, the spell, the enchantment, the urgent need to find the right name – I knew about all of these. The only thing missing was the arrival in one form or other of the prince. I suppose I'd assumed that if he ever did come, which of course he wouldn't, it would be in a form I'd recognise: a frog or a woodcutter, something sensible like that. How was I supposed to recognise him when he came disguised as an uncle?

At one time I was temporarily fooled into thinking he'd arrived in the guise of a trainee salesman from Coventry. A prince, I argued, might just as easily be turned into a trainee salesman as into a frog. Everybody else seemed to think so. Everybody else was constantly telling me how handsome Tony was, how charming, so it's hardly surprising I allowed myself briefly to be deceived. Even after we were married, I went on vaguely assuming that if only I knew how, I could break the spell and he'd turn out to be the Prince after all. But he didn't. He just went on being a salesman with a passion for machines. It was my fault: I don't blame him. Either there was no spell to break, or I wasn't clever enough, or generous enough to break it. And so reality set in – endurance, the web of lies we gathered round ourselves for warmth, the scab I cannot quite leave alone. And if all that does not, in the end, add up to love, real love, then what does? I don't know. Don't ask me. I know nothing about it.

I lay awake for hours considering these things, until the darkness softened and the sky turned a cold, exhausted grey. Puddles of light began to gather on the floor. I hung over the edge of the bed and watched them spread. Distantly, I heard a door close, a lavatory flush, the creaking of a floorboard. I lay listening. Footsteps passed my door. I knew who it was. I waited, lying on my back, staring at my watch. After ten minutes I got up and followed.

He was standing on one leg by the pool taking off his shoe. He put it tidily beside the other shoe on a patch of grass. He started to unbutton his shirt. I stood and watched. He knew I was there. He undid his watch and put it in his right shoe. I thought: how neat – this is your naval training. He looked up, squinting against the light. I kicked my sandals off. I crossed my arms and pulled off my T-shirt. He unbuckled his belt, and one of us, I can't remember which, slipped the button free and slid down the zip. One of us wrestled cack-handedly with the catch on my skirt. I have an image of him as bronze and copper. I remember being dazzled. He wasn't a handsome man: his chin was too heavy, his eyes too small, his eyebrows too bushy, his nose squashed like a boxer's, but his body was beautiful. To me, he was so beautiful it hurt. I had to shade my eyes to look at him.

What happened next was so inevitable it never occurred to me to put up any resistance. Slowly and with infinite invention we embroidered on my erotic fantasy of the previous afternoon. All I can say is that it felt like love. At the time. Honestly it did.

Hours later – so much later that the sun was high enough in the sky to burn our shoulders – he asked idly, 'So who are you?'

'I'm not quite sure,' I said.

Fitting bone to hollow, hollow to bone, we lay on his towel, and I told him the whole story from the beginning: the rue François Premier, the hotel with the adenoidal child, the drive with Chris, the prostitute in the toilets, the crash on the N20 north of Cahors. I explained to him that I'd just gone along with the majority view. There was nothing unusual in that. For years people had been telling me that I was Margaret Davison.

'And were you?' he asked.

'I don't think so, no,' I said. 'Never. I never felt as if I was.' And I explained about poor, frightened Margaret Davison who was happier weightlessly drifting among her weeds, and how Chris Masbou had turned out to be far more complicated than I'd bargained for, and now I didn't know how to stop being Chris because of what it would do to Uncle Xavier.

He was silent for a long time. I felt very bad. I felt the need to apologise to him for things I hadn't even thought of before. I had robbed Chris of her own death. I had denied her a funeral and the grief due to her. I had robbed her both of her life *and* her death.

Discomfort forced us to rearrange ourselves. I broke the long silence by asking the question I most wanted answered. 'What I don't understand,' I said, taking his small tough fingers into my mouth one by one, 'is why you said nothing last night. Why didn't you tell them straight away I wasn't Chris?'

'Because you made me laugh,' he said. 'I was very intrigued. I liked the look of proprietorial outrage on your face when you saw me in the pool.'

'I *was* outraged. This is my pool.'

'No, it isn't,' he said. 'It's mine.' He held my head against his chest. 'And then when I was introduced to you in the kitchen … ' He started to laugh. 'What a ridiculous moment,' he said. 'What a farce. You're nothing like Chris. What on earth made you think you were?'

'I didn't.' I said. 'I didn't mean any of this to happen. I was just running away.'

'And it suited you to run into someone else's life?'

I nodded.

'Well, you didn't choose too well,' he said. 'How much do you know about her?'

'It keeps changing. I know she's a secretary. I think she is, anyway. And I know about someone called Mal.'

'Mal? How do you know about him?'

'Because he contacted me. Looking for Chris. He says she's stolen £20,000 from him.'

This didn't appear to surprise Gaston. 'She was talking about leaving him the last time I saw her.'

'At Rossini's,' I reminded him.

He laughed. 'Actually it was called Salino's. I used to see her sometimes if I was in London. I was sorry for her.'

'Sorry for Chris?' Information like this continued to bewilder me.

'Well, yes. She'd had a rough time. For years there was just her and her mother. They were very close. She was a strange woman, Chris's mother. Very clinging. Very bitter. She never understood why Xavier wouldn't divorce his wife and marry her. And she hated Mathilde. I was the only member of the family who went to her funeral because I was the only one with no axe to grind. After that I used to try and see her as often as I could. She had no one in England: she was very alone. I was working on the cross-Channel ferries at the time. My wife's idea. So for a few years it was a regular thing: I met Chris for dinner maybe once a month.'

'Why didn't Chris ever come and stay here?' I asked.

'Probably because she'd inherited all her mother's resentments. She'd certainly been fed her mother's version of things. And I think she'd told too many lies. She wanted the family over here to believe them. She wanted them to think she was doing all right on her own.'

'And was she?' I asked.

'Sometimes she was, sometimes she wasn't. Sometimes she seemed to be doing incredibly well. Other times I had to lend her money.'

'But she wasn't the high-powered businesswoman she wanted people to believe she was?' I asked curiously.

'I don't know,' he said. 'I don't know what she was. She wasn't an easy person to pin down. A couple of times she wasn't at the address she'd given me. She said she'd had to leave in a hurry. Once I caught her using a false name. She covered it up very well. She came up with a very plausible story to explain why she was calling herself something else. I didn't ask too many questions. What she did with her life was her business. I just checked up from time to time to make sure she was OK.'

'And Mal?' I asked.

He shrugged. 'She was with him a long time.'

'And it took her a year to make up her mind to leave him?'

'How long did it take you?'

'I didn't make up my mind at all,' I said. 'It just happened. But even as I was saying it I knew it wasn't true. I'd been making my mind up for ages.

'It was a funny relationship,' Gaston said. 'Whatever Mal said, Chris did. I could never understand what she saw in him.'

'He's in the village,' I said. 'I've spoken to him.'

'Does he know who you are?' Gaston asked.

'I think he probably does, yes. He dropped some hints.' I explained the state of play between Mal and me.

'Be careful,' said Gaston. 'Don't trust him.' He brushed some dead leaves off my stomach. 'If he can use what he knows about you to his advantage, he will.'

Suddenly I lost control of my voice. I started to say something, but it came out splintered and distorted by tears. 'I've got myself in such a mess,' I croaked. He put his arms round me and held me and rocked me until the moment of fear had passed.

We went back to the house separately. I wandered through the car park towards the orangery and sat there for a while on the edge of the plinth where behind me the nameless dog plunged his teeth eternally into the boar's neck. I held my hands to my nose: they were rich with Gaston's smell. I breathed it in. I leant back against the glass, closed my eyes and breathed him into me. I considered whether or not I was shocked by what I'd just done.

I wasn't.

I spent some time retelling myself the story of the Acropolis Café as a kind of test; but it had lost its power. It seemed trivially irrelevant. I knew what I was doing, and it was all right. What did shock me was that I had spent sixteen years with Tony and never once felt how I was feeling now. In my head I finally closed a door which I had thought had jammed permanently open. It closed easily and with a firm and final click.

When I opened my eyes again, Uncle Xavier was peering at me through the window.

'What are you doing?' he demanded crossly, tapping on the glass to get my attention. 'Are you ill?'

'No,' I said.

He didn't believe me. He came in to check. 'What's happened to your eyes?' he demanded. Indignantly, he accused me of crying. 'Look at this. Look what you're doing to your face. Are you unhappy? What's the matter? You don't like it here?'

'Yes, of course I like it.'

'What have you been crying for, then? You've had bad news?'

I shook my head.

'So you sit here and cry for nothing, uh? What a stupid woman. What a waste of good tears.'

I laughed.

'That's better.' He came and sat beside me. 'So tell me,' he said. 'Is it this man of yours again?'

'No,' I said. 'No, I just felt sad.'

'About what?'

'About things ending.'

'What? What is going to end?' he said. 'Nothing.'

He sat beside me in companionable silence for a while.

'What did they really tell you at the hospital?' I asked.

'What hospitals always tell you,' he grumbled. 'Moderation. Don't eat too much, don't drink, don't think, don't feel.' He barked with laughter. 'Doctors! What do they know about anything.

For no reason at all, the tears started to dribble down my cheek again. (This is another lie: I knew the reasons perfectly well.)

'I'm sorry,' I said, 'I don't know what's the matter with me.'

'I know. I know what's the matter.' His solution was triumphantly simple. 'You've eaten nothing. You've had no breakfast. If you don't eat, of course you cry. You get low blood sugar. I know. I know about these things.'

He marched me into the kitchen. 'This silly niece of mine, she doesn't eat,' he said. He pulled out a chair. 'Sit,' he commanded. 'Eat. Françoise, make your cousin a coffee.'

I tried to get up to do it myself, but he pushed me down again. Across the table, Gaston was peeling an apple. He looked up. Our eyes slid past each other. 'Good morning,' he said politely.

Distantly, I returned his politeness. 'Good morning,' I said.

And so a new deception began.

We were very good at it, surprisingly good. In view of the greater deception, you probably don't find it at all surprising that I, at any rate, was so skilled at this game: but I was surprised. I didn't know I had it in me. This was different. This wasn't evasion or an inability to be certain what the truth was. It wasn't the problem of seeing such a variety of truths that I didn't know which one to choose, nor a passive acceptance of other people's truths to save the trouble of having to find some of my own. This was straightforward, honest-to-goodness deceit.

'So what are your plans for today?' Uncle Xavier asked Gaston.

Gaston shrugged. He had no plans.

Uncle Xavier had. Marie-Christine was depressed: she must immediately be un-depressed. 'What you need,' he said, is a day out. I would take you myself, but I've got some business appointments this morning. The bank. Lawyers. Tedious people.' Gaston, he said, was the only one without any commitments, so obviously Gaston was the one to take me.

'No, really,' I protested. I knew that at the slightest sign of resistance Uncle Xavier would become a tornado of determination.

Yes, yes, he said. Don't argue. It was all decided. What did I know about anything? Stay out all day. Enjoy yourself. He was not listening to any more nonsense from me. Eat more bread.

So I smiled and said coolly to Gaston: 'If there's something else you'd rather … '

'No,' he answered, equally cool. 'No. That's fine.'

I turned to include Françoise. 'What about you? Why don't you come?' It was perfectly safe to ask her because I knew she was on tour duty. She shook her head. 'Oh what a shame,' I said shamelessly.

'I'll meet you in about half an hour then, shall I?' said Gaston, pushing back his chair and standing up.

'Fine.'

I didn't know it was possible to have this kind of luck. My cheeks ached with the effort to control laughter. All the way down the drive, sitting beside him in his hired car, I was fighting the laughter.

He was wearing jeans and a faded, navy-blue shirt. I can remember every detail. The sleeves were rolled up. I couldn't stop staring at him: his hands resting on the wheel, his short, tough arms, his profile. It made him shy. I was grinning like an idiot, my cheeks stuffed full of uncontainable happiness.

'Where are we going?' I asked.

As soon as we were a couple of miles out of the village, he reversed the car up one of the forest tracks until we were hidden in the thick shade of oak trees.

'Do you want to walk?' he asked.

I didn't care what I did as long as I did it with him. We walked deeper and deeper into the woods, and talked together in a stilted, rather shy way as if we didn't yet know what to talk about, which we didn't. And then more easily, more naturally, we lay in each other's arms on the cool grass under the trees. Most of the time we just stared at each other as if somewhere in our faces or on our bodies there might be written some kind of explanation of what was happening. Sometimes we lay side by side staring up through kaleidoscopic layers of leaves, and smiling stupidly. Sometimes we lay in a muddle of limbs, holding on tight; and around us the world splintered and dissolved as if the light and the sky and the earth were all nothing more than a heat mirage, nothing more than the margins of a dream: and the only reality, the only truth, was in the flow of warmth, like an artery, between his mouth and mine.

Hours and hours passed. Thirst forced us back into the car and we drove to a shop and bought some mineral water and fruit juice.

'Tomorrow,' said Gaston, 'we'll bring some drinks in an ice bag.'

His practicality enchanted me. I hadn't thought of him as practical. I hadn't really thought of him at all, not objectively. It hadn't occurred to me that he might have any separate characteristics of his own. He was my invention.

'You had a good time?' Uncle Xavier asked when we got home. I was glowing with sun and with happiness, and with other things as well. It was manifestly obvious I'd had a good time. Uncle Xavier said triumphantly, 'You see, a day out. I told you.'

'We thought we might walk along the Gorges tomorrow,' I said casually.

He nodded. 'Good,' he said. 'Very good. Excellent.'

At dinner, I sat in my place almost opposite Gaston, forbidden to touch him, or to catch his eye, or to do anything that might break the spell. Once, his leg brushed deliberately against mine under the table and I was flooded inside with warmth, but outwardly I was very cool. Outwardly, I continued to discuss with *Tante* Mathilde the difference in taste between what the English call French beans and what the French call green beans. How pleasurable it was, this cool, polite and dangerous game played out on indifferent surfaces, while underneath every nerve-end ached to reconnect. The meal ended, we had coffee, we washed up, we sat for a while in the garden with Uncle Xavier and Celeste, spinning time out in a mutual tease.

'Well,' I said eventually, yawning. 'Bed.'

'So – you had a good day?' Uncle Xavier said as I bent to kiss him good night.

'I had a wonderful day.'

'And are you happier now?'

Afterwards I wondered if this wasn't 'my happiest day', but 'happy' is too simple a word for it. This day was alarmingly complex.

'Bed,' I said, stretching my arms high over my head.

Later, when the water had stopped clanking in the pipes, and the only noises in the house were the soft clicks as the timbers cooled, I got up and felt my way along the landing in the darkness. He was lying on the bed in his room, waiting for me.

The first day set the pattern for the second. Nobody said anything. What was there to say? Why shouldn't an uncle and a niece, both of whom are on holiday, spend a day together sightseeing? We drove into the woods again. Dazzled by the heat and by each other, we lay on beds of infinite variety: soft grass, dead leaves, damp moss, bracken. We hung on to each other's mouths as if trying to staunch some kind of haemorrhage. We made love until we were too weak to move. We spent hours examining each other, learning each other by heart.

Finally we talked. I told him my story all over again from the beginning. It was acquiring a clearer shape now. Each repetition revealed a little more of its meaning.

At night, in his room, he told me stories about the sea. We devised a mutual fantasy in which the bed became a boat and we sailed away in it, rocking quietly in the doldrums, until the wind started to blow and the boat was swept away, faster and faster, and was finally shipwrecked; but this inevitably ended in making love – in fact making love was part of it – so the story was never finished. I was never tired of hearing about the sea. I made him tell me stories about night watches, and drunken leaves in Agadir. I was obsessed by the idea that this man, whose small, gentle fingers had given me such slithering prismatic pleasure, knew how to navigate across the roughest, most treacherous seas. It was the idea that he could always find his way which dazzled me. It implied such control over the physical world.

No, he said, no, it isn't like that at all. The ship is run by computers. The sea is charted territory.

I smiled and said nothing. Together we rocked gently in the small bed-boat in which we were sailing out into infinity, into outer darkness, and I knew I was safe with him because he could read the stars, he understood how the world worked, not just the invented human world but the real world spinning in meaningless space; he knew what to do when the sky grew black and the waves hurled themselves up to meet it: and if finally the boat capsized and we started to drift hopelessly, then he knew how to survive. This was exactly the kind of knowledge I needed. I listened to him with greedy attention.

Passing through the thin, dull light of early morning back to my own room, I met *Tante* Mathilde on the landing. Her hair was in a plait. She wore a green dressing gown. She was standing there, her head slightly cocked as if she were listening for something.

'Just been to the bathroom,' I said. It seemed necessary to explain my presence on the landing, but the moment I'd spoken, I realised it was a mistake.

She nodded. 'Unfortunately,' she observed, in delicately pointed French, 'I have always been a light sleeper.'

After breakfast one morning Uncle Xavier took me into the garden. He said he was going to water the geraniums but this was patently an excuse. The geraniums were long past watering. They lay limply in fissures of cracked earth the colour of blood.

'So where are you going today?' he said, irritably, fighting with the coils of the hosepipe. He wouldn't look at me.

'I don't know,' I said. 'We haven't decided.'

'We?' he said. '*We?*'

'Yes,' I said. I tried to make him meet my eye. 'Do you mind?' I asked.

He turned the water on. The hosepipe uncurled and became rigid.

'Why should I mind? You must do what you want.'

'Then I don't know what we're talking about,' I said. 'Are you accusing me of monopolising Uncle Gaston?'

'I'm not accusing you of anything,' he said. 'Why are you so prickly?'

The water gushed over the baked pots and trickled uselessly away into evaporating puddles.

'Why are *you* so prickly?' I said.

He said nothing. He stood there stubbornly spraying the gravel with water and refusing to look at me.

'Anyway,' I said, 'it was your idea.'

'You should rest. You should not run around the countryside exhausting yourself. You are not strong yet.'

On the contrary, I was getting stronger every day.

We drove up into the hills on the other side of the river across the Causse into Aveyron. This was the fifth day we'd spent together. This was the last whole day

'What are we going to do?' Gaston said, referring not to the day ahead but to the situation in general. He said it several times.

'I don't know.'

He talked about his wife, Sandrine. He'd met her in Marseilles and married very young for reasons he couldn't now quite remember. Something to do with her persistence and his feeling that perhaps it was time to marry. Had he loved her? Not really. He wasn't sure if he knew what love was. He was fond of her. She infuriated him. They were used to each other. It was, he said, a pretty ordinary sort of marriage. They were together very little. From the beginning, despite pressure from her, he'd refused to give up the sea. Thwarted of the kind of closeness she wanted, she had channelled her energies into starting a business. Now she had two small, exclusive shops in Paris where she sold exquisite Italian fabrics and a few exorbitantly expensive lamps and *objets d'art*. He found her obsession with style as baffling as she found his obsession with stars and space. Neither of them had ever been quite what the other imagined. Nevertheless, on the rare occasions they were together, they were, he said, very gentle with each other, very considerate. They spoke on the phone almost daily as if phoning were a way of tending the wounds they'd unintentionally inflicted on each other. They'd discovered, he said, that kindness was a more than adequate substitute for love, so adequate that it felt almost like the real thing. Sometimes he suspected that it might even be better than the real thing.

'Is *this* the real thing?' he asked.

'I don't know,' I said. I left questions like that to him. I thought a man who could navigate an ocean by the stars ought to be able to find his way through whatever was happening more easily than someone who had never learned how to navigate anything.

*

We sat in a café holding hands, legs entwined, and made anxious, dazed plans. Tomorrow was Thursday. In the afternoon he had to drive to Marseilles to rejoin his ship. I would stay for the fête in the village on Saturday because Xavier wanted me to, and because I needed time alone with him to tell him the truth. The next morning I'd take the train south. I'd wait for Gaston in Marseilles. I had a picture of myself standing by the water's edge waiting for his ship to slide over the horizon. I saw myself walking along shabby, peeling streets back to the hotel, where I'd spend the blinding white Mediterranean afternoons lying alone on my bed. But it had the quality of fantasy, this vision. Nothing near the sea is ever real. It always has an impermanent, shifting feeling. It's a good place for impermanent, shifting people, but not perhaps for me. Not any more. There was something uncomfortably unreal about this plan. I couldn't get it into focus.

'We need time,' he said.

' Yes,' I said. 'Time.' We squeezed each other's hands tightly as if we felt the need to reassure each other about something.

Gaston drained his glass. 'Let's go,' he said urgently. We drove until we found a track into the woods, where we lay in a patch of grass burned by the dead eye of the sun. Afterwards Gaston slept and I lay on my side and watched him sleep and tried to be honest. It was lust, that was what the last five days had been about. I knew that. What I didn't understand was whether it was anything more. But the more I worried about it, the more the question seemed irrelevant. It was enough just as it was. I bent down and kissed him awake. He blinked in surprise. I watched him adapt himself rapidly to the fact that I was not Sandrine. He smiled. He held my face in his hands. 'I love you,' he said. But I don't think either of us really believed it. All the same, the reflection I saw in his eyes gave me courage. Whatever else, I was grateful to him for filling me with so many new and satisfyingly substantial images of myself.

*

We were late back for dinner. We sat opposite each other and politely discussed the water shortages. The absurdity of it made mé laugh. Two hours earlier my mouth had been full of him. Now I was chewing grated beetroot and listening to his views on the drought.

'What are you laughing at now?' Uncle Xavier demanded.

'Nothing,' I said.

'You laugh for nothing. You cry for nothing. You have a head like a sieve.' He rehearsed this list of my inadequacies. Twice I caught him looking at me in a confused way as if he was no longer quite sure who I was. He was unusually quiet. It might, after all, I thought, not be as hard as I feared to tell him the truth. It was the thing that worried me most, telling Uncle Xavier that Chris was dead. Obviously it would have to be done before I left, and I had to tell him myself, face to face. I owed him that, and a lot else besides. But it was the thing I least wanted to do. I dreaded the moment when his eyes would harden with pain as he grasped the enormity of my betrayal.

Later Uncle Xavier took Gaston and a bottle of cognac into the room he used as a farm office. 'I want to talk to you,' he said. 'Business. Come and have a drink.'

Françoise washed up and I dried.

'I haven't seen you for days,' she said shyly. 'You're always out.'

She was hurt by my neglect. I apologised.

'Perhaps we could go into Figeac together tomorrow,' she said.

'Not tomorrow,' I replied.

'Oh.' Timidly she suggested, 'Well, maybe next week then?'

I saw that going into Figeac with me was important to her. I'd forgotten I was her glamorously travelled and powerful cousin. I'd forgotten what Chris must represent to her. 'I'd love to,' I said, 'but I have to leave on Sunday.'

'Oh.' She pushed defensively at her glasses so her hand hid her face.

'Sunday?' said Celeste, who was carrying plates across from the table and who caught the tail-end of our conversation. '*Maman*, did you hear that? Marie-Christine says she's leaving on Sunday.'

Tante Mathilde, who had been upstairs to settle a noisy quarrel between Richard and Brigham, closed the kitchen door behind her. 'Sunday?' she said 'Well, we shall be sorry to see you go.'

'I shall be sorry to leave,' I replied formally. 'But I have to get back to work.'

'Well, yes, of course,' she said. 'Have you rung them?'

I didn't know who she meant. 'Rung who?'

'Work,' she said. 'Your company.'

'Oh.' I was confused for a moment. 'Yes,' I said rapidly. 'Yes, I rang them from the village.'

'I'm surprised you haven't got one of those mobile phones,' Celeste said.

'I have,' I said. 'In England. I have two.'

I was beginning to get sick of all these trivial and meaningless lies.

Early the following morning Gaston woke me. 'The last day,' he said, as I slipped out of his bed to go back to my own room. 'No it isn't,' he contradicted himself. 'There'll be other days. Hundreds of them.'

All the same, we couldn't stop thinking of it in those terms, final terms, and the burden was too heavy for the day to bear. It was a sad, frittered, useless morning. I couldn't get close enough to him. He was already withdrawing, already smelling the salt and feeling the wind. We could think of nothing much to say. We resorted to repeating things – plans, promises, as if repeating them would make them sound more real. I was numb when, in mid-afternoon, he carried his two cases downstairs to the hire car.

The family gathered in the drive to see him go. I kissed him on the cheek in a distant, sad sort of way as if he was someone I had once known but had long since lost touch with. Uncle Xavier held him close for a long time, then scolded him for wasting time. We waved as the car drove away, but he waved back only perfunctorily and not once did he turn round.

In the deathly heat of late afternoon I walked back into the house, moving with infinite care as if I were afraid of something breaking. I went up to my room and lay on the bed and stared at the ceiling, which I already knew in intimate detail. How cold I am, I thought. Already I was losing his face. Whenever I tried to reconstruct it – and I kept on trying – all I could see was Uncle Xavier. After a while I had a bath, for something to do, something different to think about. Everything had an empty unreality. The bath seemed to be floating in indefinable space. Five days of disorientated madness and consuming lust had produced a spell powerful enough to effect a very odd transformation. I felt as if I were recovering from a long and debilitating illness, as if I'd been ill for so long I'd forgotten what things looked like. I had that shaky, light-headed feeling you get after a high fever when everything looks strange and surprisingly beautiful. I lay in the water for ages looking at a brilliantly turquoise cake of soap. I washed one knee over and over again because the loofah was so fascinating. I felt very new and odd. With immense care I dried and powdered my body. I was extremely gentle with it because it was alive in such a strange world.

It was after ten when I woke. What was left of the morning I spent saying goodbye to things. I walked round the walls, reacquainting myself with every stone, learning the colours and what flowers grew out of the fissures and the holes where the

lizards hid. I made a complete circular tour of the outer peri-
meter. I walked every path and every patch of grass. I wandered
through every room, photographing it in my head as if my
eyelids were lens shutters.

'What are you doing?' Uncle Xavier demanded. I jumped. In
the darkness of the banqueting hall with its huge trestle table
and its two canopied fireplaces, the shadows were so deep I
hadn't seen him.

'I'm saying goodbye.'

In the gloom he looked so like Gaston that certain muscles
automatically stirred. Or perhaps it was the other way
round and what I meant was that Gaston looked so like
Xavier. Perhaps what I'd done was to project the one on to
the other.

He snorted. 'What do you mean "goodbye"?'

'I'm leaving on Sunday.'

'Yes, but you're coming back.' It wasn't a question. 'You will
come back. Soon.'

I said nothing.

'Why must you go at all?' he demanded. 'I don't understand
it.'

'Work,' I lied. 'I have to live.'

'So? Live here. You can live here.'

'No, I can't.'

He shrugged. 'If it's a matter of money ... money is the least
I can do.'

'It's not money,' I said.

After a long silence he said, 'I have to milk the goats.'

We walked over the fields together. 'I love this place,' I
said, letting a thought slip out in a carelessly unguarded
moment.

I sat on the edge of an empty water trough and watched him
work.

'I made a decision the other day,' he said.

'What kind of decision?' I asked.

He shook his head and pushed away the goat he had just milked. 'Well,' he said, changing the subject, 'never mind. Tomorrow I shall take you out to lunch.'

'Is that the decision you made?' I asked. I watched him catch another goat, I watched his hands stroke its bony rump to calm it. A brief uncensored thought slipped into my head. It so shocked me – no, that's the wrong word – it so *unnerved* me that I muttered an excuse and ran back to the house.

At dinner Uncle Xavier was himself again. He talked, he laughed, he refilled my wineglass until I lost count of how much I'd drunk, he told scurrilous and probably fabricated stories about the fête committee of which he was a member. I felt dizzy with wine and sadness and laughing too much. Tears of laughter ran down my cheeks and threatened to turn into something altogether more desperate and uncontrollable.

'I'm so sorry,' I said. 'I've drunk too much.'

Uncle Xavier took my hand and then dropped it again immediately. 'You're tired,' he said. 'You must sleep.'

I excused myself before the cheese was served and went upstairs. *Tante* Mathilde must have followed me: when I came out of my room to go to the bathroom I met her on the landing.

'You look a little pale,' she said. 'Are you in any pain?'

I supposed she meant from the consequences of the accident. 'My legs hurt sometimes,' I said.

'Do you take anything for it?'

I told her the hospital had given me some painkillers when I'd left, but that I'd finished them.

'Come into my room a moment,' she said. 'I have some Anadin.'

I followed her along the landing and into her bedroom, not because I needed painkillers, but because I was curious. I'd taken really very little notice of her since our barbed conversation on the landing at the end of my happiest day. I'd thought of her as someone to be avoided, to be treated with a distant respect. I was, in truth, a little afraid of her. She had none of the warmth of her younger brothers. It was easy both to be slightly afraid of her and at the same time to dismiss her because she was so seldom in evidence about the place. From this room, where she spent most of her day, she ran not only the domestic affairs but the whole tourist side of the business. I was very intrigued to see inside. I imagined it as a thickly woven spider's web from the centre of which she controlled affairs with an all-seeing eye. In fact, it was a light, white and gold room with brocade chairs and a large desk; and beyond it, through open double doors, a bedroom.

'Come in,' she said. 'Sit down.'

I sat on a small gilt chair. It was very uncomfortable.

'I feel I should apologise to you,' she said, searching in a desk drawer, presumably for the Anadin. 'You leave on Sunday and we've hardly spoken together.'

'I'm afraid that's probably my fault,' I said politely. 'I seem to have been out a lot.'

She abandoned her search. Perhaps it had only been an excuse and there had never been any painkillers. She sat at the desk as if this were an official interview.

'So?' she said.

It was clearly an invitation to make some kind of statement, but I didn't know what, so I smiled at her.

'You've been a little upset today, I think?' she prompted.

'Not particularly,' I lied.

She smoothed her black skirt over unimaginable thighs. 'Of course, you'll miss Gaston.' Was this a criticism? 'You enjoyed your expeditions with him?'

'Very much,' I said.

'We seem to have seen very little of you recently.'

It *was* a criticism.

I apologised. 'I didn't mean to take up all his time.'

'Oh, my dear,' she said, 'I'm sure he enjoyed it.'

What did *that* mean?

'And this morning,' she said, 'this morning I stood at the window and watched you walking about the place, and I wondered to myself: is Marie-Christine so restless because Gaston has gone and she's a little bored with nothing to do, or is it something else?'

I was considering how to answer this, and more importantly what the point of the question was, when there was a tap on the door.

'Come in,' said *Tante* Mathilde.

It was Françoise. Apologetically she said that the police were downstairs and wanted to see Marie-Christine.

Tante Mathilde turned her attention to me. 'Are you well enough to see the police?'

'What do they want?' I asked.

Françoise shook her head. 'They wouldn't say.'

I found that I was pulling at a loose thread on the padded arm of the brocade chair.

'Tell them that Marie-Christine is very tired, but that she'll see them briefly,' said *Tante* Mathilde.

I was trying to control a tight ache in my gut that was making it difficult for me to breathe normally. All the same, I was sufficiently in command of myself to admire *Tante* Mathilde's attitude. That's the way to deal with things, I told myself.

Françoise had disappeared.

'I assume this is something to do with the accident,' *Tante* Mathilde said, picking up an embroidery frame from the desk. 'I hope no one is going to charge you with dangerous driving.'

All I wanted was that they shouldn't blow it for me. Whatever else happened, I had to tell Uncle Xavier the truth myself. I didn't want anything to spoil tomorrow, the last day of his loving me.

He came up the stairs with them to show them the way. I could hear his voice. 'She's not well,' he was saying. 'You're not to upset her.'

They were polite but cool. I could picture him snapping round their ankles like an angry terrier. They closed the door on him.

It was Peyrol and his miniature sidekick again.

Tante Mathilde continued to sew quietly. She exchanged a few rapid comments in French with Peyrol. Her niece was in pain, she said, and she would prefer, unless they had any objection, to stay in the room in case I needed her. Peyrol agreed. He apologised for disturbing us.

'Sit down, *Messieurs*.' *Tante* Mathilde gestured towards a couple of hard chairs by the window, but they declined the offer. They would not take up any of my time, they said, they only wanted to return my passport.

'Thank you,' I said, taking it. I shot a quick look at *Tante* Mathilde to see whether she'd grasped the significance of this. It must have struck her as odd that I was planning to leave for England without a passport.

It had. 'Your timing, Messieurs, is excellent,' she remarked, continuing to stitch quietly at her embroidery. 'My niece was planning to leave us the day after tomorrow.'

'I have a job to get back to,' I said defensively, as if something needed explaining.

'If you could sign here – ' Peyrol offered me a piece of paper, presumably some kind of receipt. I didn't bother to read it. I pretended to, but I was too busy trying to work out the real purpose of this visit. It was something to do with the way they stood, the way they were looking at me: I didn't like it. Perhaps the return of the passport was just a ruse, an excuse to get a signature from me. Or maybe they wanted to encourage me to move on so they could follow me. Either way there was nothing I could do about it. I signed. I calculated that by the time they'd compared my signature with the specimen signature they'd obviously got from England, and decided there was not the remotest resemblance between them, I'd be in Marseilles and Uncle Xavier would know the truth. If they could just hold off for twenty-four hours it wouldn't matter what conclusions they came to.

'Thank you, Mademoiselle,' said Peyrol. He didn't even look at the paper I'd signed. He was a lot cleverer than that. He folded it up and put it in his pocket. 'Just one other thing,' he added casually. 'Do you come regularly to visit your relations in France?'

'No,' I said.

'When was the last time you visited them?'

There was no point in lying. 'Years ago,' I said. 'When I was eight.'

I watched a brief, almost undetectable spasm of satisfaction cross the sidekick's face.

'Eight,' said Peyrol. He turned to *Tante* Mathilde. 'That's a long time ago. Your niece must have changed.'

Tante Mathilde looked up from her embroidery. She smiled at him. 'Out of all recognition,' she said.

I waited for the next question. I forced myself to be calm.

'Although, of course,' *Tante* Mathilde added, 'there were frequent visits in the other direction.' Peyrol looked puzzled. 'My brother Gaston – you've just missed him, I'm afraid; he left yesterday – my brother Gaston used to see Marie-Christine quite regularly. In London.'

Peyrol and the small sidekick exchanged a glance.

'And when did you last see Monsieur Masbou?' Peyrol asked me.

'*Captain* Masbou,' *Tante* Mathilde corrected him.

'In England, you mean?' I asked. 'About a year ago.'

Tante Mathilde smoothly slipped her needle through the stretched fabric. 'They had dinner together. Funnily enough, they were talking about it only the other day.'

'And this was a regular thing?' Peyrol asked.

'While my uncle was still working on the ferries, yes,' I said.

There was a pause. The sidekick stared at his feet. Peyrol ran his tongue round his teeth. 'Mademoiselle,' he said suddenly. 'Do you know a man called Malcolm Hayward?'

I thought very carefully before I answered this. I assumed he meant Mal. The net was closing in very fast now. It seemed to me they had two choices, and neither of them looked good. Either I was Chris Masbou, in which case they'd arrest me for whatever ambiguously criminal activities Chris and Mal were involved in; or I was Margaret Davison, in which case they'd arrest me at the very least for fraudulently forging Chris's signature to obtain money. Worse, they'd contact Tony. The only thing in my favour was that they were still unsure which way to jump. I could see they'd arrived suspecting I wasn't Chris, and had been rattled by *Tante* Mathilde's insistence that I was. It made no difference to me: either way I was likely to be arrested for being someone I wasn't.

'Yes,' I said. 'Yes, I know him.'

'Thank you, Mademoiselle,' said Peyrol. He turned to *Tante* Mathilde and asked in French if he might have a private word with her.

I stood up to go, but *Tante* Mathilde gestured for me to sit down again. 'Let me show you out, Messieurs,' she said. 'We can speak on our way down.'

They were very polite. They wished me good night. They hoped I'd soon feel better. They would, they said, be in touch. Peyrol wrote down a phone number for me, 'in case I remembered anything I wanted to tell them'.

When they'd gone, I paced round the room looking at things and replaying the interview in my head. The more I thought about it, the more I realised how subtly *Tante* Mathilde had refuted the suspicion that I wasn't her niece. But what really threw me was how quickly she'd understood the implication that I wasn't. Daringly, I sat down in her chair while I considered this. I picked up her embroidery. I glanced at the piles of brochures, invoices and bills. The drawer she'd been looking through was still open. I closed it. Then, powered by curiosity, I opened it again. It was full of things like paper clips and envelopes and address labels. In one corner were some foil packets of indigestion pills. I closed this drawer and pulled out the one underneath, which was crammed full of packets of old envelopes neatly held together with rubber bands and labelled according to the correspondent. An English stamp caught my eye. Written in pencil across the top envelope of this rather thin bundle – a dozen letters at the most – was written 'Marie-Christine'. Unable to control myself, I unwound the rubber band and opened the top envelope. There was a single sheet of folded paper inside. The handwriting was big and childishly looped. In schoolgirl French it thanked *Tante* Mathilde for the birthday present of a scarf. I stuffed the note rapidly back in its envelope and opened another.

'*Ma chère Tante*,' I read. This was a more adult hand. It was an apology for not being able to take up an invitation to visit Rougearc that summer, but 'pressure of work', etc. etc. It was dated four years back.

I sifted rapidly through the other envelopes to see if I could find one with a more recent postmark. In the middle of the bundle was a loose photograph paper-clipped to a newspaper cutting. The photograph was of Gaston and Chris. They were somewhere that looked very much like Trafalgar Square; there were a lot of people and pigeons in the background. On the back of the photo was written: '*Avec Oncle Gaston – le cirque touristique*, 1990'. I turned it over. I was distracted by how disturbingly like Xavier Gaston looked. But that wasn't the point. The point was Chris. Short, slim, small boned, she stared back at me, grinning her wide Masbou smile. You could easily have mistaken her for Celeste. Easily. She could have been Celeste's twin. There was no way that you could have mistaken her for me.

I saw that I had gravely deceived myself. *Tante* Mathilde had known from the beginning that I wasn't Marie-Christine. She had this photograph to prove it. It made her smooth assurances to the police all the more bewildering. I stared at the photo in bemused fascination. I disconnected it from the newspaper clipping to which it was attached. My old passport photo, smudged and poorly reproduced, stared back at me. Underneath were a few brief lines in French about Margaret Davison, *'une femme Anglaise qui est disparue'*, 'présumée morte', etc. Hurriedly, I clipped the cutting and the photograph back together, confined the letters to their rubber band and put them back in the drawer.

Back in my room, I sat at the dressing table combing my hair and looking at the pale reflection that was probably my face. I was waiting for *Tante* Mathilde to come and say something revelatory to me. I wanted to have an answer for her: a truthful answer.

Darkness fell. Water clanked along the pipes. I heard *Tante* Mathilde call *'Bonne nuit'* to someone, but she didn't come. No one came. I kept having to remind myself that there was no logical reason why she should come. She didn't know that I'd seen the photograph and the cutting, so whatever the status quo was, and it obviously wasn't remotely what I'd assumed it to be, my discovery hadn't in any way changed it.

I couldn't sleep. After several abortive attempts I got up and started to pack. I took nothing of Chris's except the stained dressing gown of which I'd grown fond, the jeans, a shirt, and (for sentimental reasons) the green silk dress, all of which I thought of as personal gifts from Chris. Apart from these, I took only the things I'd bought for myself. Whatever else I needed, I'd buy cheaply in Marseilles. I packed and repacked these few things. And then I packed them again. And then I unfolded them and shook them out, and refolded and rearranged them – anything to stop myself thinking, anything to numb the intolerable pain of finally and irrevocably moving on.

◆ THE BEGINNING ◆

There was no one in the kitchen when I went down for breakfast. I was making myself some coffee when Françoise appeared.

'Are you only just up?' she asked.

'I had a bad night,' I said, looking at my watch. It was after ten.

'I've just been to the bank.' She dumped her shopping on the table. 'Somebody's been asking questions about you.'

'About me?'

She nodded.

'At the bank? When?'

'Yesterday, this morning. I don't know.'

'The police?' I asked.

She looked at me in owlish bewilderment. 'Why would the police be asking about you at the bank?'

Well, it was either going to be the police or Mal.

'What did this person look like?'

She shrugged. 'The cashier just said a man was asking questions. A tall man.'

Probably Peyrol, then. Although it might be Mal: he was fairly tall.

'With glasses,' she added.

'With *glasses*?' Who did I know who was tall and wore glasses?

'What, sunglasses you mean?'

'He didn't say. Just glasses.'

'What did he want to know, this man?'

She shook her head. 'The cashier just said he was asking about you.'

This was odd. Very odd. I made a decision. 'Françoise, do you know where your mother is?'

'Isn't she in her room?'

'Probably,' I said, although I knew she wasn't because I'd already knocked. 'I need to talk to her,' I said.

In the event there was no time. Uncle Xavier had a meeting of the fête committee at eleven. If I didn't mind waiting round, he said, we could have lunch afterwards. I didn't mind at all. In the scale of things, lunch with Uncle Xavier was far more important than extraneous details like the police closing in, or *Tante* Mathilde's baffling complicity in my deception, or even some unidentified person asking questions about me in the bank. All that could wait. This was the priority, this last day. I wanted to make it good for him. I climbed into the car and settled my legs under the dashboard.

'You haven't changed your mind?' he asked, taking a fierce bend under the rock so fast I had to close my eyes. 'You're still determined to leave tomorrow?'

'I have to,' I said.

He shook his head. The road catapulted downwards. 'What did the police want?' he asked.

'Didn't Tante Mathilde tell you?' I asked curiously.

'She said they'd come to return your passport.'

'That's right.' I was interested to learn what version of events she'd given him. 'They did.'

He smiled at my absurd impracticality. 'And so tell me, how did you imagine you were going to get back to England without a passport?'

'Oh,' I said airily, 'I was going to pick it up on my way north. They saved me the trouble.'

'Well, I wish they hadn't bothered,' he grumbled. A tractor appeared on the bend ahead. He braked violently, and put his hand out to stop me shooting through the windscreen. For several reasons I wished he would keep both hands on the wheel. I stared out of the window at the solid rock that lined the road so that he couldn't see my face.

The village was hung with flags. Strings of them trailed across the streets from guttering to balcony. The trees were looped with fairy lights. While Uncle Xavier had his meeting, I watched workmen erect a wooden dance floor in the square. An electrician connected the band's amplifiers to the mains and tested the sound level. Cars with racing bikes strapped to the roof started to arrive, ready for the afternoon's events. When Uncle Xavier and the rest of the committee finally emerged from the gloom at the back of the café where their meeting had convivially and vinously been held, it was to deal with the question of where to keep the fireworks until the evening. Uncle Xavier took me by the elbow and steered me across the square.

'They can sort it out between them,' he said. 'I've had enough.'

We went to the Hôtel des Falaises again and sat at the same table. I didn't know whether this was sentiment on Uncle Xavier's part or whether this was the table where he always sat.

So what did we talk about at this last meal? I don't remember. All I could think of was that from tomorrow I'd never see him again. I remember he laughed a lot as if I'd said something particularly witty or clever, which I couldn't have done because I never did, although I loved the way he always made me feel as if I had. He pressed on me various desserts.

'Yes,' he insisted. 'You like sweet things. Choose one. What will you have?' In the end I gave in and chose a *mousse aux prunes* because I didn't want this meal ever to end. I ate it very slowly. Licking the tiny portion I balanced on the tip of the spoon and watching the last moments of being Uncle Xavier's spoiled and adored Marie-Christine tick away. Tomorrow he'd despise me. Tomorrow he'd know how little I deserved his affection. Tomorrow I'd have to start again like a blank sheet of paper waiting for a story to form on it.

He ordered coffee. By mutual understanding we sat until it grew cold, then sipped it slowly as if it were still too hot to drink. 'Shall we have another one?' I asked, a little desperately, but we never got the chance to order it. A member of the committee came hurrying into the dining room carrying a megaphone. Uncle Xavier was needed at once. The cycle race was about to start.

The square was full of people now. Children perched round the central fountain and clung to the railings. Cyclists in brilliant red and green sweatshirts swooped round the square like flocking birds. The man with the megaphone handed me a starting pistol.

'Me?' I said in amazement.

'Yes, of course you,' said Uncle Xavier. 'Who else should start the race?' He grabbed the megaphone from the hand of his fellow committee member and announced to the whole village, 'My niece, Marie-Christine.' There was a lot of friendly applause. I waved and smiled as if I were used to being the sort of person who started events. I pointed the gun up into the air and fired. The cyclists shot away like a roost of frightened starlings.

Some time late in the afternoon, long after I'd awarded the trophies for the cycle race, when the *boules* contest was reaching its climax and the village was so full it was difficult to move, Françoise touched my arm.

'We're going home for an hour. To get changed,' she said.

I hadn't even realised she was there. I hadn't seen her all afternoon.

'Changed into what?' I said.

'Something for the dance.'

'Won't jeans do?'

'You can't wear jeans to a dance.'

I didn't want to leave Xavier, but I wanted to do one last generous thing for Françoise.

Xavier was standing on the edge of the dustbowl where the *boules* final was being played out, offering fiercely partisan encouragement and advice. It made my mouth dry up with pain to look at him.

'I'm going back with the others,' I said, 'to get changed.'

'What do you want to get changed for?'

'I'm going to make myself beautiful.'

He snorted with laughter.

' Be quick,' he said.

I sat in the back of the Citroën behind Celeste, who was driving. *Tante* Mathilde was in the front passenger seat. I thought once we got back to the house I might find the chance to talk to her alone, but Celeste, who'd obviously been bored by the afternoon's bucolic entertainments, was in an irritable mood.

'I don't see why we can't sell the place,' she complained, 'not that anyone would want it, and buy a little villa with a swimming pool near Paris.'

'If you want to move to Paris, Celeste,' said *Tante* Mathilde, 'you're at perfect liberty to do so whenever you wish.'

'And live on what?' Celeste snapped. 'What kind of job could I get with three young children to look after.'

I bit my tongue.

'I'm sick of it,' she whined. 'None of you appreciates how difficult it is for me. Marie-Christine's the only one who's got the slightest idea what it's like to be buried in a one-horse dump like this when you're used to cities and a cosmopolitan lifestyle.'

I wasn't sure whether Birchwood Road, Hanley, could strictly be described as cosmopolitan so I kept my counsel.

'I thought Marie-Christine was quite enjoying herself this afternoon,' *Tante* Mathilde observed.

'I was,' I said.

'Yes, but that's because she was the star,' Celeste muttered as if I wasn't there. 'She always is. Uncle Xavier's always showing her off. She can't do anything wrong, can she?' She raised her voice. 'I'm sorry, Marie-Christine, but it's the truth.'

'No, no,' I muttered apologetically, surprised by the strength of her resentment. 'If that's how you feel. It's just – well, I suppose I just like village fêtes.'

She snorted. 'Sheep shit and pig farmers,' she said bitterly. 'You must be joking. Well, I'm sick to death of it. Stuck here with nothing to do, no one interesting to talk to, no life worth talking about. It's like being buried alive.'

She kept up her complaints all the way home and then followed *Tante* Mathilde into her room to continue them. The gist of it was that her life was slipping away and why was nobody doing anything about it? Why had no one come to rescue her? Françoise and I disappeared silently into my room where, over-come by a sudden excess of generosity, I offered her Chris's clothes, the ones that I was leaving. 'You may as well have them,' I said, as if I were used to abandoning clothes and buying myself whole new wardrobes on a whim. 'And what about these?' I said, emptying all Chris's shoes out of the drawer. They fitted Françoise perfectly. She traipsed up and down, burbling with pleasure, holding shirts up against her, kicking off one shoe and trying on another.

I put on the green dress with the splits up the sides. I no longer had anything else. Celeste was waiting for us sulkily in the hall. *Tante* Mathilde, she said, had a slight headache and had decided not to come to the dance. She was going to stay with the children. I assumed Celeste's remorseless complaints had worn her out.

'I'm surprised *you*'re going,' I said.

'Well, it'll certainly be more entertaining than a cycle race and a *boules* contest,' she snapped. 'And a lot more interesting than staying here.'

When we got back to the village, the sun was beginning to cool slightly. The band had started to play. A few small girls were jigging about on the dance floor. People were sitting in the café, or round the fountain or along the wall up to the church, as if waiting for a sign before they could begin. Some bikers roared into the square and parked their black, wasp-shaped machines under the trees. Their arrival caused a flutter of alarm. I went to look for Uncle Xavier. He was drinking on the pavement outside the hotel. He caught my hand.

'You're going to dance with me?' he said.

'Of course. When it starts.'

He poured me a glass of wine and we sat together lost in our own thoughts.

As the light faded and the sun sank, I thought of winter sunsets in England, of bare black trees silhouetted against orange skies.

'What are you thinking about?' Uncle Xavier asked.

But at that moment the fairy lights came on, and the world shrank to the area they illuminated. Beyond the jewelled trees, beyond the soft glow from upstairs windows round the square, there was an impenetrable wall of darkness.

The switching on of the lights was apparently the sign everybody had been waiting for. Couples drifted on to the floor. The lead singer, an accordion across his chest, spoke a few words of welcome with the microphone virtually in his mouth. Nobody had the faintest idea what he'd said. His distorted voice crackled from speakers hung high on buildings all round the square. The bikers and the local farm-boys stood at the edges as if round the dodgems at a fair.

'Come,' said Uncle Xavier. 'We shall show them what to do.'

He took me by the elbow and led me on to the dance floor.

'I think I ought to tell you,' I warned him. 'I don't actually know how to dance.'

'I shall teach you,' he said, but the floor was suddenly so crowded, it was impossible to move. Uncle Xavier held me very firmly as if he were afraid that otherwise I might shatter. I was half a head taller than he was, but his solidity and the way he held me made me feel infinitely safe.

'I wish this could go on for always,' I whispered childishly into his ear. I could smell his skin and the sharp animal scent of his hair.

'What?' he said. But the noise from the speakers drowned our attempts to talk. Over Uncle Xavier's grizzled head I watched the other dancers. Françoise was on the floor with one of the sheep farmers from Mas Picot. Beyond her, my eye was caught by another familiar figure standing among the bikers and the spectators round the edge. Uncle Xavier had spotted him too. His hand in the small of my back tightened.

'This man of yours, he's still here. What does he want?'

'I don't know,' I lied.

Uncle Xavier started hissing in my ear. 'Is it true that you have to go back to England, or are you still running away from him?'

'He's not important.'

'Then why does he watch you all the time?'

The music stopped. Uncle Xavier took my arm and tried to push a way through the crowded dancers to the other side of the floor. The lead singer picked up his accordion and began to play something achingly and sentimentally French. I refused to let it touch me. I couldn't cope.

A voice said triumphantly in my right ear, 'Look who I've found.' It was Celeste miraculously restored to good humour.

Both her arms rested languorously on Mal's shoulders. Uncle Xavier's grip tightened.

'You look very nice, Chris,' Mal said.

Celeste was trying her narrow-eyed trick on him as they danced. 'Mal's been telling me all sorts of fascinating things about you, Marie-Christine,' she said

Uncle Xavier pulled me away sharply. He pushed me ahead of him so that it was I who bumped into the startled couples we barged through on our way to the edge of the dance floor. 'I'll get you a drink,' he said crossly. 'How did you get mixed up with a man like that?' he complained. 'Have you no taste?'

'He's nothing,' I said. 'Don't let him worry you. He doesn't worry me.'

'Then why do you run away from him, if he doesn't worry you?'

'He did worry me,' I said, 'but he doesn't now. Not any more.'

He snorted. 'You like pretty men? You like weak, pretty men with greedy eyes? Look at Celeste.' He was outraged. He couldn't leave the subject alone. We watched Celeste practising a subtle seduction technique. 'Look at her,' he said in disgust. 'What does she think she's doing?'

'She thinks he might turn out to be a prince,' I explained.

'A prince!' He choked on his beer. 'Is she blind? He's a poisonous little worm.'

After a while Uncle Xavier felt obliged to go and do his duty both as committee member and as *propriétaire* of Rougearc by dancing with the more eminent ladies of the village. I was standing at the edge of the dance floor while I finished my beer, when a hand suddenly slipped intimately across my buttocks and round to the top of my thigh. I leapt away, catapulting into a leather-jacketed biker.

'What the hell – ?' I said.

'Oh, come on, Chris,' Mal protested. 'Don't start playing silly games again. We've been lovers for years.' He laughed at my uncensored expression. 'I've just been explaining our relationship to your desperate cousin.' His hand moved familiarly across my buttocks again. 'May as well make it look authentic.'

I tried to push him off but he meant business. His hand moved round my waist. 'Shall we dance?'

'No thanks.'

He tightened his hold. 'One dance,' he said. 'Go on. For old times' sake. Or I might have to tell that besotted goat farmer who thinks he's your uncle a few truths.'

I allowed myself to be led stiffly on to the floor.

'Leave me alone, Mal,' I said. 'I've got nothing to do with you.'

'Well, that depends on who you are, doesn't it? If you want to be Chris you can't just walk out on me after eight years and not expect me to put up some kind of a fight. On the other hand if you want to be a little housewife from somewhere up north, then fine. Only in that case, you're playing a very clever game and I want a part of it.'

I could feel Uncle Xavier glaring at my back.

'So for a start,' Mal was saying, 'you can tell me what the police were doing up at your place last night?'

I was shocked. 'How do you know about that?'

'I'm watching you very carefully, Chris. I know about everything.'

'Well, in that case you'll know *why* they came, won't you?' I said, coldly. The music stopped. It was a chance to get away. 'Excuse me.'

He caught my wrist and twisted it so that a tearing pain shot through the bone. I was instantly immobilised. 'Don't play games with me,' he said.

'All right, they came to return my passport,' I said. 'Chris's passport. That's all. And if you're interested, they asked about you as well.'

He tensed. 'What did they say?'

'They asked me if I knew you. I said yes.'

He muttered something but the band started a loud, stomping

rock number and it was impossible to hear him. He still had hold of my wrist. 'Come on,' he shouted over the noise. 'We'll go somewhere quieter.'

I tried to free myself. 'I don't want to go anywhere quieter,' I protested, 'I've got nothing to say to you.'

He ignored me and pulled me away from the dance floor.

Under the tree beside the fountain, standing behind a group of noisy teenagers, I caught a sudden and confusing glimpse of a man, a tall man with glasses, whose unexpected familiarity was so totally disorientating I couldn't make any sense of it. It was a mistake. It was someone else. It was the light, a trick of the light. My stomach heaved. He was staring at the dance floor, this man. He hadn't seen me. 'Come on,' I said to Mal. 'Quick. Where's your car?'

The positions rapidly changed. He was still gripping my wrist, but I was pulling him now.

'What are you doing?' he bleated, as we crashed through the crowds.

'Where's your car?'

'Over there.' He pointed to the hotel.

I started running with him in tow. I was sure Uncle Xavier was still watching me. Celeste definitely saw us. We passed her; her mouth was tight with annoyance.

'Come on!' I snapped. 'Run.'

He unlocked the doors of his car with an alarm bleeper. I fell into the front passenger seat.

'Drive,' I said.

'Where?'

'Anywhere.'

The crowds made it hard to manoeuvre the car out of the village. I crouched down below the dashboard.

'What the hell are you playing at?' he said.

'Someone I don't want to see. Hurry up.'

He laughed. 'What a cracker-load of surprises you are,' he said. 'What kind of a someone?'

I started to shake. 'Mind your own business,' I said.

I told myself to calm down. Be calm, I said. I reminded myself that I was not instantly recognisable, not in crowded surroundings, not with fairy lights and in deep shadow. I am thin now, I said, thin and scarred and very brown, and my hair is long and sun bleached and quite different, and I am wearing a dress with a tight belt and slits. If I keep away from the square, I told myself, until it's time to go home then it'll be all right. I'll be gone tomorrow. From tomorrow I'll be untraceable.

I breathed out heavily, then took a long deep breath in. The shaking was almost under control. I sat up properly in the passenger seat. Darkness hit us as we drove out of the village. Poor old Tony, I thought, busy chasing someone who doesn't exist any more. I couldn't imagine how he'd tracked me down. Or indeed – even more unimaginable – why he'd bothered. I couldn't control an ironic snort of laughter. The net was really closing in now. Mal was chasing Chris, Tony was chasing Margaret, and the police didn't know who they were chasing but it wasn't going to take them much longer to find out.

'What's funny?' Mal asked.

Nothing. Nothing was funny. Because of a tall man in the shadows who looked a little like Tony, because of Mal, I'd lost my last evening with Uncle Xavier.

We drove in silence for about twenty minutes until we were high up on the Causse. Mal turned off down a forest track. The tree trunks crowded in towards us, thin and amber in the beam of the headlights.

'Right,' he said, stopping the car. 'So let's talk about the police. What did they want?'

'I told you.'

'Yeah, you did, didn't you, and I still don't believe you. I don't think it was just the passport they gave back, was it?'

I tensed my mouth and said nothing.

'So if you've got any plans,' he said, 'for running away again in the near future, forget them because I'll be right behind you, lady. You'll never get shot of me.'

He had switched the lights off. There was still an odd amber glow in the sky ahead. I thought it must be the lights of the village, except that I'd assumed the village was behind us. Still, what did I know? I had a very poorly developed sense of direction.

'I really don't understand what Chris saw in you,' I said. It was sad to think how badly wrong I'd got her. I wondered if she'd been frightened of him: it seemed likely. 'Well,' I said, 'I hope wherever she is, she doesn't know how little you cared about her death,' and hit a very raw nerve. He was suddenly explosively angry.

'How do you know what I care about? You know nothing about Chris and me.'

I was slightly shocked. I thought I had him pinned down. I saw a tear glitter at the corner of his eye, or perhaps it was just the odd light catching some natural moisture. 'I'm sorry,' I mumbled.

There was a long pause. 'Look,' I said eventually, 'I'm telling you the truth. I've got enough problems of my own without any of yours to worry about. So I *am* leaving. Tomorrow. But without any money. I swear it.'

He thought about this for a bit. Possibly he decided it was time to try a new approach. He offered me a cigarette.

'No, thanks.'

'You don't mind if I do?' He lit up before I'd had a chance to answer. 'So you're a secretary, right?'

I nodded.

'Yeah. It was in all the papers. Housewife and secretary from Stoke-on-Trent. They never found the body. That's you, isn't it?'

'Yes,' I said.

He exhaled. 'Funny that,' he said. 'Chris was a secretary.'

'I know.'

'Of course you do, yeah. We had a very nice little thing going, Chris and me. We supplied information. There's a very hungry market for information.'

'What kind of information?'

He shrugged. 'Anything. Whatever.'

'Industrial espionage?'

'Sometimes, yeah. That was the bulk of it. We did a lot of work for foreign companies. But we weren't fussy. It might just be the number of a safe. Or the security arrangements. Or some insider information about the market. Or they might just want a copy of a disk. That's a very common request. You can store a lot of info on a disk. Information is money and we made a lot of it when business was good. It was fun. I'm sorry it's over.'

'How did it work?' I asked.

'Depends. I found the clients and dealt with the business side. Chris did the insider job. Sometimes we had particular commissions from clients. But mostly we did it the other way round: Chris got a job, spent a few months researching the company, and then I went out and found clients who might be interested in buying what she had to sell. And then after another couple of months she'd leave the firm supposedly to get married or have a baby, or whatever. It depended what name she was working under. Sometimes it was Christine Masbou. Sometimes it was Marie Hayward. She had four or five names.'

'And she never got caught?'

'Not as such, no. We had to cool things off a couple of times. About a year ago there was a huge wages snatch at this place she was working. It was obvious they'd had inside information, and some bright spark on the force with a computer isolated Marie Hayward as the one common factor with a similar episode in Harrow five years back. So we got out of London for a bit. She took a temping job in Peterborough. Legitimately. In her own name. We got a couple of very lucrative deals out of her time in Peterborough.'

'So you sold this information to criminals?' I said.

He smiled. 'Depends what you mean by criminals. Very rarely, in fact. Mainly to businessmen. But we didn't examine our clients' motives too closely. We sold to anybody who'd pay the market price.'

There was a strong smell of cigarette smoke in the car. I wound down the window to let it out, but the smell outside was even stronger: a bitter, acrid smell. 'You said it was fun,' I said curiously. 'Did Chris find it fun?'

'Well, obviously the fun side of it was wearing a bit thin for her.' He wrinkled his nose. 'Funny smell,' he said. He lit another cigarette. 'Tell you what,' he went on. 'What about this for a deal? You could take over.'

'Take over what?' I asked stupidly.

'Take over from Chris. You're a secretary. You're bright. You've got all the skills. You're the best liar I've ever met.' His right arm slid along the top of my seat. 'You could take over her life for real if you want. I wouldn't mind.' He looked at me through a haze of exhaled smoke. 'I wouldn't mind at all.' His left hand moved to my knee. 'You've got a very nice arse,' he said. 'Nice legs. We could go into partnership, you and me.'

I pushed his hand off my knee. 'Stop it,' I said.

'Be honest, though, you don't have that many options, do you?' he said. I could smell his ashy breath. 'And you've got a real talent for the work. We'd make a good team. Think about it.'

The sky above the trees was a heavy, lurid orange. 'What is that over there?' I said, distracted by the strangeness of it. 'Is it a fire?'

He got out of the car to look. 'Christ,' he said. 'Hang on a minute.'

He walked to a bend in the track about a hundred yards ahead, then came running back, jumped into the driving seat, slammed the door shut and started up the engine. He did a rapid, screeching five-point turn and drove bumpily along the forest path and back to the road. The further we went, the worse it got. We could hear the crackle of burning wood. The air was as thick and as red as blood. Smoke caught the back of the throat.

It stung the eyes. It choked the lungs. I started coughing. 'For God's sake, we're driving straight into it,' I said. 'Turn back.'

A police car skidded round the corner, overtook us and slewed to a stop across the road in front of us. Mal braked hard. His eyes flickered with fear. Briefly – a reflex response – he'd thought the police car was after him.

'It's all right,' I said. 'They're probably just going to block the road off.'

They were. A single uniformed policeman climbed out of the car and came over to us.

'You'll have to turn back,' he said. 'I'm just going to close this road.'

Fragments of white-hot ash tipped with flame floated past us. Distantly I could hear the wailing sirens of fire engines.

'It's spreading over the hill from Breslou.' The policeman tried vainly to control his excitement. 'They're calling the helicopters out. Three farms are in danger.'

'How far's it gone?' I asked, afraid for Rougearc.

He wasn't sure. The situation changed from moment to moment, but the last he'd heard the fire had cut off the village completely on the north side of the river. Some kids on bikes, he said, probably tourists – local kids would know better – had stolen a box of the official fireworks and taken them up into the hills to let them off. It was a daft thing to do. It was spreading so fast, he said, they were going to have bring fire fighters out from Figeac.

'How do we get back into the village?' Mal asked.

We had to drive miles across the Causse and then drop down to the river about nine miles below St Julien. By the time we got back it was nearly midnight. The fête had fizzled out. A shocked silence hung in the air. Pieces of white ash floated down like fragments of tissue paper and settled on people's shoulders, in their hair, on their eyebrows. The strings of light drooped between the trees. The band was packing up. The accordionist sat alone on the edge of the dance floor, playing quietly to himself. A few people still hung around in the square, whispering together as if scared of offending the silence.

Mal parked as close to the hotel as he could.

'What do we do now?' he said.

'I go home and you go to bed.'

'And after that?'

'You go back to England and I disappear.'

Mal smiled regretfully at me. 'The trouble is, though,' he said, 'I know too much about you now. It's my business, information. And the bit I'm really good at, my area of specialisation as you might say, is knowing who might be interested and at what price. Your husband, for example. Your so-called uncle. What price would you be prepared to pay to keep me quiet?'

'Don't try threatening me,' I said bravely. 'I'm not Chris.'

I climbed out of the passenger seat and slammed the car door as viciously as I could. It was the best I could come up with. I'd have preferred some devastating comeback, some clever counter-threat that would finally get him off my back, but I couldn't think of anything he wouldn't easily twist or turn to his advantage. Slamming doors was about my limit.

I skirted the edge of the square, keeping to the shadows, my head down, in case the man who looked like Tony was still around. I was sliding as inconspicuously as possible between parked cars when Celeste pounced on me. 'Where the hell have you been?' she hissed. 'We've been looking for you for hours.'

She took me firmly by the arm and dragged me out into the light.

'Where are we going?' I asked feebly, turning my head in to her shoulder.

'Home,' she snapped.

'You go,' I said. 'I'll wait for Uncle Xavier.'

'Don't be stupid. He's out with the firemen.'

She dragged me across to the Citroën where Françoise was already waiting. I climbed into the front seat.

'You'll have to take the river road as far as Montrouge and then double back along the D311,' I said to Celeste, who was driving. 'The other roads are all closed.'

She gave me a furious look. She drove in silence, her mouth tightly drawn.

After a while Françoise managed a tentative question. She asked me if I'd enjoyed myself.

'Mixed,' I said.

Celeste let out a viperish little hiss of breath.

'What does that mean?' I asked her.

Her lips tightened. 'I don't see why you always have to monopolise everybody,' she muttered.

'Who? You're not talking about Mal, are you?' I asked. 'Because, believe me, he's not a nice man. You wouldn't like him.'

'Then why spend the whole evening with him?' she said, logically. Her voice rose to an exasperated sort of shriek. Controlling it, she muttered, 'I wouldn't actually have minded the chance to find out for myself what kind of man he is.' Bitterly, she added, 'It's so unfair. You've got everything. Everything just falls into your lap. You can do whatever you want. You could at least afford to let the rest of us have your left-overs.'

The woods round Rougearc were dark and silent. There was no sense – except for a faint, bitter, wood-ash smell – that less than five kilometres away acres of forest were blazing out of control. It was nearly one o'clock when we drove through the gatehouse.

'What a hideous evening,' Celeste said, slamming into the house. I wasn't sure whether she meant it had been a social disaster or whether she was referring to the fire. 'I'm going up to see Maman,' she said.

Françoise said quietly, 'Don't let Celeste upset you.'

'I don't,' I said. It was true. I didn't.

Françoise pushed up her glasses and rubbed her eyes. 'I wish I didn't,' she said. 'But she always manages to find the raw spot.'

Ten minutes later, when Françoise had said good night and gone up to bed, Celeste appeared and informed me with icy sulkiness that her mother wanted to see me in her room.

I climbed the stairs slowly as if my legs were still in pain. They weren't. It was just that I needed time to prepare myself. My plan was to take the initiative: I decided to surprise her with my knowledge of what she knew.

I knocked at her door.

'Come in,' she called. She was fully dressed and sitting at her desk.

'Celeste has been telling me about the fire,' she said.

'Apparently it was some kids,' I replied, standing in front of her like a recidivist schoolgirl in the headmistress's study.

She tutted. 'It seems to happen every year we have a drought. People are so careless.' She gestured to me to sit down. I sat. She folded her hands on the desk. 'And Xavier has gone off with fire-fighters, of course?' Her lips were tight with anxious exasperation. 'You should never have let him go,' she said. 'Why didn't you stop him?'

'I didn't know he'd gone,' I said.

'He'll exhaust himself.' Her clasped hands twisted anxiously on the desk. 'You should have stopped him.'

'I don't think anyone could stop him doing what he wants to do,' I said.

'Well, certainly if you can't no one else can,' she said irritably. She was pulling the second drawer open. I guessed she was about to face me with the photo and the cutting. Because I was scared she was going to take the iniative away from me, I blurted hurriedly: 'I know what that is. I know what you're going to say.'

'Really?' She looked surprised. 'I can't imagine how.' In her hand was a small box. She passed it across to me. 'I just wanted to give you this before you left. I intended to do it yesterday but we were interrupted.'

It was an old box, blue, faded, and with the name of a Parisian jeweller imprinted on it.

'Open it,' she said.

I assumed she was playing some kind of trick on me. The cutting would be folded up inside the box.

'Open it,' she said again.

I was so certain I knew what was in this box; I was so prepared for it, that what I found shocked me into silence. Resting on the rusty blue velvet was a ring, a gold ring with an old fashioned setting of four diamonds and a single garnet.

I was stunned. What was all this about?

'Try it on,' she said. 'I want you to have it.'

I looked her straight in the face. 'You know I can't accept it,' I said.

'It's a small thank-you,' she said, picking up her embroidery frame. 'For your kindness to Françoise. And for being so good to Xavier.'

'I haven't been good to Xavier,' I protested, offended by the idea. 'He doesn't need me to be good to him.' I put the ring back into the box. 'I'm sorry. I can't take it,' I said. 'You know I can't.'

'Then you'll offend me deeply. My mother gave it to me on my marriage. It's been in the family since before the Revolution. I should very much like it to stay in the family.'

She had an amazing ability, this woman, to wrong-foot me. What was she talking about? She knew perfectly well I wasn't family.

'Then you should give it to Françoise,' I said. 'Or to Celeste. Not to me.'

Gravely she pushed the box back across the desk. 'No,' she

said, staring straight into my eyes as if this were some coded message and she was willing me to break the code. 'No, I am giving it to you, Marie-Christine.'

So I took it.

'Thank you,' I muttered.

'And now,' she said briskly, 'unless you're too tired, perhaps you'd be kind enough to make me a tisane. There are some sage leaves on the windowsill in the kitchen. And then you must go to bed.'

'No,' I said. 'I'll wait up for Xavier.' After which I stammered something stupid about the ring, something like, 'I don't know what to say.'

She looked up at me and smiled. 'Then let us agree to say nothing, shall we?'

In the kitchen I filled a pan of water and waited for it to boil. I took the ring out of its box and looked at it again. I held it in my hand. I tried it on. It was a very beautiful, very subtle piece of jewellery. As I was ripping up the sage leaves and considering the extraordinarily inappropriate phrase 'keep it in the family', I realised what the coded message meant: that although she knew I was not Marie-Christine, she didn't want to be put in the position where she would have to acknowledge that she knew. More than that, she didn't want Xavier to know. She wanted me to leave quietly without ever telling him. She was protecting him from disillusionment. This ring, in fact, was payment. She was paying me off for services rendered: my kindness to Françoise, my 'goodness' to Xavier, and finally she was paying me for my silence. I pulled the ring off my finger and put it back in the box.

The Sunday-dinner smell of infusing sage leaves filled the kitchen. I was burning with humiliation. I smashed the leaves against the side of the bowl. Shut up and get out was the basic message. For which I had been handsomely paid. In advance.

It was after four when he arrived. I heard the car rolling over the gravel. *Tante* Mathilde came downstairs to greet him. His face was grey with exhaustion. He was surprised to find us both waiting for him, he kept saying, 'What are you doing? Why aren't you asleep?' His cheeks were smudged with dirt and smoke. He rubbed the tiredness from his face with his hands, pushing the skin up over his eyes. *Tante* Mathilde offered to make him a tisane, but he wanted something stronger. He seemed unable to stop talking. He sat, slumped at the kitchen table, sipping cognac and telling the story of the fire over and over again, rambling in circles, confusing himself and us. The tragedy of so much woodland destroyed seemed to have wounded him mortally. He kept repeating the estimated number of hectares of destruction. 'A wasteland,' he kept saying. 'Dust and ashes.' There had never, he said, never in his lifetime nor in his parents', been such total devastation.

I wanted to put my arms around him. I couldn't bear his pain. I needed him to comfort me. Instead I sat with my hands clasped in my lap and listened. The skin across my cheeks ached with tiredness. He rambled on and on, the same words and phrases recurring until he was stringing them together without their making any real sense any more. He was obsessed with the loss of so much life. The more distressed he grew the more his words lost coherence.

Tante Mathilde shot me a look. I knew she wanted me to help her get him up to bed. She murmured sensible things to comfort him. Fire, she said, is nature's way of clearing away the old and giving the new freedom to grow. It's all part of a natural sequence of death and rebirth, destruction and re-creation. You know this, she told him. He nodded, but he wasn't listening to her. 'All those mice,' he mumbled, holding his hands to his face. 'All those birds. You could smell it. The waste.' Tears dribbled down the folds of his cheeks.

Tante Mathilde was still trying to signal something to me, but I couldn't move. I was appalled by Uncle Xavier's grey face and the tears. He sighed heavily and got up to pour himself another cognac.

'Let me do that,' said *Tante* Mathilde, but he shook his head. I couldn't bear it: I couldn't bear to see him look so defeated.

He turned and looked straight at me. He had the bottle in one hand and the glass in the other.

'Where did you disappear to,' he said, 'with that weak-faced man of yours? I didn't see you all evening. He's still pestering you?'

I nodded.

He smiled at me, a tired, defeated smile but all the same a smile. He opened his mouth to speak, and then shut it. An expression of total astonishment slid over his face. His mouth opened again. Then, oddly, his arms lifted from his sides as though he was about to fly away. He made a strange hooting noise. The bottle he was holding crashed to the floor. He stared down at it in bewilderment, twisting his face, screwing it up tight in concentration as if the floor was so far away he couldn't see it any more. Then there was a strange and terrible whistling noise, a wet, high-pitched whistling.

I heard *Tante* Mathilde shout, 'For God's sake!' and Uncle Xavier twisted and juddered as if somebody had shot an electrical current through him.

The whistling noise stopped as suddenly and as terribly as it had started.

'For Christ's sake, Marie-Christine,' *Tante* Mathilde shouted. 'Phone for the doctor. Quick!'

Uncle Xavier was lying on the floor with the same wide-eyed expression of total astonishment. The muscles of his face twitched in spasms. I couldn't move. I had no grasp at all of what was happening. I remember him lying in a pool of moonlight, but that's a false memory because the overhead light was on. I remember feeling the uneven stone floor digging into my knees, so I must have knelt beside him, though I've no memory of getting up from the chair. I thought I was trapped there, like a stone frozen into the surface of a lake. I remember saying, 'It's all right. He's still alive.' I think it was me who said that. Somebody did, and there was no one else in the room, so I suppose it must have been me.

They took him away in an ambulance. *Tante* Mathilde went with him. I was supposed to follow later when I'd packed a case for him: washing things, a towel, anything he might need, but I was so scattered I couldn't think straight. I didn't know where anything was. I ran up and down stairs muttering to myself. I pulled five towels out of a cupboard before I realised what they were. I kept dropping things as if I couldn't remember how to use my hands any more. I couldn't find the car keys. I started sobbing in frustration at my total uselessness. I drove out of the gatehouse and was almost at the road before it occurred to me to switch on the lights. And all the time I was praying, a furious prayer, a whimpering, frantic prayer to a God who existed only because I needed one, who only ever existed out of some poor fool's need, who was always the final invention of desperation, because if you live in a world where the endless and beautiful cycle of destruction and creation takes no account whatever of the individual, even an individual as powerfully himself as Uncle Xavier, then a time will come when you need a personal God so badly you have to invent one at once. You have to find something to blame. You have to hold something to account.

They put him into a side room with pale-blue blinds and a Degas circus print on the wall.

I ran along the corridor with his suitcase banging against my leg. A nurse came and held her finger to her lips to shut me up, but I couldn't care less who I disturbed. I went on running. Against the starched whiteness of the bolster, his face was grey. *Tante* Mathilde sat in a chair beside the bed. Her hair was escaping from its pins; I'd never seen her with even one hair out of place before. A nurse fetched another chair so that we sat one on either side of him. They said he was unconscious, but he sounded to me as if he was simply asleep and snoring. We sat with him until the doctors came and made us go to another room where the seats were beige plastic. Outside the sky began to lighten. The electric strip light was very cruel. It made everything look plastic, even our skin. I turned it off.

Tante Mathilde sat bolt upright, a strand of hair snaking down her neck. 'I'd rather he died. I don't want him to go on living if he's lost his faculties,' she announced suddenly in a high, fierce voice as if someone had just put the counter-argument to her.

A doctor came and took her away for a private discussion. I stood staring out over the roofs of the town and watched the sun come up. It was going to be another beautiful day. The irony of this was like a kick in the gut. The sky should be weeping. It should be pouring rain. Instead the roofs turned gold. The smell of morning heat rose from the streets. Church bells rang. A car backed out of a garage and hit a dustbin.

Later, a nurse came to tell me I could go back into Uncle Xavier's room for a while. 'It's going to be another scorcher,' she said cheerfully. I could smell her perfume. I could smell the fresh cleanness of her skin.

Hours passed. We sat waiting for something to happen. Sometimes we sat in the room with the plastic chairs, sometimes we sat with Uncle Xavier. At some point, Françoise and Celeste arrived. They took *Tante* Mathilde away for a cup of coffee. I insisted on it. I wanted to be alone with Uncle Xavier for a while. I knew he was still unconscious because they'd told me so, but I wasn't sure what that meant. I took his hand: it was square and rough and covered with scratches. I kissed it. I couldn't stop. I kissed each of the fingers one by one, the nails, the knuckles, the gaps between the fingers. Somehow my hair, my tears, my mouth became so entangled with each other and

◆ 225 ◆

with his hands that I gave up trying to separate them. I leant so far forward that my head was resting beside his on the bolster, and my damp hair was spread over his face. His palm was pressed against the mask of my face. I had no way to tell him how much I loved him. Even if he could hear me, even if he were conscious, what could I do? Nothing was big enough. Nothing came anywhere near expressing it. There was nothing loud enough or powerful enough or enduring enough to express a half of what I felt for him. I wanted to climb inside him. I wanted him to hold me so close I was absorbed into him or he was absorbed into me, so that he'd *know*, so that there wouldn't be any need to tell him.

Perched somewhere at the back of my head, the minute, shrivelled, infinitely cold and frightened person who still lived there – and who always would live there because people don't change that much – observed with some surprise that perhaps after all I knew more about love than I'd thought. I touched his cheek. His grizzled beard was growing: he needed a shave. I kissed the roughness of it. I wanted to climb into the bed beside him and hold him: I wanted to make him warm. I wanted to give him back his energy. But I was too shy: I was afraid of a nurse or *Tante* Mathilde coming in and finding me there. So I half sat, half lay, with my cheek against his, willing him not to go away. I listened to him breathe and thought that he was the only man I had ever truly loved. He had required nothing of me, nor imposed anything on me. Whatever I was delighted him. I loved him for unconditionally allowing me to be. I thought of all the others: my real father who'd lived just long enough to leave me with an uncomfortable sense of his natural authority; my stepfather who was a good man and who'd done far more than his duty, but who, through no fault of his own, was always a father and so (not unreasonably) assumed that I should respond by being a daughter; Tony, who had no idea at all what it was he'd married, largely, I suppose, because I wouldn't let him know. How could I? Even Gaston, whom I had used shamelessly for my own purposes, had seen me as the invention of his own private fantasies, just as he was the invention of mine. But Xavier had loved me from the first moment he saw me, even with my scabby face and my newly acquired sharp tongue, and he went on loving me without strings, resentments or hidden agendas, and there was nothing I could ever do about it.

'If you get better … ' I whispered in his ear. I wanted to make a bargain with him. I wanted to offer him some huge gift, a bribe not to die. But there was nothing I could give him. Even if he recovered, nothing was changed. On every level we had missed each other, he and I. 'Oh, Uncle Xavier,' I whispered, my mouth on his lips.

Footsteps shuffled in the corridor. I sat up hurriedly. If they were surprised to find his cheeks damp with tears and his grubby, soot-ingrained fingers washed clean, if they noticed the tangles in my hair and how red and creased my cheek was, they said nothing.

Later Françoise and Celeste went home because of the children. I refused to go. The day wore on.

'You must eat something,' *Tante* Mathilde said.

I'd forgotten about food. My mouth tasted bad and I had a sharp, bitter ache in my gut, but I assumed these were symptoms of grief, not hunger. I went out and bought a sandwich and then crumbled it into the gutter for the birds. I couldn't swallow.

When I got back to the room with the Degas circus print, it was full of people. They were blocking the bed. I was so frightened I thought my chest would crack open. Nobody took any notice of me. A nurse touched *Tante* Mathilde on the shoulder. They wanted us to leave for a minute. They wanted tactfully to disconnect him from the machines and the drips.

I could see from *Tante* Mathilde's closed desperate face that it was finished: he was dead. I thought: Don't cry, don't cry. If you start, you'll never stop. But I couldn't even see far enough through the tears to find my way out of the door, and walked slap into the wall.

'Look at this absurd creature.' I could hear his voice. I could hear him chuckling with pride at yet another manifestation of my extraordinary originality (which everybody else called clumsiness). 'This one, she thinks she can walk through walls now.'

Oh, Uncle Xavier, where are you?

In the late afternoon we drove back to Rougearc in silence, *Tante* Mathilde and I. She sat staring ahead, her face completely closed. I was driving.

I was afraid of going back. I didn't know how to face the emptiness of Rougearc without Uncle Xavier there, but the moment we got through the gate we were so inundated with things to do there was no time to start testing the limits of pain. The goats needed milking. Ordinary day-to-day decisions had to be made about farm matters. *Tante* Mathilde was constantly on the phone. She held on to it as if it were a lifebelt and spoke in a sharp, clipped way about matters of business. There were official matters to deal with, people to be notified, arrangements to make. She consulted me about everything. I was embarrassed.

'You should ask Françoise. Or Celeste,' I said.

She looked at me in a distracted way and ran a pencil through her hair. 'Yes, of course,' she said. 'Yes, I will.'

I needed urgently to talk to her, to establish where I stood, but I couldn't find the right moment. She was never off the phone, and I managed to get myself stuck in the dairy where I made a number of uninformed and possibly disastrous decisions simply because decisions had to be made and I seemed to be the one people assumed would make them. Things happened in the right order. Time moved in a forward direction. The clock struck. The sun passed across the sky from east to west. When it was beginning to get dark, Françoise made a meal and we sat down at the table to eat. I started crying. The empty chair threw me. Tears streamed into my spoon. The children stared at me with shocked, awed faces.

We washed up. I willed Celeste and Françoise to go upstairs so I could be alone with *Tante* Mathilde, but the moment the dishes were put away they sat down at the table again in a bleak, miserable silence.

'I think I'll go to bed,' I said.

My plan was to wait till I heard *Tante* Mathilde come up and then go to her room and have the whole thing out with her, but it went badly wrong, this plan. I remember sitting on the edge of the bed and kicking off my shoes, and that was it. The next thing I remember was jerking violently awake in the dark, sweating with panic. The pain was so bad, I didn't know how to bear it. I wanted to howl out loud. I wanted to tear my clothes and shriek and rage against this incomprehensible and immutable loss. How could he not be there? How could he not *be*? It was an impossible concept to grasp.

I went downstairs. Movement, I thought, might ease the pain. It might be possible to dodge its intensity by keeping on the move. My eyes were swollen into gritty slits. There was a light in the kitchen.

'I couldn't sleep,' I mumbled apologetically.

She looked up. Her hair hung loose and distressingly grey over her shoulders. I was ashamed to intrude on the shocking nakedness of her loose hair.

'A tisane?' she asked.

I shook my head.

She had switched on a small table lamp. We sat on either side of the table, isolated together in space by its circle of light. She had been crying – an even more shocking nakedness.

'What will you do now?' she asked.

'That's what I need to talk to you about,'

'I've managed to contact Gaston,' she said. 'He's flying back for the funeral.' She blew her nose. 'Before you make any decisions, Marie-Christine – '

'Stop calling me Marie-Christine,' I interrupted.

' ... before you say anything else,' she went on, her voice slightly muffled by her handkerchief, 'there's a factor which I think you ought to take into consideration.'

I waited. She put her handkerchief away.

'Rougearc is now yours,' she said.

'I beg your pardon?' I said stupidly, although I'd heard her perfectly well.

'Well, the major holding. I still retain a fifth share but the rest is yours.'

My brain was the consistency of a damp sponge. My mouth fell open. 'But it can't be,' I said. 'You know it can't. You know I'm not Marie-Christine.'

'I know you're the person to whom Xavier wanted his majority share to go.'

'No,' I said.

'Of course a fifth share was always yours. You didn't know that?'

'No, of course I didn't know,'

'Your father left it to you on his death. I have a fifth share; Xavier, as the son who stayed to look after the estate, had two-fifths and eventually bought out Gaston's share. So four-fifths of Rougearc is now yours.'

I looked at her blankly.

'Xavier spoke to the lawyer the day after his hospital check-up,' she continued. 'He insisted there were to be no major alterations to the will. I argued that perhaps you wouldn't want the responsibility: your life was in England. Nonsense, he said, of course the place must go to Marie-Christine.'

'To Marie-Christine, yes,' I interrupted. 'But not to me.'

She shook her head. 'No. To you. Let us be quite clear about that. It was you he was talking about.'

'Yes, but that doesn't make any difference, does it? I'm not Chris. Chris is dead. So to accept all this ... to accept Rougearc would be a criminal fraud.'

'And pretending to be someone else for four weeks wasn't?'

'Well, it's not exactly on the same scale, is it?' I said. I rested my head in my hands to try and rub some sense into my gritty eyes. 'I don't understand,' I grumbled. 'Why did you let me go on with it?'

She snorted as if she could hardly believe anyone would be so stupid. 'You know why,' she said. 'How could I possibly disabuse him? He was so happy. I saw his face when you arrived. How could I have told him that the woman in the car with him was not Marie-Christine? Of course, then it was necessary to find out precisely who you were. So I made enquiries at the hospital, and concluded that you were probably the English housewife who went missing at roughly the same time. I assumed you simply wanted to stay missing and found this a convenient place to hide.'

'I didn't mean any of this to happen,' I said wretchedly. It felt too late to apologise now.

'No, but you didn't try to stop it, did you?' she said. 'You found a hiding place, you made your choice, and now you must take the consequences.'

I covered my face with my hands.

She reached across the table and touched my elbow. 'Don't imagine that I'm reproaching you, Marie-Christine. The situation benefited us all. Xavier was happier than he'd been in years. Françoise has blossomed. Celeste's nose has been thoroughly put out of joint, which is not altogether a bad thing. As for Gaston, well – ' she shrugged and withdrew her hand – 'from the moment he pretended to recognise you in the kitchen ... ' She gave a small, soft, knowing laugh which made the rest of her sentence redundant.

'But I am *not* Marie-Christine,' I said through clenched teeth.

She smiled. 'Oh, don't be absurd,' she said. 'Everyone knows you are. The hospital, the village, the bank, your cousins – everybody. They'd all swear to it. I will swear to it. Gaston will swear to it.' This was rapidly turning inside out: now that I was finally trying to confess I wasn't the person everybody said I was, no one would have it. 'And as a consequence of our little talk,' *Tante* Mathilde was saying, 'I think even the police might be persuaded to swear to it. We shall certainly have no problem in finding the necessary witnesses.'

'What witnesses?'

'To prove who you are. It's a legal requirement. Before you can inherit.'

'But I *can't* inherit,' I protested, so loudly that she put her finger to her lips. Lowering my voice obediently I said, 'Why did you insist to the police that I was Marie-Christine when you knew that I wasn't?'

'Would you have preferred me to say: "No, this is an English housewife who is running away from her husband?" I did it because Xavier needed you to be Marie-Christine. Don't imagine you play the central role in this story: you don't. You fulfilled a need, that's all.'

I stood up. 'I have to leave,' I said.

She raised an eyebrow. 'Now? Don't be ridiculous. You will at least have the courtesy to stay for the funeral. It would look very strange if you didn't.'

'Yes, of course,' I mumbled, 'I'm sorry,' and sat down again.

After a moment she broke the silence by saying in a softer, almost cajoling voice, 'Let's look at it logically. How can it possibly be criminal fraud if no one ever contests the will? And no one is going to. Of course not. We've told the world you're Marie-Christine: we're hardly going to turn round and deny it now.' 'Besides,' she went on, 'is it technically possible, I wonder, to defraud someone of a debt? Because that's in effect what you've inherited. The estate is bankrupt. If you tried to sell your share you'd make a crippling loss. So there you are. What have

you, in fact, inherited? A time-consuming, uneconomic mill-
stone. But it's all we have, and Xavier loved it.'

'I love it,' I mumbled into my hands.

'I know you do,' she said.

'What about Gaston?' I asked.

'Gaston? It's the last thing Gaston wants. He sold his own
share in the estate to Xavier years ago. He wanted the money
to set Sandrine up in business. No, the sea is his life; he'll never
leave it. Celeste can't wait to get to Paris. She'll go with the
first man who'll take her. And Françoise? Well, she's a good
girl, but … ' she shrugged. 'He was a very practical man, Xavier.
He understood these things, and he wanted *you* to have
Rougearc. No one else. He entrusted it to you. Remember that.'

'Thank you,' I whispered. I was afraid to look at her in case
I started to cry again, but she was in no mood to let sentiment
get in the way of business. She pointed out that I, of all people,
had very little room for moral quibblings.

Personally, she said, she could see no reason whatsoever
why for the general good I shouldn't continue to be Marie-
Christine.

'I'll tell you why I can't,' I said. 'Because Chris was on the
run too, and her past's rapidly catching up with her. I think in
the next couple of days I'm likely to be arrested.'

I was impressed by how efficiently she controlled her shock.
Or perhaps I was mistaken and she wasn't shocked at all.
Perhaps she had a far better idea of who Chris was than I'd ever
had. 'I see,' she said.

'In which case,' I pointed out, 'I've got no choice. I'll have
to tell the police who I am.'

She nodded. She was thinking hard.

'But that's complicated too,' I explained. 'Because Margaret
Davison's past is catching up as well.'

She surprised me, as she frequently did. She laughed.

'So I'm in a mess,' I said. I stood up. 'I'll stay for the funeral
… '

'Yes,' she said rather vaguely as if she was too busy thinking to speak. 'Yes, the police are hardly likely to make a move until after the funeral.'

' … but then I'll have to go. I'm sorry. I wish I could have stayed. I wish it *was* mine.'

Saying this – realising that looking after it for him might almost be as good as having him there, might in a muddled way be almost the same thing – made my loss doubly unbearable.

Tante Mathilde stood up. She kissed me on both cheeks. 'He trusted you to do what was right,' she said, and added as if the idea amused her, 'after all, my dear, in the end what is a name? Nothing.'

It was a beautiful morning, fresh and cool. The thin grass on the lawn was wet with dew. Drops of water rolled into the throats of parched flowers. The sun glittered on the windows. I wandered barefoot over the wet grass, my dressing gown brushing against the nettles and the brilliant blue spears of viper's bugloss. I wanted to walk the boundaries of the place before anybody else claimed them. I blinked up at the silvery towers. He had given me all this. The stones, the trees, the bushes, the weeds, everything from the vast construction of castle to the pea-sized stones of the gravel – it was all mine. Everything within sight was mine. The cliffs, the woods, the rock pool, the fields, the smallest creature, the tiniest plant, everything that lived and breathed, the goats, the chickens, the butterflies, the crickets, even the ants, even the worms, he had given them all to me. They were mine. I had inherited his kingdom. And although there was nothing I could do about it, it was still mine.

For the next few days, until after the funeral, the castle was closed to visitors. Of necessity I had to spend most of my time dealing with farm business. I either shut myself up in the office, or strategically put myself out of reach in the fields or the dairy. *Tante* Mathilde was right: out of respect the police were unlikely to start asking further questions until after the funeral, but there was no knowing what Tony might do: if indeed it *was* Tony I'd seen. I was convinced at the time, but it's easy to make mistakes about people. He was in the shadows, the man I saw, and at the back of a crowd: I was in a particularly nervous state of mind. I could have been mistaken. And the man who was asking questions about me in the bank didn't necessarily have to be Tony. Why should it be? Why would Tony ask questions about Marie-Christine Masbou in a French bank? It was far more likely to be one of Peyrol's colleagues.

I was irritated by having to think so much about all this: none of it seemed to have anything to do with me any more. There were far more important things to worry about; for example, how easily the world went on without Xavier, as if it hadn't even noticed his loss, as if he'd never been there. The goats should have fallen into a decline and refused to eat. Stunned by grief, the birds should have plummeted from the trees. The river should have stopped flowing. It wasn't so. Nothing cared. The self-obsession of the natural world, its selfish, insistent, perpetual thrust forwards, its failure to understand the extent of the loss it had suffered, enraged me. In my head I could hear him scolding me. 'What's the matter now, uh? Why waste your energy being miserable?' And in my head I tell him that I'm miserable about things ending. He laughs and tells me that for somebody so clever I'm remarkably stupid. 'What is ever going to end?' he says. 'Nothing. Nothing ends. There are no such things as endings.' Or perhaps that's me talking. It's difficult to tell. Then he says – and this is definitely Uncle Xavier – 'I know what's the matter with you. You don't eat. Go and eat something.'

*

On the morning of the funeral Gaston's wife, Sandrine, arrived from Paris. I was surprised by her. She was small and slim, a tiny-boned woman with huge eyes. She was exquisitely and discreetly dressed in black. She kissed us all, looked at me with critical interest and said how delighted she was to meet me at last. I liked her, which embarrassed me. I found it difficult to connect her with Gaston. He arrived separately. I avoided him. I was afraid to look at him.

After the funeral mass we followed the coffin in procession to the cemetery on the edge of the village. Half the population of the Causse was there. It was a pity, really, that Xavier wasn't available to organise it. *Tante* Mathilde headed the mourners, the priest on one side of her and Gaston on the other. I kept my head down and concentrated on the wild flowers in the grass verge: vervain, wild marjoram, soapwort, common centaury. Ahead of us, six farmers in tight, shiny, navy-blue suits, their faces respectful and pickled in wine, carried the coffin on their shoulders. Behind us, their wives followed in their best summer dresses. On their plump, cellulite arms they supported aged mothers in black, who had known Xavier since he was a baby, and whose faces were carved in lines of suffering dignity as if over the years they'd built impenetrable defences against age and pain and loss. Dogs, and children on bicycles flanked the procession. Look how much you were loved, I said to Xavier.

The edges of everything blurred and went out of focus. I concentrated on the hole in the earth, grimly controlling my bottom lip with my teeth. I studied the details of the moment, and refused to think about the coffin being lowered, slightly crookedly, into this obscene, earth-smelling hole. I refused absolutely to think about what was in the coffin. Around me people wept and held handkerchiefs to their eyes. I blinked and stared upwards at the rooks in the trees, and considered the way the wind turned the leaves so that their paler undersides caught the sun. Once, by accident, I caught Gaston's eye across the grave. I looked away hurriedly.

Afterwards, at Rougearc, we drank ratafia and port and ate small almond biscuits. When I went down to the cellar to fetch up another bottle, Gaston followed me.

'I can't talk to you,' I said. 'Not now.'

I was annoyed with him for looking so much like Xavier, for being so much like Xavier and yet *not* being Xavier. 'If things work out,' I said, 'I'll be in Marseilles in a couple of days.'

But even as I said it, I knew I wouldn't. Things had gone beyond that. Between us, Chris, Margaret and me, we had spent a lifetime running away. It had to stop.

He looked at me in surprise as if he wasn't expecting me to come to Marseilles either. 'But what about this place?' he said, with a sudden flicker of panic in his eyes. I could see he was afraid that if I didn't take it on, *he* might be expected to shoulder the responsibility.

'I can't,' I said. 'I've got no right.' I didn't tell him *Tante* Mathilde had known from the beginning I wasn't Marie-Christine. I didn't tell him anything. I found it painful to talk to him at all.

The cellar door opened. 'Marie-Christine,' Françoise called. 'Are you down there? We need another ratafia and a cognac.'

After that there was no further chance to be alone. It was a relief, really, because Gaston's presence confused me. He kissed me when he left as avuncularly as an uncle ought to kiss his niece. 'Phone me,' he whispered into my ear. My throat ached as if something hard were stuck there. I thought I probably would phone him, because he was the one link with Xavier that I needn't lose, and we were good together. We could go on supplying each other's fantasies.

I stood with the others and smiled sightlessly until the car disappeared through the main gate. He didn't turn, he didn't wave. I understood how shot through he was, like me, with the instinct to run. He could never finally be pinned down. He wasn't, in fact, at all like Xavier. He would always leave everything early, and never look back because he'd already forgotten what was behind him and was speeding towards the sea and the endless shifting horizons where he felt safe, where he was not defined by solid realities. It might even have been what we first recognised in each other, this instinct to run. Except, if that were so then we were deceived. His impermanence was part of his nature. Mine was just a knee-jerk response to panic.

The morning after the funeral *Tante* Mathilde came into my office. Already, in unguarded moments, I was thinking of it as 'my' office, and sat with my feet up on the desk flipping through intriguing-looking books on the diseases of sheep.

'I should like to go through the financial affairs of the estate with you before we see the lawyer,' she said.

She sat down in a chair opposite me so that now I was the one in authority.

'I need your advice,' she said. 'You know about these things.'

'No,' I said patiently. 'I'm not Marie-Christine. And even if I were, it wouldn't help. She was just an ordinary secretary. Like me. The rest was a story she told. Neither of us is a financial expert.'

'A secretary?' There was a long pause while she digested this. 'And is that now an arrestable offence? What else was she?'

'Are you sure you want to know?'

Her lips thinned into a brief, tight smile. 'At the moment,' she said, 'I'm more interested in you. If you're determined to stick to what you insist is the truth, then the lawyer will have to know.' She sighed and stood up. 'It will cause enormous problems,' she complained. 'Of course,' she remarked from the doorway, 'there's your truth, and there's Xavier's truth.'

'No,' I said. 'There's only the one truth.'

'Are you sure?' Before I had time to answer this, she added, 'It's a little arrogant, don't you think, to assume that your truth is the only one that counts? And to insist on inflicting it on everyone else simply to make yourself feel morally cleaner? You should never start things you're not prepared to finish.' She paused in the doorway. 'Anyway,' she said, with brisk formality, 'let me have your decision as soon as possible.'

I thought about that. How much was Rougearc worth to me? Was it worth the distress and discomfort of a prison sentence and everything that went with it? Well, of course it was: there was no question. I'd do it gladly if that was all there was to it, but it wasn't that simple. And what I could not do, not even for Rougearc, not even for Xavier – particularly not for Xavier – was to go on being Chris Masbou. It seemed to me that what I most owed to Xavier was the courage to take off all the masks, to jettison the assumed names, and to start from there.

So I sat in my office with my feet on my desk and thought for a long time until I came to a sort of decision.

The problem, though, about making decisions is that other people refuse to behave in the way you planned for them to behave. They knock you off balance by assuming that they're the ones taking the initiative.

I went into the kitchen.

'Does anyone need the Renault?' I asked.

No one did.

'Good, because I have to go to Figeac,' I said. 'To the bank. I won't be long.'

'Take care,' said *Tante* Mathilde. She meant it more literally than the phrase is usually meant.

I did. I took enormous care, but there was no one waiting at the bank to arrest Chris; nor was there any sign of anyone who looked remotely like Tony. I completed the necessary business, and was home well before lunch, in plenty of time to talk to the rep who supplied packaging for the cheeses and afterwards to discuss the application of Swedish Tar to a ewe's foot.

That afternoon the château reopened to tourists. It was a Friday and particularly busy. Celeste had taken the children into the village for their music lessons; *Tante* Mathilde walked down to the gatehouse with her cash-box and a roll of tickets; Françoise was on tour duty. I was planning to go down to the farm, but as I came out into the sun I saw the crowd of tourists drifting in groups across the courtyard ready for the two o'clock tour. Sitting on the edge of an ornamental stone urn, his feet perched on another, sat Mal.

'Hi,' he said, as I walked past him. 'How are you? Sorry to hear about your uncle.'

I was very annoyed: *I'd* planned to catch *him* off guard, not the other way round.

'I threatened I'd do the full tour one day, didn't I?' he said cheerfully. 'And when I woke up this morning, I thought: Yeah, why not?'

Across the courtyard I could hear Françoise summoning her flock.

'These geraniums are very dead,' he remarked. 'You should water them.' He took a notebook out of his pocket, and pushed back the sleeves of his fashionably baggy jacket. 'I brought this with me,' he said. 'So I can jot down a list of the things I've got potential buyers for.'

I hated him. I hated his studied arrogance, his colourlessness, his charm, his certainty that he was frightening me, his beige trousers, the light, perfect tan on his disgustingly smooth arms, the way his hair flopped across his forehead, his relentlessly fashionable sunglasses. I loathed him so much it made me feel slightly sick. And I despised Chris for ever having been deceived by him, or worse still for *not* being deceived by him and yet still sticking with him for so long.

'Nothing's for sale,' I said coldly.

'Really?' He smiled at me in boyish surprise. He did boyish surprise very well. Then he lowered his voice. If I hadn't been so consumed with dislike I might have been amused by his techniques. 'That's a pity,' he whispered nastily, 'because you owe me, lady. You owe me twenty grand. Which according to the local grapevine you can well afford now. What a clever girl, eh? I'm speechless with admiration.'

'You sound it,' I said.

'No, I am,' he said. 'You must be sitting on a couple of million quids' worth of antiques and paintings and stuff here. So twenty grands' worth's not going to be missed much, is it?'

'I told you. Nothing's for sale.'

His smooth, bland face hardened to enamel. 'I don't think we're communicating very well here. I tell you what, let me put it another way ... '

Françoise was tentatively approaching us. I was so grateful to her for interrupting that I greeted her too effusively and confused her. She nudged nervously at her glasses and backed away. 'It was just ... is the gentleman here for the tour?' she asked. 'Only we're just starting.'

'No,' I said. 'He's leaving.'

'Who said anything about leaving?' Mal turned the full force of his charm on to poor, flustered Françoise. 'I wouldn't miss this for the world. I've bought my ticket. Look. No, I'm stopping.' He slid off the stone urn. Halfway across the courtyard he turned, waved his notebook at me and winked.

I couldn't gauge whether this was still just a threat or whether it was a statement of intent to help himself. There was plenty of room in his jacket for a couple of small, valuable and easily accessible items. I waited until I reckoned the tour was properly under way, then tagged myself on to the end of it. They were in the banqueting hall. I stayed partly hidden behind the heavy curtain looped across the entrance, and listened to Françoise go through her usual spiel. Mal was very interested in the paintings. I noted his speculative concentration in a group of four sixteenth-century miniatures. He could easily smuggle all of them out in his pocket. I watched to make sure he left the room with the rest of the tour. I wondered if I ought to find a way to warn Françoise.

The French spiel ended and she started her English paraphrase. The English and the Dutch listened politely. My attention was suddenly caught by a thin man who was listening to Françoise with his head slightly bent in a way that was familiar to me. Painfully familiar. I hadn't expected this. Partly, I suppose, because I'd convinced myself I was mistaken about the man I'd seen at the fête, but mainly because I'd planned that when I next saw him, it would be on my terms and at a time of my choosing. From my cover I observed him look up towards the ceiling where Françoise was pointing out the coats of arms painted on the beams. I was a little shocked by his appearance. He'd changed in some fundamental way. Superficially, he was thinner, much thinner and his face was different, but it wasn't that. Whatever it was, it was very puzzling. I couldn't work it out. I moved in closer to get a better look at him and hovered behind a large Dutch woman on the outer fringes of the group.

'This is believed to be a portrait of Diane de Poitiers,' Françoise was saying. 'And this one over here is a portrait of our great-great-great-grandfather, Jean Yves Masbou.'

It was a mistake, moving into the body of the room. Françoise had seen me, and with a typically generous gesture included me in the grand-daughterly relationship. The party turned to see whom she was including.

'If you would like to follow me,' she continued, 'we'll move into the Library.' She raised her voice to attract the attention of the French. '*Mesdames, Messieurs, voulez-vous me suivre …* '

Chattering among themselves, the party filtered through the carved doorway.

Tony was in a state of shock. He had gone very white. His

feet wouldn't move. He stood there winded, all the certainties knocked out of him. I waited for him to recover a little, and said nothing. The room had emptied; Mal had moved on with the rest of the party. In the distance I could hear Françoise droning away about *des manuscrits enluminés*.

'Maggs?' Tony said tentatively. His voice was so familiar. I was touched to hear it again.

'Maggs?' he said again. His face buckled. 'I don't understand. Who are you?' He looked ill. His face was pale with confusion.

I wasn't ready for this, but there was no avoiding it now. 'This is my home,' I said evasively.

He shook his head as if trying to clear it. 'I've looked for you everywhere,' he said, his hands twisting and fidgeting with nothing. The cuffs of his shirt were dirty. 'Everywhere. All over France. Everywhere.'

We stared at each other for a long time. He was someone else. I didn't know him. He wasn't the Tony who represented in my mind whatever it was I'd spent sixteen and a half years trying to escape. He was a thin, sad-eyed, shy man.

'I don't understand anything,' he said helplessly. 'Any of this. Any of it. What have you got to do with this Masbou family?'

'This is my home,' I repeated gently. 'I live here.'

His face crumpled. He put his hands up to cover it. When he took them away, he'd recovered himself a little. I tried not to look down or avoid his eyes. 'You've changed,' he said.

I smiled. 'Well, yes,' I said. 'I expect I have. I'm someone else now.'

'Oh, don't start playing silly games, Maggs,' he snapped, and I saw that after all he was Tony; he was the man I'd left in the rue François Premier.

'Why did you go on looking for me?' I asked. I was very curious about this. I couldn't understand what made him think he wanted to find me.

'Why?' The question obviously annoyed him. 'Because I

never believed you were dead,' he said. 'That's why. There was no body. I wouldn't believe it until I actually saw the body.'

I smiled. He was still unfailingly literal.

'Yes, but the person you're looking for *is* dead,' I said. 'She walked out of the Ladies' room and just went on walking.'

He refused to allow this. This was exactly the sort of imprecise phraseology he most disliked. This was an example of what annoyed and baffled him most about me. '*You* went on walking,' he insisted.

'All right, *I* went on walking.'

'And then what happened?'

I shook my head. I wasn't going to tell him any more. The rest was my story; I wasn't going to let him have it. I wasn't going to let him pick holes in it and reinterpret it to fit his way of looking at things. Once he got hold of it, I might start not to believe in it either. I changed the subject. 'Were you asking about me in the bank the other day?'

'Yes,' he said. 'Well, no. I was asking about Marie-Christine Masbou.'

'Why?'

'Because I was getting nowhere. And last week I was in Limoges: I was searching through back numbers of the local papers for anything, any clue at all, when I found this report about a woman who was killed in an accident on the N20, an English hitch-hiker. It was dated about two days after you disappeared. It was a bit of a long shot – the name was wrong to start off with – but I thought it might be worth a try. The hospital was useless, so I decided I'd try to find the driver, this Marie-Christine Masbou.'

It was very odd listening to all this. 'Why the bank?' I asked.

He shrugged. 'Well, I don't know really. I arrived in Figeac, I went to the bank to change some travellers' cheques, and I just happened to ask the cashier if she knew the Masbou family.'

'Yes, we bank there,' I said.

He looked at me with the kind of exasperation I remembered very well. He'd always been intensely exasperated when I persisted in seeing things differently from the way he perceived them.

'What else did you ask?' I said.

'Just about the family. That's all. I wanted to see Mademoiselle Masbou that afternoon, but the cashier said no one would be in: there was a fête on. And then I heard her uncle had died, so I thought I ought to wait until after the funeral.'

'And here you are,' I said.

He looked slightly embarrassed. 'Well, the woman at the gate wouldn't let me through unless I bought a ticket. I thought I'd have a word with the guide afterwards and see whether it would be appropriate to try and speak to Mademoiselle Masbou yet or not.'

'You *are* talking to her,' I said.

His face went bright red. 'Stop it,' he said. 'Stop that. Stop saying that.'

'Go back to England, Tony.'

He shook his head miserably. 'I can't. Not now I know where you are.'

I made him sit down. 'You don't know anything,' I said, sitting beside him at the refectory table. 'Except that the person you're looking for died in an accident.'

He wasn't listening to me. I could see he wasn't. He didn't want to hear. It was a pity because I was telling him the truth. For once, for the first time, I was offering him a real truth about myself. He put his hands up to his face. I thought maybe he was weeping. I waited for him to recover himself. I put my hand on his shoulder. 'Go home,' I told him.

We'd been so long alone in the banqueting hall that the tour had finished without us. Françoise came back to see what had happened.

'I'm so sorry,' I said to Tony. 'You've missed the tour now. This is Tony,' I explained to Françoise. 'We used to know each other in England. We once had a mutual acquaintance.'

He looked as if he had been hit. I was sorry for him, but there was nothing I could do. Françoise offered him her hand. Like an automaton, he shook it. I thought what a pity it was he couldn't take Françoise home with him. She'd suit him very well. He was a good man. He deserved none of this.

She looked at him a little uncertainly. 'Would you like to join the next tour?' she asked him.

'No,' I said, firmly. 'I don't think so. Would you, Tony?'

I kissed him on the cheek. His smell was unfamiliar to me. His skin was cold with shock. 'Goodbye,' I said. 'Better not to come back. There's nothing for you here. Nothing you'd want.'

He allowed me to usher him out. When he'd gone I collapsed on a wooden chest and waited for the shaking to stop. I think what upset me more than anything, what moved me, was his dogged perseverance, his determination to find me. He had hacked his way through forests of bureaucracy and indifference. How could I not be moved? But there was nothing I could do about it. There was no way in which I could make it easier for him. His pain was no longer my pain. He was a grown man. He must manage for himself. I had other responsibilities. He must find a way to make himself whole without filling himself with huge chunks of me.

I was still sitting there at the entrance when Françoise came round with the next tour.

She touched me on the shoulder. 'Are you all right?' she whispered.

'Yes,' I said.

'Your friend was very upset.' She tried not to look too curious.

'I know.'

'Will he come back?'

'I don't think so, no.'

But the point was that it wouldn't matter if he did.

I'd completely forgotten about Mal. I went into the kitchen to get a cold drink and took it out into the garden. He was sitting there on one of the sun-loungers, leaning back with his hands behind his head.

'This is a private garden,' I said coldly.

'Is it?' He opened his eyes and grinned at me. 'Well, that's good, then, because this is a private visit. We never got round to finishing our conversation, did we, so I thought as a friend, as an ex, you wouldn't mind if I waited in your garden for you.' He nodded at the glass of orange juice I was holding. 'That looks nice,' he said. I ignored the hint.

'You'd better come into my office,' I told him.

He chuckled. 'Your office,' he said as he loped along the passage behind me. 'You've got your feet well and truly under the table here, haven't you?'

I led him down the various passages, and opened the door to the farm office. 'Sit down,' I said.

He sat, his legs sprawled out in front of him, his hands in his trouser pockets.

'I ought to frisk you,' I said.

He laughed. 'Actually, I made a very useful list of things that could easily disappear. Do you want to see it?'

'You touch anything and I'll have the police on you faster than you can count to one.'

His eyes flickered rapidly to hide his surprise. 'Hang on a minute,' he said. 'I don't think you're in any position to threaten me. I think I'm the one who holds all the cards when it comes to making threats. Because if you're not in the mood to share your amazing windfall with your business partner, then I shall tell this precious family whom you're intent on defrauding of their estate, exactly who you are: an ageing housewife from Stoke-on-Trent.'

'Do,' I said. 'Unfortunately it won't get you very far because they already know.'

There was a pause. I watched the complexity of his reaction mirrored on his face. 'Christ, you're good,' he said finally.

'You're fucking amazing. I actually believed you there for a minute.'

'Well, I should go on believing,' I said, 'because it's true. And shortly the police will know as well. I'm going to tell them everything. Including your connection with Chris, and where the money came from.'

I watched his face. He was nothing really: a rather vicious little shell. It distressed me to think that Chris had probably never grasped how easy and painless it would be to tell him where to get off. But then perhaps she loved him; or had been bound to him by a tangle of contradictory and painfully interwoven threads similar to those which had imprisoned Tony and me.

'I'd leave now if I were you,' I told him. 'Drive through the night. Get as far away from here as possible.'

I waited to see how he'd react. I don't think I expected physical violence but I did still expect him to be cleverer than I was. I thought he'd have an answer: I thought he'd have a last word hidden up his sleeve. He had nothing.

'You're bluffing,' he said, warily. 'You're a liar.'

I sat with my hands on my lap and waited.

'Christ,' he said, 'you really are the best. No question. We could've done brilliant things together, you and me. Big-time stuff.'

I smiled and went on waiting.

'You *are* lying, aren't you?' he said with a little less certainty this time.

I slid open the drawer.

'What are you doing?' he said nervously.

I took out an envelope. I handed it to him.

'What's this?'

'Seventy thousand seven hundred and forty-five francs,' I said. 'It's everything that was left in Chris's bank account. I closed it this morning. Take it. Think of it as compensation.'

Gingerly he took the envelope and opened it.

'Oh, for God's sake,' I said, 'you don't have to count it. Just take it and get out.'

He looked at the money doubtfully. ' You are bluffing about the police, aren't you?' he said.

'No.'

'You're deliberately giving up all this?' He couldn't believe it. He shook his head. 'What the hell for? I thought you were cleverer than that.'

'I'm not giving up this. I'm giving up being Chris.'

'Yeah, but it amounts to the same thing, doesn't it?'

'I'm afraid it probably does,' I said.

He was very rattled but he covered it well. He looked at me as if he'd realised I was a lot less interesting than he'd supposed, and was no longer worth his attention. 'Well,' he said, holding up a fistful of notes. 'Cheers. It's not exactly what I hoped for, but under the circumstances it's better than nothing. I'll see you around some time.'

The rest of the afternoon I spent getting things in order. At half-past six, when the goats were back from the fields, the poultry had been fed, the sheep watered and the dairy workers were packing up ready to go home, I walked slowly back to the house and phoned the number Peyrol had given me. Then I went into the kitchen. A rich smell of garlic hung in the air. Through the window I could see the children playing in the late afternoon warmth. Celeste lay on the sun-lounger, smoking. At the table indoors *Tante* Mathilde was chopping tomatoes. Françoise was at the sink washing beans in a colander under the tap. This is my family, I thought. I opened my mouth to speak and couldn't. I couldn't trust my voice.

Tante Mathilde looked up. I shook my head. With delicate tact she looked away and continued chopping. I steadied myself by leaning against the door jamb. 'I'm going up to my room for a bit,' I managed to say finally. 'I've rung the police. When they come, take them into the office. I'll see them there.'

She nodded.

I took off the T-shirt I'd worn all day and the skirt I'd had to borrow back from Françoise, and washed myself very carefully as if I were preparing for some important ceremony. I wanted to be clean and thoroughly prepared, inside and out. It was an odd time, a nameless time. Technically I was no one. I had cast off all my old names. Back in the cool, dim, half-shuttered room with the blue cabbage roses, I sat in front of the mirror and looked for the last time at the woman on the other side. I introduced myself to her. 'Marina James,' I told her. She looked at me gravely, waiting for more. So I repeated it: 'Marina James,' I said. There was no flicker of disbelief, no twitch of sceptical amusement, nothing to make me lose confidence and start to falter stupidly and mumble a retraction. 'I shall have to make it official,' I told the woman on the other side who was brushing her hair. She seemed to think this was a good idea.

There was a sharp tap at the door. I took a deep breath. 'Come in,' I said. I had put a little lipstick on and drawn a faint grey line round my eyes.

'They're here,' said *Tante* Mathilde. She came into the room and closed the door behind her. 'You know, don't you, that I consider this quite unnecessary?'

'Yes, I know,' I said.

'It's going to cause a great deal of totally unnecessary trouble – to you, to me, to Rougearc. If Xavier could speak to you now he would say the same.'

His name made me wince. There was no point in explaining to her that I was doing this for him, and because of him.

She came and stood behind me. She held my head in my hands so I was looking straight into the central panel of the triptych mirror. 'Who is that?' she said.

The woman on the other side smiled and whispered her new name silently to herself.

'That's you,' she said. 'You. No one else. You. You can call yourself Marie-Christine, or Margaret, or Frou-frou, or Napoleon, anything you want. It doesn't change what's there.'

'I know,' I said. 'But I'm not any of those people.'

She sighed. 'You're as stubborn as your uncle,' she complained. I laughed. 'All right,' she said, sitting on the edge of the bed beside the case in which I'd repacked the few things I was taking. 'All right, let's be practical then.'

I got up and went and sat beside her. I loved and admired her for her unsentimental practicality, for her infinitely flexible way of looking at things. 'So what will they do,' she said, 'the police?'

I had no idea. I assumed they'd take me in for questioning and charge me with fraud.

She shook her head. 'Why should they charge you with anything if we refuse to prosecute?'

'Because I forged Chris's signature for gain. I've used her money. And they'll probably charge me with wasting police time and resources. They spent weeks dredging ponds.'

She tutted and waved her hand dismissively. 'Rubbish,' she said. 'In France we expect our police to be more intelligent than to search for a body that doesn't exist. If they wasted their time, then that's their affair.'

'Well, I know nothing about French law,' I said. 'But I suspect fraud is fraud wherever you are.'

'I shall expect you back,' she said, testily. 'I can't run the farm as well as everything else.'

Amused, I suggested she could hire a manager. She looked at me. 'Don't be absurd,' she said. 'Xavier didn't leave Rougearc to you so that I could hire a manager. Besides,' she added with unfailing practicality, 'I can't afford a manager.'

I slid the ring she'd given me on to my finger and stood up. 'Do I look all right?' I asked.

'You look very nice,' she said crossly. After a moment she added, 'When you're ready to come back, let me know. Your room will be waiting for you.'

'If I come back, it will be with a different name,' I warned her.

'I don't know what's the matter with you,' she grumbled. 'You're obsessed with names. It was you he loved. Your name had nothing to do with it.'

'No,' I said, 'what I meant was that if I ever come back, I shall come back as me.'

I kissed her on both cheeks. I wasn't quite brave enough to hug her. Nor was I brave enough to say goodbye.

I walked downstairs slowly, practising what I was going to say. 'Messieurs –' this was the abridged version – 'Once upon a time, Messieurs, there were three sisters. For ages I deceived myself into thinking there were only two, but the third, the youngest sister, was there all the time. So, you see, it's all right: the story can end properly now.' Not that they'd understand a word of that. They weren't, after all, very bright, or they'd have worked it out for themselves.

They were waiting for me in the office. 'Good evening, Messieurs,' I said. I gestured to a couple of chairs but they shook their heads. They preferred to stand.

I settled myself in the chair behind the desk. I took my time. I was very calm. 'Forgive me for contradicting you,' I said, smiling at them, 'but I think it would probably be better if you sat. I'm afraid I've got a long and rather complicated story to tell you.'

They exchanged glances. They sat down.

'Listen,' I said.